A Picture of Innocence

A Picture of Innocence

Lew Matthews

PIATKUS
CRIME

Although Hampstead exists, as do many of the locations described in this novel, all characters are entirely fictitious and no reference is intended to any living persons, any more than the *Hampstead Explorer* is intended to represent the *Hampstead and Highgate Express*

Copyright © 1996 by Matthew Lewin

First published in Great Britain in 1996 by
Judy Piatkus (Publishers) Ltd of
5 Windmill Street, London W1

The moral right of the author has been asserted

A catalogue record for this book is available from the British Library

ISBN 0-7499-0354-6

Set in 11/12pt Times by
Action Typesetting Ltd, Gloucester
Printed and bound in Great Britain by
Biddles Ltd, Guildford & King's Lynn

Chapter One

*Although he had stopped struggling, the pain in his wrists
and ankles was still intense. But then even that began to
recede as the drowsiness pushed him deeper and deeper
into the seat of the car.*

*He could still hear the engine running, he could still
smell the exhaust and feel the tightness in his chest from
breathing the toxic fumes, but in the last few minutes it
had become almost pleasant to sit there in the dark.*

*His mind touched, very briefly, on the image of a
young girl with a wide mouth and wild red hair, and he
smiled. Then he let himself be led gently into the deepening darkness where he could no longer feel pain or smell
the fumes, and where all was silence.*

'You're nicked,' said the large policeman with ears like satel-
lite dishes.

I was standing in the doorway of my hotel suite, clad only in
a pink brushed cotton dressing gown four sizes too small for
me. It was half past six on a Thursday morning and I was still
half asleep, but I was nevertheless alert enough for some adroit
repartee.

'I beg your pardon?' I countered deftly.

Minutes before I had been woken by heavy pounding on the
door. For a moment I thought the room service waiter had
gone criminally insane and brought me my coffee an hour and
a half early, but then I realised that he had a key and would not
have had to bang. I threw on the first garment that came to
hand, and went to the door.

1

There were two of them, in uniform, one rather thin with a long nose, and the other big, with the ears. They immediately wanted to know if I was Horatio Thorpe Parker, formerly of 240 Estelle Road, NW3.

I winced and again wondered why my late mother had to have been a fan both of naval fiction and a previous leader of the Liberal Party, and I nodded sleepily.

That was when he had delivered the puzzling phrase which had sparked off my smart rejoinder.

'Nicked,' he repeated. 'You are under arrest.'

'What for?' I knew my legal rights.

'Non payment of fines.'

'What fines?'

'We'll discuss that back at the station.'

The other one was looking at my pink dressing gown. 'I suggest you get dressed, Mr Parker.'

'Give me three minutes,' I said, and I closed the door. I hung the pink dressing gown on a hook in the bathroom, experiencing a pang as I remembered its previous inhabitant, the small but exquisitely formed Samantha McDuff, who not only had a black belt in karate, but had also been the first manager of my hotel, which I had bought the year before. I shaved quickly, brushed my teeth and threw on some clothes, all the while searching desperately through my thirty-five-year-old memory banks for some clue as to what fines I was supposed to have incurred.

I opened the door, half expecting the two constables to have disappeared, the whole thing having been a bizarre nightmare, but they were still there. By this stage I was intrigued. I had never been arrested before, and I was finding the experience rather interesting. I closed the door behind me and put my hands out, wrists together, in time-honoured fashion, for the handcuffs.

'That won't be necessary,' said the big one in an irritated sort of way. 'Just come with us.'

The night receptionist's eyes bulged as we emerged from the lift, me sandwiched between the two policemen. 'They caught up with me at last, Simon. They found the body perfectly preserved inside a shark, covered with my fingerprints.'

'A shark was covered with your fingerprints?' he gulped.

2

'No, the body. And the carving knife.'

'That's enough!' snapped the big one, shouldering me forward.

'Do you want me to ring someone, Mr Parker?' Simon called as we headed for the door.

I thought briefly of waking Ambrose Pendleton, the elderly solicitor who handled my complicated affairs, but decided it was too early in the morning for him. I could always call him later if this nonsense turned out to be serious.

'No,' I called back. 'I'll take my punishment. If you can't do the time, don't do the crime, as they say.' Then I was led firmly through the door, a meaty hand on the upper part of each of my arms, as if they expected me to do a runner as soon as we hit the street.

At that time in the morning, Chalk Farm Road was still relatively deserted. They led me to a red and white jam sandwich, and Big Ears got into the driver's seat. I sat in the back with Skinny and, looking at the back of Big Ears's head, I realised that his ears only looked big because be had an unusually small skull.

He drove up Haverstock Hill, and in the absence of any traffic it took precisely three minutes to reach Hampstead police station, a nick well known to me as the crime reporter of the local weekly *Hampstead Explorer*. He drove into the car park at the back, and a few minutes later I was sitting in one of the interview rooms where, I remembered, some wag had once written in felt tip pen on the wall a list of Rules For The Fabrication of Evidence. It had contained such useful instructions as: Always leave occasional blank pages in your notebook, and: Always tell your prisoner that his wife/mother has also been arrested and is in another cell, singing like a canary. I noticed that the wall had a fresh coat of paint.

My captors left me alone and locked the door. No doubt they were going back out to arrest some other major criminal. I'm not sure how long I sat there dozing despite the hardness of the chair, before a sergeant I had never seen before came in and put a thick file down on the table.

'Morning,' he said briskly. 'I'm Sergeant Hall.'

'Good morning, Sergeant. I'm Horatio Parker of the *Explorer* – you may have heard of me – and I hope you don't intend to keep me here very long since I have to be at work at nine o'clock.' I just wanted to see what the reaction would be.

He gave me a steely look. 'I don't care if you're Horatio Hornblower of the *Bounty*, you'll stay here for as long as I need you.' We eyed each other in a guarded sort of way. Then he cautioned me; you know, all that complicated new stuff about how things I didn't mention now could have aspersions cast against them if I wanted to bring them up in my defence later. I had the feeling that had I said 'Pardon?' he wouldn't have been able to explain it to me.

Instead I said: 'It would help me to answer your questions if I knew what all this was about.' But he ignored me. He opened the file and started asking the usual stuff.

'You are Horatio Thorpe Parker?'

'Guilty.'

'Just say yes or no.'

'OK.'

'Formerly of 240 Estelle Road, NW3?'

'Yes, until it was burned down. Arson, you know.' No response.

'Now residing at the Chalk Farm Hotel?'

'Yes.'

'You are thirty five years of age?'

'Thirty five and three quarters.'

'And the owner of a green Triumph Herald convertible, registration mark BIG 57 D?'

'No.'

'No?'

'No.'

That flummoxed him for a moment, and he shuffled through some papers. 'Well, according to the Driver and Vehicle Licensing Centre in Swansea you are indeed the owner of this twenty-seven-year-old vehicle, which has been the recipient of no less than fifty-three parking tickets in the last two years.' Aah, things were beginning to make sense at last. I began dimly to remember scores of summonses which I had instantly binned.

'Well, DVLC is wrong,' I said. 'I gave it away, two years ago.'

'You gave it away?' It was more like a sarcastic sneer than a question.

4

'Yes, I gave it away. It was a lovely motor, but it was beginning to fall to pieces, and the starter motor particularly was giving me a lot of grief.'

'I don't suppose you could tell me who you gave it to?'

'I don't suppose I could, for the simple reason that I never knew her name.'

'You don't know ...?'

'All I know is that she was a traffic warden.'

'A traffic warden?' Sergeant Hall was beginning to lose his cool slightly, but it was true. I had given my old car to a traffic warden who had, come to think of it, just given me a ticket.

I could remember that day with brilliant clarity, since I had just been given the utterly confounding news by Ambrose Pendleton that a childless elderly friend by the name of Edwina Llewellyn had left me the unimaginable sum of fifty-two million pounds in her will.

Edwina and I had been friends for years, during which time I had somehow got the idea that she was actually rather short of dosh. There had even been a time when I had quietly, yet nobly, paid one of her gas bills. It turned out that her late husband had been the last in a line of rather obscure but rather wealthy Llewellyns who had started off in coal, moved into shipping and finally into just watching a great pile of cash get steadily bigger in gilt-edged shares managed by N.M. Rothschild, Mrcnt Bnkrs of St Swithin's Place, EC4.

I had emerged from this astounding conference in the Gray's Inn chambers of Ambrose Pendleton, who had been her lawyer and was the executor of her estate, in a somewhat hazy state. The traffic warden had just given me a ticket, so I gave her the car. My last words to the stunned woman had been: 'You'll have to pay the parking fine.' Obviously she hadn't.

The policeman stared at me, hard. I stared back. 'I'm afraid it's true, Sergeant. I gave the car to a traffic warden, but I haven't the foggiest notion who she was.'

'Did you sign the change of ownership section on the registration document?' he asked.

'I did.'

'And did you detach that section and send it to DVLC?'

'No. Come to think of it, I just signed it and handed her the whole document.'

5

Sergeant Hall sighed. 'Well, someone has run up fifty-three parking and other traffic violation tickets on this vehicle, with fines amounting to more than two thousand quid, and as far as DVLC and I are concerned, you are still the legally registered owner of this vehicle and, despite the fact that you may not have been the driver, you are ultimately responsible for the offences. You have also ignored scores of summonses and court orders to pay, and you were top of the list when the traffic division decided to crack down on persistent fine evaders.'

'Oh come on, Sergeant, this is obviously a technicality. I am clearly not the owner of this car, I am not the person who committed the traffic offences, and you should be out there looking for a rogue traffic warden in a green Triumph Herald.'

He was unimpressed. 'I'm afraid you'll have to pay these fines, totalling two thousand, two hundred and forty-six pounds and seventy-two pence, or you will be held in custody pending a hearing in the magistrates court next door later this morning.'

'This is nonsense, I'm not paying.'

'Then you'll have to argue with the magistrates. Come with me, and I'll book you in to our hotel.' He led me out into the corridor where, thankfully, we collided with the large bulk of Inspector Theodore Bernstein.

'Theo!' I exclaimed happily.

'Parker,' he sighed mournfully, looking for all the world as if my presence caused him a lot of pain. My theory was that Theo Bernstein only pretended to dislike me. After all, we had been through a lot together, and some of my efforts had directly contributed to his promotion to the rank of Inspector.

He was an unusual breed of policeman, one of the few Jewish officers in the service, and probably the only policeman in the northern hemisphere who was an authority on the contents of the Talmud, the ancient deliberations of the exiled Babylonian rabbis. Or the southern hemisphere, come to think of it.

'How did you get here so fast?' he asked.

I found it a puzzling question, and so did Sergeant Hall, who explained: 'He's been arrested in Operation Yellow Lines. Fifty-three tickets.'

6

I expected concern about my predicament to crease Theo's brow, but I was dismayed to see a smile creep across his face. I even distinctly heard a chuckle.

'Hey, Theo,' I protested, 'I need some assistance here, and I see no reason whatsoever for mirth of any kind. This is all an idiotic mistake, and I'm sure you can sort it out without any further wasting of everyone's time.'

I told him as quickly and succinctly as I could, standing there in that dreary corridor, that I had given my car away, that I had assumed the summonses were an error on the part of authorities, and that, as he well knew, I was an honest citizen, an upstanding member of the community, and a supporter of the police to boot. I was irritated to see the smile get a little wider.

Perhaps he was getting me back for that dreadful day when I had passed on information I had received about a planned bank raid in Willesden. He and I, and about thirty armed police, had waited in the freezing cold all day outside the bank – while the raid had gone down, wholly unmolested, two miles away in Harlesden. He never did quite accept my apology for getting that single syllable wrong.

Theo was grinning broadly now, but then the smile began to fade, as if he had remembered something. He turned to the sergeant and informed him: 'Parker's coming with me.'

'But I was taking him to be processed ...' The sentence tailed off under an icy stare from Theo.

'I'm sure you can find other criminals to process, Sergeant Hall,' he said crisply.

'Yes sir,' Hall said meekly, and moved off down the corridor, my bulky file under his arm.

I was feeling better now and turned to thank my protector, but there was a grim look on his face. 'Don't say anything, just come with me to my office.'

We went through a door, up one flight of stairs, through another door and into a room which would have been depressing had Theo not stamped his personality on it. There was a Persian rug on the floor, pleasant prints on the wall, and a bookcase packed with impressive looking tomes along one wall. He waved me to a chair and sat down at his desk.

'What did you mean when you said "How did you get here

7

so fast"?' I asked him. 'Don't tell me you knew they were going to nick me and you did nothing about it.'

'No, I had no idea they were going to pick you up. When I saw you I assumed you had heard the news.'

'What news?'

'About your friend, Albert Wallis, you know, Wheezy.'

'What about Wheezy? Has he been arrested again?'

'No, I'm afraid he's dead.'

Chapter Two

The breath went out of my body and an icy chill clamped my heart. Bad news like that sometimes has the impact of an express train hitting you in the guts. It wasn't that I was winded, just that I didn't breathe for a while, and I must have gone very pale.

'You OK, Parker?'

'Yeah.'

'Hang on, I'll get you a cup of tea.'

He went out of the office and I heard him bark something at a minion. When he came back, I asked him: 'How?'

'Suicide. Driver of a patrol car noticed a car with its engine running in that dark lay-by in Swain's Lane near the entrance to Highgate Cemetery. When he investigated he saw the hosepipe from the exhaust running to the back window. Wheezy was in the front seat, with the doors locked. They had to break a window to get in but he was dead. The ignition key had been broken off in the lock, presumably in case he tried to change his mind. Doctor at the Whittington Hospital said he'd been dead at least an hour.'

'What time was this?' I asked.

'He was found at about quarter past four this morning.'

'Maisie know yet?'

'His wife? Yes. One of the officers thought he knew Wheezy, but in any case his wallet was in his coat pocket, and it was his car. The duty sergeant went round and broke the news to her.'

'How's she taking it?'

'OK, considering.' Theo paused. 'They had four kids, you know.'

I knew. I was the godfather of one of them. She was four months old. I felt sick.

'Who identified the body?' I asked.

'No-one yet. I was hoping you would.'

'Me? I'm not family.'

'No, but you'll do until we get a chance to get one of them down to the mortuary later today.'

I didn't like the idea, but I couldn't see any justification for refusing. 'OK, but I'll have to phone the office first.'

'Be my guest. I'll be waiting in the car in the yard,' Theo said, and he walked out of the room.

I dialled the number of the *Explorer* and asked to be put through to the editor, a large and very irascible South African by the name of Arnie Bloch. Our relationship was a complex one; well, for me at any rate.

You see, although he was the editor, and I was merely the paper's crime reporter, I also happened to be the owner of the newspaper, and therefore Arnie Bloch's boss. He didn't know that because I had gone out of my way to ensure that no-one knew about it – apart from Ambrose Pendleton, a man at Rothschilds, the former owner and one or two of my close woman friends.

The *Explorer* had been my first acquisition after Edwina had dropped her fifty-two-million-pound-bombshell on me. I bought it secretly through an offshore company in Jersey called Golden Daffodils Limited, retained my anonymity by using Ambrose as a figurehead, sacked some people, hired some others, made Arnie editor, gave everyone a big pay increase and a fifty per cent share of the profits, and carried on working as a simple crime reporter. I enjoyed my job too much to become a financier or newspaper tycoon.

After that I had bought a few other things, including the famous Bluebelle Restaurant in Mayfair (that was in a fit of pique after being thrown out by the maître d') and, of course, the Chalk Farm Hotel where I now resided for the time being, my own house having been burned down in a nasty arson attack in which I and one or two other people had nearly been killed. My colleagues had been told that the insurance company was footing the hotel bill pending the rebuilding of my house.

10

I had also set up the Edwina Llewellyn Memorial Trust, which helped me dispose of my astonishing income of nearly forty-five thousand pounds a week (after tax, of course), in the direction of the needy who fall though the usual benefits and social security nets.

'Yew're bleddy late, man!' Arnie growled at me on the phone in an accent as thick as it was the day, many years before, when he had swum across the Limpopo River with some of Pretoria's finest snapping at his heels.

'I'm at Hampstead nick, Arnie,' I explained patiently.

'Ha! You been arrested?' There was an irritating note of glee in his voice. The fact that I had indeed been arrested only served to increase my irritation.

'I'm working, Arnie.'

'At this time in the morning?' He sounded unconvinced. He also sounded as if he was eating something, but then it was always a safe bet to assume that Arnie was eating something.

I explained that Wheezy Wallis had been found dead and that I had been asked to go and make a preliminary identification of the body. He grunted sympathetically. 'OK, but I want you here by eleven, and don't mess about or I'll fire you again.'

It was true; a year before, Arnie had fired me, in the process creating a rather ticklish problem for me: could I sue for wrongful dismissal at an industrial tribunal without disclosing the fact that I owned the newspaper? Luckily I was rehired before having to deal with that conundrum.

In the car, on the way down to the mortuary in one of the depressing back streets behind St Pancras Station, my thoughts turned inevitably to the subject of Wheezy Wallis.

His nickname had nothing to do with the state of his chest and a lot to do with his occupation which, without putting too fine a point on it, was burglary. He was good at his job, was said to have been able to squirm his way into virtually any premises not guarded by a hungry Rottweiler, and had become known as The Weasel, later contracted to Wheezy.

He had on two or three occasions found himself as a guest of Her Majesty, but usually for short periods, and as the result of minor misdemeanours. He had been an old-fashioned crook, stealing only from people whom he genuinely believed already

11

had too much in this world, and he was implacably opposed to the new and violent breed of criminal.

Wheezy had also had a particular hatred of drug dealers, and had had no qualms about becoming one of the most useful police informers on that particular subject.

As far as my own work was concerned, Wheezy had been my ticket to the underworld, taking me to places I would never otherwise have found (not to mention emerged from alive) and introducing me to people I would never otherwise have been able to approach.

Everything had a price, of course, and my association with him had cost me a packet over the years. But behind the business side of our relationship we had also developed a peculiar kind of friendship and loyalty – the sort that can only exist in very particular circumstances between people who come from utterly different worlds.

We never took each other home for dinner, and most of our meetings took place in pubs and dark alleys, but I had once or twice been invited to family occasions such as weddings, and I had thus met most of his family.

A few months before, Maisie had given birth to their fourth daughter and Wheezy, suspecting shrewdly that I had more dosh than anyone else he knew, thought he would do his new child a bit of good by asking me to be her godfather.

The fact that he was dead had not begun to register properly with me yet, but even so I began to wonder about what could possibly have driven this determinedly cheerful little bloke to suicide. The answer was not long in coming.

One of the coroner's officers led us into the mortuary and asked over his shoulder: 'Which one is it?'

'Wallis. The suicide,' Theo said.

The officer consulted a ledger-type book on one of the stainless steel tables and looked puzzled. 'There is a Wallis here, but it's not listed as suicide. It says here "probable murder".'

'What?' Theo said. 'What are you talking about, man?'

He looked aggrieved. 'Don't ask me, guv, nothing to do with me. Ask the pathologist; I think he's still here.'

'He's done the autopsy already?'

'Nah, just the prelim. Hang on, I'll get him.'

We waited in that creepy room for about five minutes,

knowing that in each of those metal cabinets there was the body of a person who was likely to have met with some unusual form of death. I shuddered more than once.

Eventually a grey haired Asian man wearing a white coat breezed into the room. 'Morning Inspector,' he said to Theo with his hand out. He ignored me completely. 'I'm Dr Rushdie, no relation, ha ha, the duty pathologist. I gather you want to see our Mr Wallis?' He didn't wait for an answer. 'He's over here.'

One of the big metal drawers was pulled out, and there was poor Wheezy, wrapped up in what looked like a big plastic bag with a zip. Like they say, the faces of the dead are serene, but also terribly pale and bloodless. Being serene and bloodless didn't suit Wheezy's perky face, and a painful dart of emotion and loss went through me.

'Do I gather that you think he was murdered?' Theo asked.

'I do,' the man said briskly.

'I thought he gassed himself in his car.'

'Aah, wait a minute,' the pathologist said. 'I'm not saying that the cause of death wasn't due to the inhalation of carbon monoxide. I haven't done the autopsy yet, but I'm pretty certain that it was the toxic exhaust that killed him.'

'So?' Theo prompted.

'So, what I am suggesting is that his presence in the car was not entirely voluntary. Look.' He pulled some of the plastic sheeting away, revealing Wheezy's pallid, naked body, and pointed to the wrists. 'Where have you seen bruising and laceration like that before, Inspector?'

Theo didn't have to look for long. 'Handcuffs,' he said quietly.

'Indeed. These bruises and lacerations are precisely what one finds on people who have attempted to escape from a set of handcuffs. And, given that there is bruising around his ankles which suggest that they were similarly handcuffed, I am inclined towards the preliminary view that he was handcuffed in place and left to suffocate in the car. At some stage, probably when he had lost consciousness, the handcuffs were removed.

'No doubt examination of the vehicle will reveal further evidence of my theory. He must have been secured in such a

13

way that he could not reach door or window handles or even kick out at the glass.'

'Anything else we should know at this stage?' Theo's voice was grim.

'Not at this stage. As I said, I haven't done the autopsy yet, but something tells me my findings are going to be no different. If not, I'll let you know, of course.'

On the way out the coroner's officer said to Theo: 'You want to take his possessions, clothing and stuff?' Theo nodded, and was handed a large plastic bag.

I hadn't said a single word since entering the building, and I was still silent until we were in the car and halfway back to Hampstead.

'Mind if I have a look?' I said, meaning Wheezy's things on the seat between us.

'Yes, I do mind,' he said in his distinct don't-mess-with-me tone of voice.

I left it at that. But he couldn't stop me looking at the bag and, since it was transparent, I noticed something that puzzled me. A piece of paper with the words Rupert Cornwell Fine Arts scrawled on it in pencil. Wheezy wasn't the kind of person who went to art galleries.

'Jesus, Theo, who the hell would want to kill someone as inoffensive as Wheezy Wallis?'

'Oh, I don't know. Any one of the scores of drug dealers he shopped to us, I suppose. Or their accomplices. He did help us put away a lot of pushers, you know, when he wasn't breaking into houses. That sort of thing can't be kept entirely secret for ever, and no doubt one of them finally caught up with him.'

'But still,' I protested, 'what kind of person would handcuff a guy in a car and watch him die?'

'Any number of people.' Theo was silent for a few seconds. Then he added: 'In the Talmud, Rabbi Hanania put it this way: "Were it not for the fear it inspires, every man would swallow his neighbour alive".'

14

Chapter Three

When we arrived back at the police station, Theo set off to find the Chief Super, no doubt to inform him that their simple suicide had turned into a murder inquiry, and to arrange for an incident room to be set up.

I used Theo's telephone to call Frankie Price in his taxi which, I knew, would still be waiting for me outside the Chalk Farm Hotel. Frankie was one of my few luxuries: an independent cab driver who worked for me during the day. Between nine o'clock in the morning and six in the evening on weekdays he was at my beck and call. Outside of those times, he was free to seek other fare-paying passengers, and he did. It was an arrangement which suited us both perfectly. For my part I had instant transport during the day, whenever I needed it, without the problem of having to find parking. Taxis, as everyone knows, can hang about on double yellow lines with apparent immunity from traffic wardens. The cab was fitted with a telephone, fax machine, air conditioning and even a small fridge in the front for occasional emergencies.

The arrangement suited Frankie perfectly too. He was something of a scholar, having already taken a BA in psychology through the Open University, and he was now working towards his Masters degree. Our deal enabled him to sit around in the cab for hours on end reading his books, writing his papers and planning his research projects; while being paid handsomely by me.

The only drawback was that he was a greedy sod who would switch the taxi's meter on at the stroke of six; and I also had to endure his particularly cheeky brand of Cockney humour.

15

Mind you, in the two years I had known him, Frankie had also proved himself to be a loyal friend who, on more than one occasion, had put his life and liberty on the line to help me out of a jam.

None of his cheeky Cockney humour was on display that morning when he collected me from the police station. I had immediately told him about Wheezy, and the drive to the *Hampstead Explorer* took place in a shocked silence.

When he drew up outside my office he asked me: 'Do they know who did it, Mr P?'

'Not yet, as far as I know.'

'Think they'll find the geezer?'

'I haven't a clue, Frankie.'

'They better had,' he said darkly.

I went inside to confront Arnie Bloch and steeled myself, as always, for the encounter. I am not a small feller, being around five feet eleven in my socks and respectably muscly in appropriate places, but I somehow always felt dwarfed by Bloch, even though he was a good four inches shorter than I. Partly it was to do with his bulk, but his brooding presence and dark scowl contributed a lot to the effect.

'So?!' barked my employee who was also my boss. 'Wotchoo got?' Fine particles of croissant sprayed the air between us.

I told him about Wheezy and, like a good newspaper man, the first thing he did was check his watch – to see whether there was still enough time to get something into that week's paper. The newspaper was printed late on Thursday afternoon, and the printers could often handle last minute changes in the morning.

'Five hundred words, fifteen minutes,' he said, retreating into his office and slamming the door.

The piece quickly took shape: a suspected suicide that had turned into a murder after the scene of the crime – and many possible clues – had been trampled over by a load of unobservant plods. I knew Theo would hate it. I also put in some background about Wheezy, glossing over his main career achievements somewhat in favour of his role as an undercover informant in the police's endless war against drugs. Wheezy, I

16

knew, would not resent being labelled posthumously as a grass on this subject; he had always been quietly proud of his role in putting druggies away.

A last minute check with Theo elicited the irritable response that no, the police did not yet have any suspects nor indeed any leads since, as I was well aware, the investigation had only just got under way, and yes I would be informed when and if there was anything the press should know about.

I had just finished my piece and sent it winging its electronic way towards the printers when my phone rang and Arnie's voice growled at me: 'Come in here, I want to talk to you.' My heart sank.

'Grab a cup of coffee,' he said as I walked into his office, gesturing towards his filter coffee machine. That shook me a little; Arnie didn't often entertain his staff with refreshments. He also pushed a plate of chocolate biscuits across his desk towards me. Not having had breakfast that morning I took two, and waited patiently for this unprecedented largesse to be explained.

'Phillips is leaving. He's got a job on the *Financial Times*,' he announced. Ed Phillips was our news editor, an irritating but talented young man who had done the job admirably since the departure of Andy Ferris eighteen months before.

'Ah. Good news for the *FT*, but bad news for us,' I responded.

'Yes, he's done well,' Arnie said. I waited. 'That leaves us without a news editor.'

'Yes.'

'Any suggestions?'

I pondered for a few moments. 'What about Roger or Paul? Both of them could do it with a bit of training and guidance.'

'What about you?' Arnie said.

'*Me*!?' My alarm was genuine. The last thing I wanted was to be tied down to a desk job. And I certainly didn't need the money.

'Why not? You've been here longer than any of them, and you could do the job with your eyes shut if you pulled your lazy finger out for a change. You'd also earn an extra five thousand a year.' He popped a whole chocolate biscuit into his mouth and grinned at me. The effect was disconcerting in the extreme.

17

I didn't know how to answer him. On the one hand I could not envisage doing the job, being stuck in the office most of the time, telling people what to do all of the time, and still carrying on running my other enterprises, not least of which was the Edwina Llewellyn Memorial Trust. But to turn it down flat would have been both insulting and highly suspicious – what impecunious journalist would instantly reject an important promotion and a five thousand pound increase?

'Arnie, I'm overwhelmed.' I wasn't joking. 'Have you cleared this with the general manager and Pendleton?' Ambrose was their only contact with my mysterious company which owned the newspaper through a complicated set of offshore concerns registered in Jersey.

'Not yet, but they've always accepted my recommendations in the past. Pendleton always just tells me to get on with it and do what I think fit.' I saw a ray of hope.

'I'm very honoured, and very grateful for the offer and, pending confirmation from Pendleton, I'd be delighted to do the job.'

'Good.'

'I presume Phillips will still be around for a few weeks?'

'Yes, there'll be time for him to show you the ropes.'

'Uh, Arnie ...'

'Yes?'

'Let's not say anything to any of the others about this. Until ... you know, until it's all confirmed, OK? You know how funny Pendleton can be sometimes, and I wouldn't want us to have egg all over our faces if he turns down the idea.'

'Why would he do that?'

'Still, just in case ...'

Arnie looked puzzled, but in the end he said: 'OK, if that's how you want it.' Then he clapped me on the shoulder as I left his office, leaving a bruise that would last for four days, and gave me another of those toothy grins. I flinched. All I could see were the remains of the chocolate biscuit, and instinct told me that there was maybe a thirty per cent chance that he might bite me.

I went back to the cubicle they called my office, closed the door securely, and dialled Ambrose Pendleton's private line.

'Help!' I said when he answered.

'Goodness me, what's the matter?' His voice was soothing.
'Bloch wants to promote me to news editor,' I complained.
'Congratulations!'
'You don't understand. I don't want to be news editor.'
'Why not?'
I explained. There was a short silence.
'Well then, I'll just veto the idea, shall I?'
'No, that's no good,' I groaned. 'Arnie would regard that as unacceptable interference in his editorial decisions, and would probably resign. At the very least it would put you at logger-heads with him and I don't want that. We need him; he's the best local newspaper editor I've ever seen.'
'Well, what then?'
'You'll just have to delay your decision when he comes to you with the suggestion. Stall him. Tell him that the owners are considering expanding the editorial staff and that no promotions can be made before all that is sorted out. Yes, Arnie will like the idea of getting more journalists. And in the meantime I'll think of a way of screwing up a bit here. I'll make some mistake that will convince Arnie that I couldn't do the job although, hopefully, not bad enough so that he'll fire me again.'
I put down the telephone and noticed that I was sweating. This could turn out to be a major spanner in my carefully contrived and balanced works.

Chapter Four

Lunch is normally a quiet sandwich with my feet up on my desk, but that day I was in need of comfort and solace.

'The Bluebelle,' I told Frankie as I climbed into the cab. I was rewarded by a happy grin for once. Frankie loved it when I ate at the Bluebelle, since it would give him a good hour in the Slug and Lettuce, his favourite hostelry and part, I was sorry to hear, of a popular and growing chain of pubs of the same name.

For the life of me I couldn't understand why anyone would voluntarily enter a place with a name like that, let alone order a salad there.

My manageress at the Bluebelle, Hazel Cowan, who of course didn't know she was my manageress, greeted me with a warmth befitting one of her best customers. Hazel was an old friend who used to work as a journalist on *Spotlight*, the theatre magazine. When I bought the restaurant, I got Pendleton to offer her the job as manageress, not only because of her wide contacts in the world of theatre, television and films, but also because of her personality – which was an appealing blend of bubbling bonhomie and efficiency. She had hesitated for less than a second before accepting the job, and although she had known nothing about the restaurant business, she had had all the right instincts, and the once fading eatery had gone from strength to strength.

What helped, of course, was that I paid wages higher than any comparable establishment in the catering world, with half the profits going direct to staff, as well as a fat bonus for every year that they managed to retain the top three-rosette rating in

20

the Michelin Guide. In spite of all this, the Bluebelle made a fat profit, which was transferred instantly to the coffers of the Edwina Llewellyn Memorial Trust.

Thus was the ill-gotten wealth of the rich redistributed to the poorest.

The place was usually fully booked, but Hazel kept a table free at all times for the odd celebrity who might pop in unexpectedly, or for her best customers – of which I was one.

'I don't know how you can afford to eat here so often,' Hazel said as she led me to a table, 'you being a penniless scribe and all that.'

'I know the owner,' I said, 'and he just gives me my money back.'

She laughed. 'I wish you did know the owner. I wish *I* knew the owner, for that matter. All I know is that there is this charming elderly man who comes by every now and then to look down my cleavage.' I made a mental note to mention that to Pendleton and watch him turn red.

'But of course, he's not the owner either, just some sort of lawyer. Nice man, though, and I must admit that they let me get on with it. And, seeing that we're not doing too badly, they must be pleased with what I'm doing.'

'I'm sure they are,' I said soothingly. 'But enough of this chit-chat. I am a hungry customer in need of the service this establishment is so famous for. Send over the waiter immediately.'

The food, as always, was excellent. I started with an individually baked onion tartlet served with a pot of grainy French mustard and the crispest Sancerre in the cellar. I kept the main course simple, and just had six enormous langoustines, lightly grilled, with a few fresh vegetables.

I also took it easy with the wine, since I had work to do that afternoon – one particular task being to visit the Rupert Cornwell Gallery in the chic St Christopher's Place shopping precinct, to see why Wheezy might have been carrying that piece of paper around with him.

I was thus perfectly sober and alert when Frankie dropped me at the entrance to St Christopher's Place an hour later. The gallery was one of those brightly lit, minimalist places with lots of space and nowhere to sit. But there was nothing minimalist about the art on the walls.

The works ranged from boring, but probably fabulously valuable old master type portraits, to paintings by Kokoschka, drawings by Hockney and relief works by Ben Nicholson which were much more to my taste. There was also a little alcove, somewhat less brightly lit, which contained a few original French impressionist paintings. No wonder there were three very large and very aggressive looking security guards prowling around and watching my every move. They seemed to be glaring at me with particular hostility but, knowing myself to be pure of heart, I dismissed them from my consciousness.

Apart from the guards there were one or two other browsers and a young woman sitting at a desk, pecking away with two fingers at a word processor. I noticed her immediately because she was an extremely attractive young woman, mid-twenties I estimated, wearing an interesting skirt made from what looked like crumpled silk – just like the one I had noticed in the window of the Whistles fashion shop next door. She was also wearing a loose black silk top with three-quarter length sleeves, scooped fairly low in front, showing off to perfection her smooth, tanned skin. I smiled at her; my warm, genuine one with lots of eye crinkle. She smiled back. I felt a whole new interest in art growing in me.

The whole focus of the gallery, however, was a large four-sided glass case in the centre of the floor, about six feet high, inside which was an old wooden easel holding an unframed canvas, about two feet high by eighteen inches across.

It was an oil painting of the torso of a young woman against a roughly drawn landscape. The girl was not beautiful in any classical sense – her features had a ruddy, country rudeness about them – but she stopped me in my tracks.

She had a grin on her face which could have been the teasing smirk of a tart; but could just as easily have been the naive grin of an innocent farm girl. The startling face was topped by an unruly halo of wild red hair flecked with small pieces of straw, which also thrust an inevitable ambiguity into the mind of the viewer: had she been rolling in a haystack, or diligently working in the fields? She wore a dirty red peasant smock, suspiciously creased, or naturally worked in, depending on how you wanted to look at it. The smock was unbuttoned at the throat; one button more than pure chasteness would demand, but one button less than wantonness would require. There was an alertness and freshness in her eyes that insisted on the viewer's attention and, as in all great paintings, the overall effect was far more powerful than the sum of its parts.

I knew little about painting, but even I could see the genius in the work. The paint had been applied not in the careful, almost disguised manner of the classical masters, but boldly and instinctively, with sweeping brushstrokes, which made even more remarkable the subtlety and depth achieved.

There was no signature on the painting, but a small plaque on the easel read:

François Bretton (1838-1879)
Portrait of Silvie c. 1858?

I wasn't a complete ignoramus. I had, of course, heard the name, and had seen many reproductions of his paintings, including the two in the National Gallery and the three in the Louvre. But I had also seen this one before somewhere. I tried to think where, but nothing came to me. I must have stood there gazing at it for a good ten minutes.

Then I became aware of someone standing next to me and I turned my head. He was a tall, thin and ascetic man, dressed in a plain black suit with a classy little brass Rupert Cornwell Gallery plaque on the lapel. He looked slightly perturbed, nay, even a little anxious, and I wondered for a moment whether my reaction to the painting had been unusual in some way. I instantly dismissed the thought and decided that, being a conscientious gallery worker, and one who could recognise a wealthy art collector at a hundred paces, he had come forth to schmooze and to solicit my opinion.

Thus when he inclined his head towards me with the clear intention of saying something in a discreet manner, I too inclined my head.

'Perhaps you are unaware,' he whispered, 'but I regret to say you have tracked dog mess all over the gallery floor.'

There followed one of those petrified tableaus in which, for a good few seconds, I looked at him uncomprehendingly,

23

wondering desperately whether he had actually said the words I thought I had heard.

But time passes, and eventually I had to look down. And yes, there was a horrendous lump of dog shit adhering to my right shoe, and yes, there was a meandering series of brown shoe prints nicely contrasting with the pale ash wooden floor.

I don't think Oscar Wilde himself, the all-time master of repartee, could have produced a jaunty rejoinder in such circumstances, and nothing much occurred to me.

'Ah,' I said, hoarsely.

'Yes.'

'I'm terribly sorry,' I added.

'Yes, but perhaps you could, er ...' – he was pointing vaguely towards the door – 'deal with it. Outside, I mean.'

A dignified gait is not easy when you are being stared at with hostility by three security men, frowned at by a gallery employee, gaped at by four customers and giggled at by a disturbingly attractive young woman, and you have what feels like a gigantic mound of excrement attached to your foot. But I got to the door somehow without falling over. Outside, I sort of limped nonchalantly up St Christopher's Place, hoping madly that the gorgeous salesgirls at Whistles weren't watching my progress, and I did what had to be done against a lonely tuft of grass at the corner of Wigmore Street.

I noticed Frankie looking at me impassively from where he was parked on a double yellow line.

'Just one word, even a single word, and you're fired,' I remarked as I got in the back. He said nothing, although I swear there was a hint of a smirk on his lips, and the bastard opened both front windows.

'Where to, guv, Hampstead?'

'No, Wheezy's place. Let's go and pay our respects.' That took the smile off his face.

Chapter Five

Wheezy's house was in Kelly Street, a delightful road full of two-storey Victorian houses which formed the only conservation area in the whole of Kentish Town. A number of the houses were owned by the council, and some by a housing association, but Wheezy's, in the middle of the terrace, had been his own.

The family had had a property in Kings Cross somewhere, left by his father, but Wheezy had sold it years ago and moved up market to NW5. I don't think he ever had a mortgage, and I always suspected that the house was the result of one of his more successful jobs, but Wheezy had never volunteered information about his financial affairs, and I had never asked.

All I did know was that there were frequent periods when Wheezy had been completely skint, including one occasion when he – together with the rest of the regulars in his local pub – had been tricked out of thousands of pounds by a clever con-man who had thought up a darling of a betting wheeze with a specially modified tape recorder. I had had to bale him out that time, through the Edwina Llewellyn Memorial Fund, of course. I wondered how Maisie was going to manage with four children, one an infant, without him.

The house was, as always, immaculate on the outside, and looking very pretty in the June sunshine. The curtains were drawn, and there was no sign of the mourning and grief that I knew was being experienced inside. Frankie parked the cab and came with me up the garden path.

The door was opened by Wheezy's brother, George, who I knew lived nearby somewhere, and ran a market stall in

Queen's Crescent on Thursdays and Saturdays. A lot of his merchandise had come from Wheezy's activities, and I wondered how he was going to survive without his brother. He looked pale, and his eyes were red.

'Mr P, Frankie, nice of you to come.' He led the way to the front room which, although smoky and crowded with people, was full of quiet sadness. Maisie was sitting on the couch with three of her children, the baby on her lap and one child on either side of her. The oldest boy, Nicholas, who was about twelve, was standing with a man I recognised as Uncle Herbert, the brother of Wheezy's late father, who lived with them. A woman was pouring tea from a large teapot.

I went over to Maisie and put a hand on her shoulder. 'I just wanted to say how sorry I am,' I said.

She looked at me in that desperate way that people have when they are recently and shockingly bereaved. Her eyes were also red, and she dabbed at them frequently with a handkerchief she held crushed in her hand.

'The Bill say that he killed himself, Mr P. That he put a hose in the car and didn't leave a note. Do you believe that?' Her voice was cracked, but she was in control.

'No,' I replied. I had spoken softly, but the impact of the word spread through the gathering like a forest fire and there was suddenly a deep quiet. 'I was at the mortuary this morning, and it wasn't suicide.'

I looked at George and nodded towards the children. He spoke quickly into the ear of a woman next to me who gathered them together and took them out of the room. The baby stayed with Maisie. Everyone was looking at me expectantly.

'The simple fact is that Wheezy was murdered,' I said into a shocked silence. 'The pathologist found bruising on his wrists and ankles, which suggest that he was handcuffed into the car while the engine was running. It was made to look like a suicide. I thought you ought to know.'

The silence lasted a few more seconds, and was then broken by George. 'I knew it! He'd never do that to hisself. Not Wheezy.' There were murmurs of agreement from all over the room. Maisie was looking at me intently.

'Do they know who did it?' she asked quietly. The room fell silent again.

'No, they haven't a clue yet. And because they initially thought it was suicide, some of the forensic evidence may have been lost.'

'The Bill should've come here to tell us, shouldn't they?' George said.

'They should have,' I agreed, 'and I'm sure they will. They'll also want to ask a lot of questions, of course.'

'They always do,' Maisie said wearily. I was sure she had endured many visits from policemen asking questions during her years with Wheezy. The conversations started up again, a little louder now that there was new information to discuss, and an enveloping group of people closed round Maisie.

Someone put a cup of tea into my hand, and I found myself talking to George. 'You got any ideas about this?'

'Not a clue, so help me God,' he said.

'Did he seem worried lately? Acting strangely? Anything like that?'

'Not that I noticed. He was just Wheezy, you know? He hadn't even been busy for a couple of weeks, if you know what I mean.'

'How's Maisie fixed? I mean as far as money goes?' I asked.

'She's OK for now. Seems Wheezy did a bit good a little while ago and there's some dosh in the building society.' That seemed like something that deserved some further investigation, but I didn't think then was the right time. I spoke to a few more people, none of whom could think of any reason why Wheezy could have been murdered. More than a few uttered dark threats about what they might do to the person who did it.

I looked around the room to see if there was anyone else I knew, but my glance was arrested by a dark patch on the wall above the mantelpiece. It was the sort of dark patch a picture causes as the light fades the paint around it, and it measured about eighteen inches by two feet. Now I remembered where I had seen that portrait of the girl with red hair before. But, not knowing it was by François Bretton, I hadn't taken much notice of it.

I felt that excitement at the pit of my stomach that you get when you start putting things together, and I knew then that this picture had something to do with Wheezy's death. But what? Wheezy must have had a copy of the painting, and

27

perhaps he had seen the one at the gallery, the original. That didn't quite make sense; Wheezy wasn't the type to browse through posh art galleries. Anyway, it wasn't here now, and I wanted to know why.

I went over to say goodbye to Maisie, and she grabbed my hand and thanked me for coming. 'By the way,' I said as casually as possible, 'what happened to the picture that was on the wall over there?'

She looked puzzled for a moment, and there was no guile or deception in her face. 'I don't know. I think Wheezy sold it for a few quid.' There was no doubt in my mind that she was speaking the truth, but I was concentrating on something else. In the corner of my eye I saw someone stiffen, turn round and listen closely to what she said. It was Uncle Herbert, and when I looked up he was staring at me intently. But now was not the time. I smiled warmly at him, offered my condolences again, shook hands with a few more people, and then Frankie and I left.

As we walked out of the gate, I saw Theo and the DCI getting out of their car. We waited for them to walk up.

'You should have been here hours ago,' I said quite sharply. Theo sighed his patient sigh, the one he used for humouring pesky journalists.

'You're right, I suppose. In an ideal world we would have been able to tell her immediately, and we would also have found the murderer and extracted a confession. The fact is, however, that this is the real world, and there are other demands on us too. We came when we could.'

'You're not going to get a very friendly reception inside there,' I warned him.

'We're used to that,' the DCI said, without any humour.

Theo winked at me: 'Happy is he who hears an insult and ignores it; for a hundred evils will have passed him by.'

'Tell them about the Talmud,' I suggested.

'I might just do that,' Theo said.

Chapter Six

'Did you have a good lunch?' Arnie Bloch growled at me sarcastically when I got back to the office at about half past four. It was uncanny the way he was able to haunt every corner of the building; there was only about one chance in a million of slipping in or out of the newsroom unobserved by his ever-roving glance.

'Been working, Arnie,' I said lamely. He had this way of making you feel guilty even if you were as pure as the driven snow.

'Oh yeah?'

'I've been speaking to Mrs Wallis, Wheezy's wife, and other members of the family.'

'They know anything?'

'They hadn't even been told that it wasn't suicide and that the police were launching a murder inquiry,' I explained.

'That's a good story in itself,' he said.

'Yes,' I said, hoping he was finished with me. I had some phone calls to make. But Arnie was not finished.

'I've got something I want you to do.'

'Me?'

'Yes, you! Do you see me talking to somebody else?' I hated it when he raised his voice like that. It made everyone stop work and look over in our direction, that look of vague relief on their faces, pleased that they weren't on the receiving end. 'I want you to sort out the photographer's diary for tomorrow. Roger will show you how to do it.' He walked away.

My heart sank. This, I realised, was the beginning of the process of instruction that would lead towards me becoming news editor.

It took Roger about three minutes to explain the mysteries of the photographer's diary to me. Essentially it was a process of finding out from the production staff how many pictures would probably be required over the next few days, and then choosing the most likely jobs from the many possibilities that had been put into the diary.

I could have done it in my sleep, but the thought of having to do such boring administrative tasks made me shudder with horror. I looked carefully at the photocall options listed, and at the weekly diary of the mayor's activities supplied to us by Camden Council, and I made some highly creative choices.

Then I went to the glassed-off recess in the wall that was laughingly described as my office, and picked up the phone. I dialled the number of the *Daily Telegraph* and asked to speak to Nigel Regan, the arts editor, who had started his career on the *Hampstead Explorer*.

'Is this going to cost me a lunch?' he asked when he heard my voice. I hadn't spoken to him for some time, probably not since my inheritance, and I had forgotten that there had been times in the past when I had been forced to scrounge the occasional meal from slightly more pecuniously advantaged friends.

'No, Nigel, in fact the next lunch will be on me – at a restaurant of your choice.' There was a suspicious silence.

'You won the pools, then?'

'Not quite. You might have read about my house burning down and, well, I am expecting the pay-out from the insurance company any day now.'

'Ah yes, I do remember something about it. An arson attack, wasn't it?'

'Yes.'

'So we had better schedule this lunch sometime soon; before you spend all the money, that is.' There was a pause while he chuckled. I wondered how he would chuckle if he knew I had more money than I could ever spend. 'So, what do I have to do for this lunch?'

'Just tell me about François Bretton,' I said.

'You mean now, on the phone? That's all?' He still sounded suspicious.

'Yup.'

30

'Well, I assume you're referring to the business about the Bretton at the Cornwell Gallery?'

'Tell me about it,' I said.

'It was in all the papers, Parker, even the tabloids. It's been the event of the decade in the art world, and everyone is terribly excited about it.'

'I must have missed it. No offence, but art is not my speciality. I have been known to skip a few pages every now and then.'

I heard him take a deep breath. 'I suppose you've heard of Bretton, though?'

'Yes, and I've even seen some of his paintings. There are a couple in the National Gallery and three in the Louvre.'

'Very good! So you know enough to understand why the sudden appearance of a new Bretton, or rather the reappearance of an old Bretton, is big news in the art world?'

'I think so,' I lied. I didn't fool Nigel for a second, and he sighed again.

'OK, I'll summarise from the beginning. Listen carefully. You have François Bretton, a virtually self-taught artist, born somewhere around 1840, brought up in a small town in Brittany, arrives penniless in Paris around the age of twenty with a bagful of charming paintings of rural landscapes and country folk. Although his style and technique are highly unorthodox, Paris takes the yokel to its breast and his pictures start selling like hot cakes.

'After a while he's so popular that he can name his own price for portraits and commissions and his coffers are overflowing. The trouble is he becomes more interested in making money than painting pictures, and within a few years he stops painting altogether. He becomes a property developer, a very successful one, and absolutely filthy, stinking rich.

'Had the story ended there he would have gone down in history as a popular and gifted artist whose main claim to fame was that his ideas and techniques were way ahead of his time. But the story didn't end there. As he got older and richer he became more and more eccentric, and his most enduring eccentricity was his passion for buying back his paintings. It was more than a passion, it became an obsession and he would pester and hound owners, many of whom had previously been valued patrons, until they sold him the pictures he wanted.

'Then he seemed to go completely mad – possibly alcohol, possibly syphilis, probably both – and that's when he committed the deed that ensured his everlasting fame, or notoriety, depending on how you look at it. He burned the lot. Every painting he had. Nearly three hundred canvases, piled onto a huge bonfire and set alight. Parisian society was scandalised.'

'Wow!' I said.

'Wow, indeed. Bretton died only a few years later, aged forty-one I think, which supports the syphilis theory. But the point is that there are only something like thirty or forty of his paintings still in existence. And, as you know, what is scarce is very valuable, and on the incredibly rare occasions that they come onto the market, they fetch astronomical sums.'

'What sort of astronomical sums?' I asked.

'Millions. The Getty museum bought one a few years ago in a private deal with a collector, but the figure was rumoured to have been over four million.'

'So what about this one at the Cornwell Gallery?'

'Ah, well, as I've explained, the appearance of any Bretton is going to cause a stir in the art world, but this one was especially newsworthy because it had last been heard of in 1966 when it was stolen in a burglary. There was quite a lot of publicity about the theft at the time because, apart from the fact that it was a Bretton that had been stolen, it turned out that the painting had not been insured.'

I was amazed. 'Who would have a Bretton and not insure it?'

'His name was Munro Forbes, and the reason he didn't insure it was that he couldn't afford to. Mr Forbes, it seemed, was the tail end of a once very wealthy family with a big house in Suffolk which had become progressively impoverished through a series of failed business deals and death duties. He had a number of valuable pictures, but instead of paying thousands a year in insurance premiums, he spent some of his dwindling loot on burglar proofing and alarms. Fat lot of good that did him.'

'So how come it has suddenly turned up again now?'

'Well, this is the mysterious part. Rupert Cornwell claims that Munro Forbes had managed, secretly, to buy the painting

32

back from the burglars, which is not an altogether uncommon occurrence. The story he tells suggests that they, the burglars, must have realised that the picture was unfenceable – so well known and so valuable that the thieves knew they could never get rid of it. Cornwell claims they sold it back to Forbes for some paltry amount, twenty thousand pounds or something like that, and that Forbes put the picture in a cupboard and never told a soul that he'd got it back. Frightened it would be stolen again, the story goes.

'Apparently, the first anyone knew of all this was when old man Forbes died a year or so ago and the painting was discovered by his daughter, carefully wrapped up together with a written account of its recovery. There had also been a son, but he was killed in a car accident about ten years ago. Anyway, this daughter brought the painting to Cornwell, who is planning to auction it next month. Some people say it could sell for around six million pounds or more, which would mean a cool million or more for the gallery, depending on what kind of commission they're on.'

'It's genuine, of course?' I was ever the cynic.

'Oh, no question about that. Cornwell wheeled in some French professor who is recognised as *the* world expert on Bretton who had no hesitation in pronouncing it the genuine article.

'Cornwell is an excellent PR man, and he's milked every inch of the story for coverage. He even managed to interest the tabloids in the affair, selling them the "painting too valuable for thieves to get rid of" angle, and the *Sun* then ran a list of twenty famous burglars – all dead – who could have been the ones wot done it.

'Privately, I've heard less gullible people suggest that this Munro Forbes was a very odd gentleman indeed, and that there is a good chance that the paintings were never stolen in the first place. They think he hid them to stop them from being stolen, and reported the theft in order to keep the burglars away ... well, you understand the reasoning, I'm sure.'

I could understand the reasoning, and I could understand why the art world was agog at the discovery of a painting believed lost in the 1960s. I could understand why everyone was excited about the auction. But what I couldn't understand is how Wheezy Wallis fitted into all this.

I thanked Nigel Regan, promised to ring him about lunch, and hung up.

It had been a long and distressing day. I had been arrested, forced to look at the murdered body of a friend and humiliated in an art gallery. I was puzzled and bewildered, and on top of it all I had been threatened with promotion at work.

I went back to the hotel, skipped dinner, had a long hot bath and was fast asleep by nine o'clock.

Chapter Seven

The next day was Friday, usually a quiet day at the *Hampstead Explorer*, except for the complaints that roll in on publication day from advertisers claiming we got their ads wrong, from people telling us we got our facts wrong, and from PR people wondering why we hadn't run stories about their clients.

I took one call from the grandmother of a man from Camden Town who, we had reported in that day's paper, had been given a long prison sentence for raping and murdering his former girlfriend.

''Ere, you got your bleeding facts wrong!' she complained.

'Which facts, exactly?' I inquired. I had covered the case myself and had sat in court questioning whether I really was against the use of capital punishment for men like him.

'Well, your articule says that my grandson held a blanket over her face.'

'Yes.'

'Well, that's not true. It were a towel.'

I waited in silence, but that was it. She didn't say anything else.

'That's it?' I said.

'You should get your facts straight!'

I considered some sort of sarcastic rejoinder about how difficult it would be for him now to hold his head up in prison when it became known that he had used a towel instead of a blanket, but I said nothing. Realising that your grandson is a monster is hard enough without some journalist adding to the grief. I told her we were very sorry about the mistake, and that I appreciated her call.

Then I put the telephone down and went back to working on my story about a series of break-ins in Hampstead which, I was sure, were being committed by the same burglar.

The event that I had been praying for took place just when I was becoming desperate, at about half past twelve. Someone telephoned the newsdesk to report that a house was on fire in Belsize Avenue and four fire engines were on the scene.

A reporter was dispatched immediately and Arnie shouted: 'Where's Wyndham?' Michael Wyndham was our photographer.

There was a short but uncomfortable silence before Amanda Popplewell, one of the reporters, looked in the photographer's diary and replied: 'He's in Milton Keynes.'

'*He's where*?' Arnie bellowed.

'Milton Keynes,' she repeated nervously. I took a deep breath in my cubbyhole of an office and waited for the shit storm to break over me. I was ready for it.

'*Who the almighty fuck sent him all the sodding way to Milton Keynes*?' Arnie shouted. All eyes turned to look in my direction, and two seconds later Arnie appeared in my doorway with an alarmingly purple face.

'Why did you send a photographer to Milton Keynes?' he hissed, desperately trying to keep his temper.

'National Association of Labour Mayors meeting, Arnie. Camden's Mayor is there and I thought it would be a good idea ...'

He looked at me for a few seconds, his eyes threatening to pop from his skull, then he turned on his heel. 'OK, get whatshisname, Irving, the freelance, onto it,' he called to poor Amanda. There was another uncomfortable silence.

'Irving's in Richmond, Arnie,' she said, 'Some Camden schoolchildren visiting ...' She didn't get a chance to finish. Arnie turned again and looked at me.

'You sent Wyndham to Milton Keynes and Irving to bloody Richmond? At the same time?' They weren't so much questions as statements of wonderment.

'I thought ...'

But Arnie clearly didn't want to hear what I had thought. He stormed off towards his office, pausing only to yell at poor Amanda: 'Get someone, *anyone*, who knows how to use a camera!' And then he slammed the door so hard that I expected the glass to leap out and shatter on the floor.

Arnie never spoke to me again about the incident and, I can happily report, he never again asked me to organise the photographer's diary. The only comeback I had was a note scrawled across my next expenses claim when it was returned to me, unpaid. It read: 'Your expenses were used to send photographers to Milton Keynes and Richmond.' I considered the money very well spent.

Everyone smiled at me sympathetically when I left the office at about two o'clock. Arnie had his head down in some papers and pretended not to see me pass his office. No doubt he couldn't trust himself to speak to me without making a grab for my throat.

I directed Frankie towards St Christopher's Place again. I had made an appointment to interview Rupert Cornwell about his amazing painting and, despite the short notice, he had readily agreed.

When I walked into the gallery I got a brilliant smile from the receptionist, determined scowls from the security guards and a horrified look from the effete man in black who instantly moved his glance down my body to check my shoes.

'It's OK,' I called across to him, gaily. 'Absolutely no dog shit this time! I checked!' A look of real pain crossed his face as a number of art browsers looked up in alarm. I ignored them all and walked up to the receptionist's desk. I gave her another of my warm smiles. Thirty per cent eye crinkle. Didn't want to overdo it.

'Hi,' I said.

'Hi.'

I liked the way she could smile and speak at the same time. 'What's your name?' I asked.

'Erica.'

I handed her one of my cards. 'My name's Parker, and I have an appointment to see Mr Cornwell.' Her eyes widened slightly.

'From the *Hampstead Explorer*, right?' she giggled. Erica really was gorgeous, but I wondered how much grey matter there was between the ears.

37

'The very one,' I said.

She got up, looked over her shoulder at me and said: 'Walk this way please, Mr Parker.'

There was no way I could have walked that way. For a start I wasn't wearing a very short skirt and very high heels, but in any case there were fundamental differences in our anatomies that would have made it very difficult for me to get the same rhythm to the wiggle. But I did my best, concentrating intently on her behind, where most of the movement seemed to be centred, and I followed her through a door behind her reception desk, up a staircase (where my concentration never wavered), and along a corridor. We stopped outside a door, and she knocked.

A voice said: 'Who?'

'Mr Parker for you, Mr Cornwell,' Erica said in the kind of sing-song voice that I thought only secretaries on television had. A moment later the door was opened and I was confronted by one of the most handsome men I have ever seen.

His face reminded me of actors like Paul Newman and Rutger Hauer, not just because of the strong, clean lines and even, well-proportioned features, but because he had those dramatically piercing pale blue eyes which are so much more arresting when they are possessed by men with tanned skin and dark hair.

He was wearing a dark blue Paul Smith suit with an exquisitely subtle silk tie, all of which hung on his slim and athletic frame as if the designer had had him in mind for the clothes in the first place. He put out a slender, perfectly manicured hand and drew me into the room. His teeth flashed, brilliantly white and perfectly even, when he smiled at my guide.

'Thank you, Erica. We'll have some coffee, please.' She blushed deeply to the very roots of her hair which, I had noticed, were somewhat darker than the rest of her hair, and closed the door behind me. Cornwell waved me towards a chair.

'I know the *Explorer* well, of course. You're my local paper,' he said. The only thing that jarred with me was his accent: far too rounded and bursting with over-ripe plums for my liking.

'Oh? Where do you live?'

'Just up from Wyldes Farm, on the Heath. Do you know it?'

I nodded. I knew it; an exclusive little enclave of stunning properties on the edge of Hampstead Heath, behind the famous Old Bull and Bush pub.

'You are, presumably, the arts correspondent,' he said pompously, settling in his chair behind a leather-topped desk covered with piles of photographs and exhibition catalogues.

'Uh, not exactly arts, but I'm very interested in the François Bretton you have downstairs,' I replied. He beamed at me and the thought of more publicity for his auction.

'What do you want to know?'

'Everything.'

He was charming, I had to give him that. He began to tell me the story I had heard from Nigel Regan the day before, but a somewhat longer and more detailed version. I took notes. During the tale Erica arrived with coffee, and blushed deeply again when he thanked her and touched her hand. She was so obviously smitten with him that I was surprised she had had the sensual energy to respond to my own paltry smile earlier on.

Eventually, he summed up. 'All in all, the particular circumstances of the discovery of this picture, quite apart from its inherent artistic merit, make this the most important artistic find of the century.'

'It's a very powerful painting,' I agreed.

'Oh yes, very fine. Quite a wench that Silvie must have been!'

'Is anything known about her?'

'Quite a bit, apparently, according to Professor Beaumanoir. His theory is that Bretton was in love with her and he left for Paris only when she spurned his affections.'

'Professor Beaumanoir, he's the man who authenticated the painting?'

'That's right, Robert Beaumanoir. He's widely accepted as the world expert on Bretton. He came over from France and had no hesitation in declaring it one hundred per cent genuine.'

'Would I be able to talk to him?' I asked. Cornwell hesitated, but only for a second or two.

'I don't see why not. He's a perfectly jovial sort of chap, full of interesting anecdotes and that sort of thing. Hang on, I'll give you his telephone number.' He opened an address book, found the name, and read me a string of numbers, which I wrote down.

'Is that his office number?' I asked.

'He's retired now, of course. Lives in a delightful spot called Cap Ferret.'

'On the Mediterranean?'

'No, that's Cap Ferrat. This is Cap Ferret, a lovely town at the end of the Arcachon peninsula, on the Atlantic coast, about fifty kilometres due west of Bordeaux.'

The interview had gone really well, and Cornwell and I were getting on famously. But I hadn't come a step closer to the information I really wanted. I felt as though I was looking into a perfectly clear pool where, although the water was absolutely unclouded, there was absolutely nothing to see. In situations like that, the only thing you can do is take a sharp stick, stir up the mud at the bottom and see what swirls into view. I took a deep breath.

'What had Albert Wallis to do with all this?' I asked.

I was watching him carefully, and I didn't miss the signs. Cornwell's eyes changed focus and seemed to lose some of their brightness. It was as if a portcullis had crashed down in front of those sparkling peepers and dulled them. There was no sharp intake of breath, no blink or change of expression, but his complexion did pale by one delicate shade.

'Who? I beg your pardon?' There was innocence and puzzlement in his voice, but guilt in his eyes and pallid brow.

'Albert Wallis, a burglar, sometimes known as Wheezy. Someone murdered him the night before last. Handcuffed him into his car and gassed him with the exhaust.' Cornwell's face greyed another shade, his eyes dulled a little more.

'Do you know, I haven't the faintest idea what you are talking about,' he said, his voice entirely normal.

'Of course you do,' I said quietly. He shrugged, as if perplexed.

'You did say that you were the arts correspondent?'

'No, that's what you said. I am the crime reporter, and I'm working on a murder story. I know Wheezy Wallis was here, and that he must have spoken to you and I'd like to know what it was all about. If it was something innocent and above-board you wouldn't be lying to me now.' Cornwell was looking at me as if I was talking gibberish, his brow furrowed with an apparent effort to understand.

'Mr Parker, I assure you again, I haven't the faintest idea ...'

'The police also know he was here.'

His composure was unwavering. The perplexed look on his face deepened as we looked at each other for a few seconds. Then he stood up.

'I'm sorry. Look, this has gone off at an extraordinary tangent and, quite frankly, you've lost me completely. I do, however, have lots of things I need to do, so perhaps we can finish now. I'll show you out.' The last phrase was very pointed.

I made no effort to resist, and followed him down the stairs and through into the gallery. On my way out I winked at Erica, and she smiled. The eyes of the burly security men, and those of the somewhat less burly black-suited man, followed me across the gallery.

Cornwell opened the door for me. 'I'm sorry I don't know your Mr Wallis. But I can't see what all this has to do with the Bretton, which is what I thought you wanted to speak to me about this afternoon.'

I looked at him levelly. 'Never mind, Mr Cornwell. I'm sure I'll be seeing you again. Maybe we can discuss it further.' He shrugged and shut the door behind me.

When I was sitting in his office I was wholly convinced that Cornwell was lying. By the time I got into Frankie's cab I was beginning to wonder whether I could have made a mistake. And by the time we were halfway home I was wondering whether I had made a massive fool of myself.

I had a fantasy about being cross-examined in court. 'Tell the court, Mr Parker, why you thought the plaintiff, who is suing you for slander and is seeking damages of fifty-two million pounds, was lying.'

'His eyes dulled, your honour.'

'His eyes dulled?'

'Yes, they seemed to lose their focus.'

'Lose their focus?'

'Yes. And then he seemed to go a whiter shade of pale, your honour ...'

41

It sounded absurd, and I knew it. Maybe Cornwell never had heard of Wheezy. Maybe Wheezy had just gone there to have a look at the original of the copy he had at home; he could have read about the painting in the papers and recognised it. Anyone would have been interested enough to do that. Why had I assumed that the people at the gallery would have had to have had some dealings with him? And, even if I was correct, why had I just tipped Cornwell off to the fact? Why hadn't I just spoken to Theo and left it all to the police for a change?

By the time Frankie had fought his way through the Friday evening traffic and dropped me at the hotel, I was feeling thoroughly depressed and confused.

I checked my diary and found no social engagements at all for that weekend (how's that for the busy life of a multimillionaire?) so I telephoned Professor Beaumanoir in France. He spoke perfect English, was perfectly charming and, when I suggested I might be in the Bordeaux area the following day, he was good enough to invite me to visit him.

The next call was to Air France to book a seat on the Saturday morning seven o'clock flight to Bordeaux's Merignac airport. I shuddered at the thought of having to get up so early in the morning, but one has to make sacrifices for art. Then I rang a car hire company which told me that if I wanted to hire a Porsche I would have to take a taxi into Bordeaux itself, since such items were not usually kept at the airport.

I was just about to order dinner in my room when the telephone rang.

'Mr Parker?' A woman's voice.

'This is indeed he.'

'This is Erica, you know, from the Cornwell Gallery.' Walk this way ...

'I remember you well,' I said.

'I was just wondering if you were free this evening.' She sounded nervous.

'I am entirely untethered and unencumbered,' I replied.

'Pardon?'

'I'm free.'

'Oh good, because I am going to be in Hampstead this evening and I thought it would be nice to have a drink with you.'

'A delightful idea. Should we meet somewhere?'

'Or I could come to your hotel. There's a bar there, isn't there? Because I'm picking something up at Camden Lock and I'm going to be in the area anyway. It's right there.' The words gushed out.

I wondered how she knew where I lived, but I said: 'Of course, my hotel is fine. I'll meet you in the bar and I might even buy you dinner if you're good. What time?'

She giggled. Perhaps with relief. 'About eight?'

'I can't wait,' I said. She giggled again. 'See you then,' I said, and managed to hang up.

That would give me just enough time to have a bath, pack for my little trip to France, and get downstairs in time to meet a startlingly beautiful young woman. It would be an interesting evening. Not very stimulating, perhaps, but interesting. And so what if she bleached her hair?

Chapter Eight

In fact I was a few minutes late, and I was telephoned by the front desk.

'There's a young lady to see you, a Miss Erica Kennedy. She's waiting in the bar.'

'Thanks, I'll be down in a sec.'

'Mr Parker?'

'Yes?'

'Wow.'

'I know, I know.'

The first floor bar of the Chalk Farm Hotel is normally a jolly sort of place, humming with well oiled conversation by people who appreciate my cut-price alcohol. But when I walked in there was an unusual hush, and I suspected it had something to do with Erica, who had perched herself on a bar stool and was being gurgled at by Ben, the barman.

Erica was wearing black tights with a hint of glitter in them. Her legs seemed to stretch into eternity, disappearing at the very last moment under a tight and extremely short black outfit apparently made of some sort of stretchy material. The bottom half of her was arresting enough, but it was the top half that held almost every gaze in the room. The top half of the heretoforeabovementioned outfit was strapless, backless and almost frontless, the garment being held up by what I assumed was a small nuclear reactor. Nothing else could have had the strength to keep that bosom covered. To be fair, she was wearing a silky and diaphanous wrap around her shoulders, but given that it was an almost transparent garment, it actually added to the overall effect. Which was spectacular.

When I say that Ben the barman was gurgling at her, I mean that he was probably asking her whether she desired to order a drink, but he was being somewhat tongue-tied about it. 'We'll have champagne, Ben,' I said as I walked up. Erica turned, flashed me a brilliant smile, pulled me down by the hand and planted a kiss on my cheek as if we were old, old friends. Rays of hatred from just about every man in the room burned holes in the back of my jacket.

I led her to one of the vacant booths along the big windows overlooking the famous Round House theatre and the wasteland known as the Chalk Farm railway lands. Behind me I heard Ben pop the cork from a bottle of a 1982 Gold Label Veuve Clicquot. It's not that I recognised the pop, you understand, but I knew Ben knew what I liked to drink.

'You do live here, don't you, in this hotel, I mean?' she asked.

'At the moment I do. I had a house, but it burned down so I moved in here.'

'Oh.'

Why did I have this feeling that she didn't really care where I lived?

'How did you know that I lived here, anyway?' I asked.

Panic momentarily flashed across her face. 'I telephoned your office. They told me,' she explained.

It was a lie. Giving out a journalist's home telephone number, let alone a home address, to a member of the public, was one of the worst crimes you could commit at the *Hampstead Explorer*. But I let it pass; I was much more interested in finding out why she had come to see me.

Ben poured the bubbly and looked disgusted, as always, when I stuck a finger in my glass and wiggled it about to get rid of some of the fizz. We then clinked glasses.

'So, to what do I owe this very great pleasure?' She blushed, and the results were slightly disconcerting, since she was wearing so much make-up that the natural colouring only showed through in a few uncovered blotches. Why such a naturally beautiful woman would want to plaster herself with bright green eye shadow (outlined heavily in black), lipstick and about half an inch of cream foundation and rouge was beyond me.

'Well, as I said, I was in the area, and I thought it would be nice to have a drink with you.'

'It is nice,' I agreed, 'but I can't help wondering why.'

She sipped her Champagne in what could have been interpreted as a sexy way. 'Didn't you want to have a drink with me?'

'Of course I do,' I said. Let it go, Parker, I told myself. If there is any ulterior motive, it will become apparent.

Erica proved to be one of those people who generate an air of empty desperation around them, not by being morose or silent but by chatting on gaily about things that would even have bored the dirty raincoat off a reporter from the *Daily Star*. She drank more than her fair share of the Veuve Clicquot, and as the bubbles carried the alcohol swiftly into her bloodstream, her already loosened tongue came adrift completely.

She told me how wonderful Mr Cornwell was; how she had first come to the gallery as a temp; how impressed Mr Cornwell had been with her typing; and, in detail, how he had insisted to the agency that she come to work for the gallery full time. She prattled on about the gallery and its customers, mentioning names I had never heard before with a deep reverence, and minor names I had heard of with an almost religious adoration.

After a while I took her through to the restaurant where she also failed utterly to appreciate the subtleties of the steamed sea bass with samphire and potatoes prepared by my chef, Claude Delors (no relation), whom I had liberated from a restaurant in Reims with flattery and ridiculous amounts of money. 'Lovely fish,' she agreed, when I asked her how she was enjoying the food, 'but the sauce has made the chips soggy.'

These were not chips, but delicious morsels of pommes de terre Dauphinoise in a subtle cream and gruyère sauce.

We drank, or rather she drank and I sipped, a delicate and very expensive Chablis and, with dessert, a golden honeyed Loupiac from a winery aptly named Domaine du Paradis, while she told me her favourite wine was 'Leebfrownmilk' and her favourite drink was Malibu with lemonade.

I was regaled by tales drawn from the private lives of gallery staff, including some of the marital problems of the security guards (one had a wife who just did not understand him), her considered thoughts on supermarket shopping, and the relative attractions of various Spanish holiday resorts. By eleven o'clock I was close to running amok and killing someone. Preferably Erica.

When I suggested coffee and cognac in the lounge she hesitated, took a deep breath, summoned up a sultry look and said, 'What about somewhere a little more private?' And she added a nervous little smile.

Taking women back to my room was not one of my common habits, but this was all in the line of duty, you understand, definitely to be listed under the heading of Essential Research. Our Erica clearly had some business in mind, and if finding out what it was meant having to take a gorgeous woman back to my room, well, that was the sacrifice I was going to have to make.

As we waited for the lift I could feel, even if I couldn't hear, the repressed buzz of speculation among the hotel staff, and as the lift door closed I just had time to receive a knowing smile from the clerk behind the desk.

Erica loved my suite, especially the little bottles of shampoo and bath foam in the bathroom, not to mention the small, individually wrapped bars of soap, the complimentary ladies' shower cap in a little cellophane bag and the hair dryer which was attached to the wall.

Eventually, after she had wandered around, inspecting all the goodies, fixtures and fittings (she just adored the mini-bar) she joined me on the couch, sitting just a little closer to me than other new acquaintances might have done. I could see that she was nervous; all that pacing around the rooms had been one telltale sign. But there was also a sense of purpose now, something which could almost be described as grim resolve.

She smiled at me softly. 'You're very nice.'

'So are you,' I lied. Gorgeous, yes, but nice, no.

Then she kissed me. She didn't have far to travel; she just leaned forward and put her slightly open and luscious mouth, which tasted faintly of strawberry-flavoured lipstick, on mine and kissed me long and deep. One of her hands was on my arm and I could feel her fingers trembling.

47

When it was finished she drew back slightly, made a kind of forward shrugging movement with her shoulders and, just as mysteriously as it had stayed in place, the backless dress also became a frontless one, and Erica was half naked on my couch, lovely to look at, her eyelashes fluttering seductively. The script called for some lustful grabbing, some more kissing and taking off of clothes. But nary a frisson was stirring in my breast; nor in my groin, for that matter. There was a slightly awkward silence.

'Oh dear,' I said gently.

'What's the matter?'

'Well, nothing really, it's just that this is all very unexpected.'

It took a few seconds for it to become clear to her that I was not going to make a grab at her, and then an even more uncomfortable stillness descended on the room while we just looked at each other.

Eventually I said quietly: 'Cornwell told you to do this, didn't he?'

The stillness persisted, but now her eyes were swimming with tears which soon overflowed, mixing with her eye-liner and forming a murky delta under her eyes from which emerged dark-edged tributaries which splashed down onto her breasts. She sniffed and her shoulders began to tremble, and she looked as utterly miserable as it was possible for a half-naked girl to be when sitting in a hotel room with a man she hardly knew, feeling humiliated.

I put my arm around her and drew her head to my shoulder just as the sniffing developed into heaving sobs. I had no doubt that my new short-sleeved Jonelle shirt with its smart button-down collar, would be completely ruined.

It was really some time before the mortified weeping subsided sufficiently for me to let go of her and get her a box of tissues. I stroked her back in a sympathetic, brotherly sort of way.

'It's true, isn't it? He did tell you to do this, didn't he?'

'Yes,' she snuffled miserably.

'You love him desperately, don't you?' That brought forward new waves of anguish, and again pounds of make-up silt were deposited on my shirt. I waited until speech was possible

48

again. 'He wanted you to get close to me, and find out things.'
She nodded.

'What sort of things? Anything specific?' I was still stroking
her comfortingly.

'About ... about the painting.' It was only just audible
amidst the snivelling.

'The Bretton?'

'Yes.'

'OK. You can tell him the truth. I know very little about the
painting, although I will be going to see Professor Beaumanoir
in France tomorrow. Maybe he'll be able to tell me more. But
my real interest in coming to the gallery was to find out what
happened to a friend of mine, a Mr Wallis, who, I think, also
came to the gallery some time in the last few weeks. I know he
had a copy of the Bretton painting, and he was murdered a few
days ago. I just wondered if his murder had anything to do
with the painting. That's it, really. That's all I know.'

'Murder?' she looked at me, her face a smear of merging
colours.

'Yes, he was murdered. He was handcuffed into his car and
exhaust fumes were piped in through a window.' Her eyes were
wide now. 'Did you know him? He was known as Wheezy
Wallis, although his real name was Albert.'

'No.' She sounded thoroughly dejected.

'Right,' I said brightly, 'you put those away' (indicating her
chest) 'and go and wash your face in the bathroom. I'll have
some coffee sent up, and you'll feel much better in a few
minutes.' The smile she gave me could, I suppose, have been
described as wan.

The room service waiter was visibly disappointed to find me
fully dressed in the sitting room of my suite, and I suspected
this episode would do nothing for my reputation with the staff.
He poured the coffee and left, probably hoping that a hot drink
might help me along in my quest.

Erica emerged from the bathroom red-eyed but otherwise
repaired and, in my view, a lot more attractive than she had
been earlier on.

'You look lovely without all that make-up on,' I told her.

'Really?' I could see she was not convinced. Years of smear-
ing on green eye shadow would not be reversed by the opinion

of one solitary male, and particularly one who had just spurned her not inconsiderable charms. She drank some coffee.

'You know, you are very nice, Mr Parker.'

'No-one nicer,' I agreed.

'No, I mean really nice. You could have ...'

'Now, now, never mind about all that.' I didn't want to be reminded about what I could have done. 'You just tell Mr Cornwell that you did what he asked, and you tell him what I told you. That'll be OK, won't it?'

'Yes.'

'You might also want to think about whether you really could love someone who asked you to do something like this.'

'Yes.' To give her credit, I think that thought had already occurred to her.

We didn't talk much while we finished the coffee. I was too busy congratulating myself on my instincts. I had to be right about Cornwell; why else had he sent Erica to pump – or hump – me for information?

After a few minutes I wrapped her in her transparent shawl and escorted her downstairs where the doorman summoned her a taxi. We stood in the warm evening air in front of the hotel, and she kissed me good night.

'Are you sure you don't want me to stay?' she whispered in my ear.

'I'm sure,' I said unsteadily. But I was not sure at all.

Chapter Nine

The seven o'clock flight to Bordeaux was so short that the stewards were hard pushed to serve the awful coffee and worse breakfast and sell the duty frees before everyone had to buckle up again for the landing. It was only by skipping both the breakfast and the duty frees that I managed to grab about thirty minutes' sleep during which I continued the dreams of the night before.

They all seemed to be about beautiful half-naked women offering themselves to me in hotel rooms while I was paralysed by that terrible inertia one experiences in dreams. And life. And then, shortly before the plane touched down, a nightmare came along, in which I saw Wheezy Wallis trapped in his car, vainly struggling for life.

Merignac airport was one of those quiet provincial places where it takes exactly eight minutes to get your luggage and four minutes to go through sleepy immigrations and customs. By nine-thirty, local time, I was at a rather swanky car-hire place in Bordeaux where they scrutinised me, my passport, my driver's licence and my credit cards with great diligence before they let me drive away in a shiny black Porsche. I got the distinct impression that they were renting me the car against every instinct, let alone their better judgements.

But by ten o'clock I had negotiated myself around the Rocade, the ring road around Bordeaux, found the road to Cap Ferret, and was heading due west through the pine forests towards the peninsula.

It was a perfect early summer day: hot without being oppressive, not a cloud in the sky and the air full of country smells and the strong scent of the trees. I opened the sun-roof and broke a few speed limits on long straight roads and one perfectly delightful stretch of new dual carriageway with hardly a car in sight and not even a hint of traffic policemen.

After about fifty kilometres the road veered south onto the peninsula between the Atlantic coast and the Arcachon Basin, and I began to drive through a series of resort towns on the shores of the bay. The further down the peninsula I went the more chic became the little towns, the more trendy the restaurants and shops in the high streets, the more luxurious the yachts and power boats in the sparkling marinas, and the more spectacular the developments of holiday villas, some of them up on bluffs overlooking the water.

Although tourism and boating were clearly the main occupations now, it was also obvious that this was a major centre of the seafood industry and, in particular, oysters and mussels. Glimpses of the bay from the road revealed acre after acre of oyster beds in the water, marked out by squares of sticks that protruded from the water even at high tide. And if that wasn't clue enough, there were the endless roadside shops and stalls advertising fresh, live oysters. My mouth began to water.

Cap Ferret itself was a pleasant little town with a charming old section and trendy new shopping centres, all dominated by a distinctive red and white striped lighthouse. I stopped to ask directions and received clear and polite instruction from a gendarme who appeared not even to notice my terrible French and even worse accent.

I drove through the town, back onto the main road leading down to the point of the peninsula, went past two roundabouts and then took the first road to the right. This led me meandering through the foothills of the vast, endlessly long sand dune that hides the Atlantic coast from the road, before I came to a gatepost marked 'Beaumanoir'. I drove in, followed the road for about a hundred metres and then found myself at a dead end; a little hard standing of bricks, where a small Citroen was parked. Nothing more.

I got out of the car and looked around. There was a paved pathway which became a staircase up into the dunes and I began to climb. The path was steeper, and longer, than it had appeared from below, and by the time I got to the top of the dune I was panting freely and perspiring genteelly into my fashionable Marks and Spencer blue shirt and checked sports jacket.

But the reward was the view: in front of me a piercing blue-green Atlantic, with long lines of rollers pounding in to what had to be the longest and whitest sandy beach I had ever seen. To my left was the point of the peninsula at the opening to the Arcachon Basin; another broad expanse of beach, this one dotted with crumbling Second World War blockhouses. Behind me was the ubiquitous pine forest, and to my right was the professor's house, a brown wood and glass affair with an enormous patio overlooking the sea, and perched on solid-looking wooden stilts which, I presumed, dove deep into the sand to concrete pilings. It was the sort of house I had always wanted, where you could lie in bed and hear waves thundering tirelessly, where you could sit on a patio and gaze at the endless turmoil of the sea, where the beach was at the bottom of the garden, and yet where one was only a few minutes away from good wines and fresh seafood.

Professor Beaumanoir answered the door with a broad smile. He was a tall, thin man of about seventy, wearing brown corduroy trousers, beige shirt and a tweedy brown tie. 'Mr Parker? Welcome!' and he grabbed my hand warmly with long, slender fingers.

'It's very good of you to make time for me at such short notice,' I said.

'Oh it's nothing, I'm just a retired old professor with nothing else to do, who loves having his ego flattered by showing off his knowledge. I'm delighted to have you here.' His English was lightly accented, but flawless.

He led me into a hall where one wall was dominated by a huge aerial photograph of a typically turreted and crenellated French chateau. Nearly three metres long, it was not the sort of thing you could walk past without gawping at, and I gawped.

'My ancestral home,' he said proudly. 'It is the castle at Josselin in Brittany.'

'Your family owned that?' I was very impressed.

'Well, perhaps not exactly the ancestral home in the sense of owning it,' he corrected himself, 'but it is certainly the seat of our family's honour.'

I raised my eyebrows in polite inquiry, and he ploughed on.

'In 1351 a Jean de Beaumanoir was captain of the chateau at Josselin when he and thirty other Breton noblemen defeated a similar number of English and Flemish knights led by a certain Richard Bembro who had had a mind to take over the castle. The event, known as "The Battle of the Thirty" is commemorated still by a granite obelisk nearby which carries the names of the victors. Unfortunately, however, Beaumanoir's name was inscribed as Robert, in error.

'It was my father's idea of a joke to call me Robert, since he always said my conception had been an error.'

'Ha ha,' I laughed politely.

'I never quite saw the joke myself,' Beaumanoir said, and the grin died on my lips. I had mistaken the bitterness in the professor's voice for mirth. Great start, I told myself, rub salt in the wounds of the guy's psyche. He did not seem to be offended, though.

'But come, I'm sure you don't want to hear about my family. You have come all the way from London to talk about Bretton, and here I am talking nonsense.' He led me into a big room, one wall of which was a sheet of glass overlooking the beach and the sea. The glass was, however, heavily smoked, and I quickly realised that this was to stop strong light from fading the many oil paintings hanging on the other three walls.

'I will order some coffee, and perhaps some croissants?' he said.

I smiled gratefully, not having eaten yet that day, and he left the room. I didn't have to be told that many of the paintings were by François Bretton; even to my Philistine eyes, the style was distinctive, the broad, bold brush-strokes and the clever way he had of suggesting detail without having actually to paint it. And I was just marvelling at the fact that one man appeared to have so many priceless paintings when he came back into the room.

'They're all Brettons?' I said breathlessly.

'Good heavens, no!' he laughed. 'Although you could be excused for not knowing that. No, they are all copies, except for one. See if you can identify it.' I began to look at the pictures, most of which were paintings of what appeared to be high society women in mid-nineteenth century formal attire, although there were a few men, posing pompously with guns, horses and dogs.

Professor Beaumanoir was still chuckling. 'Goodness me, if these were all genuine Brettons I would sell them and become rich enough to buy the Chateau Josselin!'

A few minutes later a young woman wearing an apron brought in deliciously aromatic coffee and croissants, just as I found what I thought was the original painting. I chose it not because I could see any discernible difference in the style or technique, but because of the subject matter – it was the only painting that was not a portrait. It was small, only about eighteen inches square, and was a painting of a dead bird – some kind of hawk or buzzard, lying on its back and partially decomposed so that there were exposed parts of its skeleton harshly contrasting with the soft grace of its feathers. Not an obvious choice of subject, yet somehow it managed to capture all the poignancy of broken power and decayed elegance.

'This one,' I said.

'Very good! Although you will accept that it was an easy choice, it being the only one of its kind in the room. Yes, that is my original Bretton, my pride and joy. A very early painting, of course, done when Bretton was a very young man, and before he confined himself mainly to painting human figures.'

'May I ask how you happen to have it?'

'But of course. It has been in the possession of my family for generations. That's why it survived Bretton's great act of destruction. It never left Brittany until, when my father died, I brought it here. It was this picture, hanging in our dining room when I was a child, that awakened my interest in art and then, of course, it was only natural that when I was a student I would concentrate on Bretton.' He shrugged, as if to suggest that the rest was history.

He poured coffee into delicate white cups and for a while I was aware of little more than the taste of real coffee and delicious croissants which were warm and fresh, still hot from the oven.

'Tell me about the other pictures,' I said eventually.

'They are copies of some of the known existing Brettons, some in private hands, some in museums and art galleries. One or two are by quite well known copyists, and perhaps quite valuable because of that. And there are a few fakes, too.'

'What's the difference?'

'Between copies and fakes?' I nodded, and he continued, 'It is a question of intent to deceive. Look at this one, for example,' he said, indicating a portrait of a woman holding a baby. 'This is clearly a copy because the artist has, firstly, signed his own name in very small letters down here in the corner and, secondly, he has made a deliberate error – here, on the baby's shoe – that would be immediately apparent to anyone acquainted with the original which, incidentally, is in Zurich. It is an exact copy, painted by a highly talented artist who has captured most of the detail and brilliance of the original, and most people would be proud to own it, as I am.'

The professor was in full flow now, and I could picture him in a lecture theatre, showing slides and speaking fluently and with passion on the subject that he had made his life's work.

'Now look at this one; this is a picture which purports to be an actual Bretton. It is a forgery. It is a copy of a painting in an art gallery in Chicago, and the artist has attempted to reproduce it exactly so that he could sell it as an original. As it happened, in this case, the painting was offered in the 1930s to a dealer in Moscow who, contrary to the hopes of the forger, knew where the original was and was able to check with Chicago before he bought it. The forger ended his days in some gulag or other, which is a pity in a way, because he was a very talented painter who could have done some interesting work.

'And here, this is another forgery. This is not even a copy; Bretton never painted this subject. The forger has cleverly copied Bretton's style and technique to produce a painting in the style of Bretton. When it is done well, this type of forgery is very difficult to detect because there is no original to compare it to. Many people have been deceived by paintings like this one.'

'But not you?' I asked.

'Well, most of the time an expert, someone who has spent a lifetime looking at genuine Bretton paintings and studying his technique, will recognise a forgery like this.' He walked across to a small bureau and came back with a large magnifying glass.

56

'The way a painter paints, the way he applies the paint to the canvas with his brush or with the palette knife, is very individual. It is as different and as distinctive as people's handwriting. 'Look here.' He held the magnifying glass over a section of the painting, and I noticed he had a wooden toothpick in his other hand which he was using as a pointer. 'Let us confine ourselves for the moment to the horizontal brush-strokes and we can see that the paint was applied from left to right.'

'We can?' I said.

'Oh yes. Look at the ridges in the paint, and you will see that they get slightly thinner towards the right, as the amount of paint on the brush reduced. It is also a question of the shape of the stroke; it is something one learns to recognise.

'Now, we know that Bretton also painted from left to right, as it were, and our forger here has been careful to duplicate that style, but he has made some mistakes.'

'Where?' I said, peering at the magnified section.

'Look here, at the end of this brush-stroke, as he lifted the brush off the canvas, he has left little tails of paint which point upwards, towards the top of the painting. That's entirely wrong. Bretton, when he allowed that to happen, left these little tails of paint pointing downwards. *Voilà*, a forgery!'

'You can tell from such a small detail?'

'Think of it this way,' he said. 'Pretend that I am a superb handwriting forger and, after months of study I become able to forge your handwriting perfectly, even to the extent that you yourself cannot tell the difference. Except for one letter of the alphabet. That is enough. You will look at my writing, and as soon as you come across my faulty "t" or "x" or whatever it is, you will know, with certainty, that you did not write that sentence.

'Well, my friend, I have studied the "handwriting" of Bretton's paintings all my life and these mistakes are like big signposts to me, even though they may only be tiny details.' His eyes were shining, and I realised he was enjoying himself. Evidently his claim that he loved showing off his knowledge was not just a polite remark designed to put me at ease.

'But in the end it is a question of your knowledge and opinion,' I said. 'Are there ways of proving, conclusively, that this is a fake?'

57

'Yes, you are right. Often it is a question of an expert's opinion. But there are also times when the forger makes other mistakes. Sometimes they will use paint and colours that were not available at the relevant time. Sometimes they will paint on a particular type of canvas that is wrong. Often there will be something in the painting which will be an anachronism. There are chemical tests we can do to analyse the properties of the paint and varnish.

'Nowadays we can even X-ray the paintings, and look at them in infrared light, to see what is underneath the paint, and you'd be amazed at what has been found. In one case they found, beneath the forgery of a Picasso, an earlier forgery of a Modigliani! And we frequently find paintings which turn out to be nothing more than painted photographs.

'Sometimes the clue will be in the frame, or in the wood used to stretch the canvas. Sometimes there will be conclusive scientific proof, but frequently the last word will come from someone like me. Sometimes we even argue with the scientists!

'Always there is reputation and vanity involved. The expert does not want to be proved to be wrong. The buyer does not want to discover that he has bought a worthless fake. An auction house will have a fiduciary stake in contending that it did not sell a forgery.'

'What about Mr Cornwell's painting, is that genuine?' I asked.

'Yes.' He walked away and gazed through the smoky glass at the sea, his back to me. 'It is a fine example of Bretton's early period, exhibiting many of the artist's most characteristic mannerisms and what you could, I suppose, call his "hand-writing" in oils. Some of these mannerisms became more pronounced as he matured as a painter, but they can be seen quite clearly in this work.'

'No question about it?' I asked.

'None whatsoever.'

'You examined it, of course?'

'Of course.'

'Is it a well-known Bretton?' I persevered.

'Yes, it is.'

'Could you tell me about it?' I asked softly. 'Please.'

He turned towards me and began to speak, excitement in his eyes, and a lilt of animation in his voice.

'It is a well documented picture. It is known, as you probably know, as the "Portrait of Silvie". It is an early work, painted some time around 1857 or 1858 when Bretton was only nineteen or twenty, and before he went to Paris. Silvie appears to have been his first love and he gave her the picture. Some art historians believe that his feelings were not reciprocated by this young farm girl and that it was for this reason that Bretton went to Paris, but that is conjecture and not well documented.

'For some reason, when Bretton's mental state deteriorated, and he started obsessively buying back his paintings, he did not pursue this one; which is one of the reasons why it survived the artist's terrible act of destruction.' He paused. 'Perhaps the story is true, that he loved this woman, but she did not reciprocate. Whatever the case, shortly after his death she sold it in an auction for a very great deal of money. Well, that is to say, a very great deal of money for those days. It is nothing to what it is worth now.' He chuckled.

'And as I said, it is well documented. We know exactly who bought it at that auction, and who all the owners have been ever since.'

'Had you ever seen it before you were asked to examine it a few months ago?' I asked.

'Yes, I was lucky enough to have seen it many years ago, when it was owned by Munro Forbes, before the burglary. I wrote to him asking if I could come and see it, and he agreed. This was before it was stolen, of course. You know about all that? That it was stolen and then recovered and hidden by Mr Forbes?' I nodded.

'Yes, so I saw it before, and there is no question that this is the same painting that I saw then.'

I couldn't think of anything else to ask and there seemed nothing more that he wanted to say. Professor Beaumanoir smiled at me in a friendly way and then picked up an almost empty cup and drained it of its last few drops of cold coffee.

I thanked him for the most interesting lecture on art forgery; we shook hands, and he showed me courteously to the door.

Chapter Ten

I left Professor Beaumanoir more educated about painting and forgeries, but no closer to unravelling the mystery of Wheezy's death than I had been in London.

But I was in a good mood. The weather was balmy: a hot sun but a friendly breeze coming in off the Atlantic and carrying with it the scent of the pine forests that stretch along the length of the Cap Ferret peninsula, behind the dune. It was about one o'clock and I had a whole day and a half to explore the area before my flight back the following evening.

I opened the roof on the Porsche and drove down to the point of the peninsula, where the vast volume of water which feeds the tides in the Arcachon Basin flows twice daily through the relatively narrow canal between the long spur of the peninsula and the mainland.

I sat in the car on a bluff and watched a fishing boat fighting the powerful current from the outgoing tide on its way into the bay from the open sea, its stern almost obscured from sight by a cloud of seagulls whose screeching and bickering could just be heard across the open water. I guessed that the fishermen were already busy gutting their catch and throwing the guts overboard.

An even louder sound emanated from my stomach: a bitter complaint at the lack of proper food since the night before. There was a restaurant at the point, but it looked windswept and deserted, so I started the car and drove back along the main road towards the town. About a hundred metres on I saw a sign advertising another restaurant and, at my stomach's bidding, I went to explore what Chez Hortense might have to offer. This was a sheltered and appealing place, with an encouraging number of diners sitting on a terrace overlooking the channel and the remarkable Pyla sand dune just south of Arcachon, on the opposite side of the water.

A woman with a strangely fixed smile, perhaps Hortense herself, brought me an excellent *soupe de poisson* with suitable accompaniments, followed by the house speciality, *moules farcies* – the mussels tossed in a pan with garlic and what appeared to be minced pork. With it I had a delicious white wine from Pessac, a Château Le Louvier, full of fruity body and a hint of the oak in which the wine had been matured.

The meal left me full of the joys of living and I decided to mosey on back up the peninsula, possibly to find a hotel, or maybe drive into Bordeaux. This time I drove up a road that hugged the Basin side of the land, a route studded with clusters of attractive, mainly wooden-frame houses, most of which appeared to be deserted this early in the season. I assumed they were weekend or holiday homes belonging to rich Bordelais.

The roads, too, were empty and it was probably that fact which drew my attention to a green Renault 25 behind me which I thought I had noticed once or twice before that morning. Wondering if I was being followed, I pulled off the road into the parking ground for a pleasant marina at a place called La Vigne. The Renault passed by without hesitation and disappeared around the next bend, without the slightest flicker of interest from the driver. I decided that I was being paranoid but, having stopped, I got out to look at the sparkling craft rubbing gently against each other in the marina.

There were some graceful yachts and a few very large and sleek cabin cruisers and for a moment I wondered whether I should buy myself something of the sort. Then I remembered how large the sea was, how small the boats really were, and how little I knew about sailing and boating in general, and abandoned the idea before it had even matured. Next to the marina was a small sandy beach dotted with a handful of sunbathers.

Feeling the effects of the meal and the wine, I decided to indulge myself in a little sloth. I removed my shirt, rolled up my trousers, and sat down on the beach. Then I thought I

61

might lie down on the warm sand for a short while, merely to rest my eyes briefly, you understand, and in less than a second I was asleep.

I must have been snoozing for about half an hour before I was woken by the sound of someone flapping a beach towel near me. I opened one eye dreamily and then the other snapped open jealously. About ten feet away, one of the most attractive women I had ever seen was preparing to sunbathe within easy ogling distance, and I didn't even have to turn my head to look at her.

She wasn't very tall, about five foot six or seven, but the proportions were exquisite – particularly if your feminine ideal is slightly on the slim side – with long limbs, long fair hair, long eyelashes and a supple grace that made the shrugging off of her wrap-around skirt and T-shirt an almost heart-stopping experience. Beneath the clothes she was wearing a clinging, beige, one-piece lycra swimming costume deeply cut at the back and the sides leaving little need to speculate about what was beneath it.

She sat down, reached into a large handbag and brought out a tube of suntan lotion which she proceeded to rub into her arms, legs and shoulders while I lay somewhat breathless, watching her movements and the way the muscles played beneath her smooth skin.

I thought about the beauty of the paintings I had seen earlier that day, and contemplated the difference between the emotions I had experienced then and the sheer contentment of witnessing the physical beauty of the real woman I was watching now. She appeared not even to be aware of my presence and, in a single, wholly unselfconscious movement, she peeled off the top half of her bathing costume.

The woman, who appeared to be somewhere around her mid-twenties, was now lying back, with her torso propped up on her elbows in order to catch the sun. From her collarbones there was a graceful ski-slope of line leading to nipples jutting pugnaciously skywards.

Then she started smoothing suntan oil onto her body. I lost my composure. A sharp intake of breath on my part was involuntary, and I managed to sniff up a nose-full of soft white sand.

It was my distressed hawking and spluttering that drew her attention to me for the first time and she gave me a guileless smile. Small, straight teeth showed briefly behind lips. Eyes looked at me with the faintest trace of concern.

'*Vous sentez bien, monsieur?*' The voice was slightly deeper than expected and tinged with concern.

'*Oui, ça va, merci,*' I replied, still choking, in my most carefully pronounced accent-less French.

'Ooh, you are Eengleesh!' she said in an accent so appealing that it made my pulse race.

'Yes,' I admitted, still spluttering and trying to get the sand out of my nose.

'You are on 'oliday 'ere in ze Cap Ferret?'

I made an attempt to master my excitement at finding myself in conversation with my delightful apparition, and explained that I was just there for the weekend after a business meeting in the town.

'You are staying in an hotel near here?'

'I don't know. Perhaps. Or maybe I'll go to Bordeaux later. I have no plans,' I said.

'OK,' she said happily, 'so now we can talk and I can practise my Eengleesh?'

'It would be my pleasure,' I said with genuine feeling.

She moved her towel next to me, lay down again propping herself up on one elbow and put out her hand. 'My name is Eve Dupont,' she said. Her hand was cool and smooth and the tiniest bit oily from the suntan lotion, and was it my imagination that the handshake lasted a hundredth of a second longer than it strictly had to?

I took a deep breath, and said something I didn't often admit to: 'My name is Horatio.'

' 'Oratio? That is a strange name.' I could only agree.

And then we chatted. She was, she said, an agent for a company that let holiday villas to visitors in the summer, many of whom were English families. She lived in Bordeaux and came to the cape whenever she could. 'I love ze beach,' she explained. And, speaking as a senior representative of the rest of humanity, I assured her that the beach loved her.

She giggled. 'You are so funny!' Funny? I felt hilarious. No-one could tell them like I could, and I was positively basking in the attention of this woman, and proudly hoping that everyone else on the beach would assume that this exquisite being was with me.

She spoke animatedly in her charming, heavily accented English about the area, about the Arcachon Basin and its vast production of oysters and mussels; about its dwindling fishing industry in the face of ever-increasing use of the water by anglers, holiday makers and their pleasure craft; and about the wonderful sandy beach on the Atlantic coast which stretched virtually unbroken for hundreds of miles all the way down past Biarritz in the south.

Suddenly she looked at her watch and then at me with a bright expression. 'Would you like to go on a boat on the basin?'

'Now?' I was slightly flustered.

'*Mais oui*, why not?' She looked at the water, and I noticed that the tide had turned and water was beginning to flow back into the bay. 'My father has a *pinasse* at Le Canon. It's not far. I could show you the oyster beds and the Ile d'Oiseaux, which is, how you say, a sanctuary for the birds.'

'A *pinasse*?'

'That is the traditional boat of the Arcachon Basin. Verry beautiful,' she purred, her guttural 'r's rolling appealingly out of her lovely throat. She was looking at me expectantly, the sun glinting on her eyelashes, and try as I might I could not think of a single reason why I should not go out alone in a boat with the most gorgeous woman in the whole south west of France, if not the world.

'OK, you're on.' I put on my shirt and shoes while she covered her perfect body with her clothes.

'You have a car?' she said, as we walked past the marina. I pointed to the Porsche and she squealed with delight.

'Ooh, you are very rich?' I told her modestly that it was only rented, but of course I enjoyed the effect the car had had on her. We drove a few miles to Le Canon, the next small town on the basin, and I parked in a shady spot next to the little post office.

'First the picnic,' she said, and I followed her into a little supermarket where, with admirable decisiveness, she bought a couple of baguettes, a bottle of wine, some cheese, smoked ham and a tin of foie gras. I insisted on paying and then we walked down to the little harbour where about thirty or forty boats were moored.

The *pinasse* was indeed a beautiful craft. It was long and graceful, with a shape that reminded me vaguely of the gondolas in Venice, except that it was much wider, and there was a low flat cabin which covered the front half of the boat. With a practised efficiency, Eve boarded the boat, extracted a key from a hiding place near the dashboard, stowed the purchases in the cabin, cast off the mooring rope, started the motor, and within a few minutes we were chugging smoothly out into the basin. When we were about a hundred yards out, we both stripped down to the waist again.

For an hour or so she showed me the sights including the acres and acres of oyster beds in the shallow sections of the bay, still visible before the incoming tide would eventually cover them, leaving only the rows and rows of wooden poles sticking up out of the water to warn of their presence. She collected a few wild oysters adhering to the poles, opened them deftly with a slim knife and we ate them, fat and juicy, there and then. I had never tasted oysters like these before. I wondered whether what they said about oysters and the libido was true.

Then she circled the Ile d'Oiseaux, pointing out various birds wading around the mud flats. After a while she dropped the anchor in a relatively shallow channel and switched off the motor. The silence, with only the water slapping against the sides of the boat, was delicious.

'I want to swim,' she said. 'You too?' I shook my head. I had no swimming costume and I was, well, too damn shy to strip off in front of her, lovely as she was. She smiled, shrugged her shoulders, pulled up her bathing costume, and dived like a fish into the clear water. Esther Williams fans eat your hearts out. This was a display of grace and economy which, could it have been captured on film, could well have sparked off worldwide interest in a new kind of Olympic synchronised swimming.

Then she pulled herself effortlessly out of the water, and breathing only slightly more quickly than before, dried herself off with a towel from the cabin. 'So, now we sunbathe, yes?'

I nodded agreeably. Frankly I didn't mind what we did, as long as this day went on and on. There were, I admit, a few occasions during the afternoon when I wondered why this woman, who could have picked up just about any man on the beach, had chosen me. I also marvelled a few times at her total unconcern about me. For all she knew, I could have been released the day before from a long prison sentence for kidnapping, grievous violence and sexual assault. But as these thoughts appeared I pushed them aside. Sometimes, as Freud said, a cigar is just a cigar. She stretched out full length on the roof of the cabin, lying on her back, and motioned for me to join her.

It was after seven o'clock now, but the sun was still shining strongly, if obliquely, down onto the water. Eve turned to me, held out the bottle of oil, and made my year. 'Would you put some on my back? Would you mind?'

Oh Lord. Mind? A nuclear explosion wouldn't have deterred me, and never mind that it was by now not really hot enough to require oil on the skin. I kneeled next to her, poured some oil on my hand, and began to apply it. Her skin was warm and smooth, and she made a contented 'Mmmmmmm' sound as I worked the oil in diligently around her back and shoulders. I took much longer at my task than I needed to, but there was no sign from her that anything was amiss. And was it my imagination again that when I was smoothing the oil into the lower part of her back, perhaps even the beginning of the rise of her bottom, that she pressed her pelvis almost imperceptibly up against my hand? I don't know, but all too soon, there was no more back to oil and I was forced to desist.

We chatted again, this time about me and my work. She was easy to talk to; a good listener who seemed genuinely interested in what I did, and what I had to say. To report that I was enjoying myself would have been an absurd understatement.

The sun remained warm, and when a little while later she suggested another swim, I threw caution to the winds and stripped off. We swam in the clear water for about twenty minutes, and when I finally heaved myself out of the water and back onto the boat it must have been close to eight o'clock.

'Are you hungry yet?' she asked, rubbing herself dry with a towel.

'Very,' I replied, and she brought out the food she had bought. We spread foie gras directly from the tin onto pieces of fresh baguette, and sipped at the strongly aromatic white wine she had opened. We ate the thinly sliced pieces of smoked ham with our fingers and I honestly could not remember ever enjoying food more.

Then it was back to the roof of the boat to catch the last of the sun, me in my underpants and Eve in her rolled down swimming costume. Lying there on the roof of the boat, feeling warm and content, I began to get drowsy again, the combined effect of the hours of hot sun on my pale skin, the wine and the intoxicating female I was with.

'You have got burnt,' Eve said to me after a while. 'Let me put some of this cooling lotion on you.' Thinking back on that moment, I still cannot decide which experience I enjoyed more – putting oil on her back, or having her return the favour. She smoothed the liquid on in long, flowing strokes, during which she pressed down on my back muscles with the palm of her hand in a massaging motion. I was dreamily in heaven.

Too dreamily. I was suddenly indescribably exhausted, and when I lifted my head I saw her looking at me with a strange expression on her face – somewhere between concern and anticipation. I remember feeling a sharp frisson of alarm before an inexorable warmth stole across my body, blotting out the sun, the feel of her hand and the light. I submerged helplessly into unconsciousness.

Chapter Eleven

My awakening could not have been more shocking. The first sensation was icy wetness and I opened my eyes to total darkness. Waves of insistent nausea surged through me and I vomited blindly in the dark. I found myself kneeling in numbingly cold water reeking of oil and for some seconds I had not the faintest idea where I was. I made a blundering attempt to stand up and pounded my head painfully on hard wood.

I remembered the boat ride with Eve, but could not reconcile that perfect afternoon with the sudden nightmare I was experiencing now. Where the hell was she? Where the hell was I, for that matter?

I was wracked by further waves of nausea but eventually my head began to clear until I realised that I was in the forward cabin of the *pinasse*. I found to my confusion that I was wearing my trousers and shirt again but I couldn't work out where all this water had come from.

The water! I realised with a sickening jolt of fear that it was getting deeper at an alarming rate. The air was also foul with the stench of diesel fuel. I knew I needed to get out but I didn't even know which way I was facing. Frantic scrabbling in the direction I was facing took me into an even narrower space, and I realised I had moved even further into the cabin. I turned around and crawled through the water in the opposite direction. The cabin became wider and at last I found the door.

I pushed against it, aware that the water was getting deeper more and more quickly, but the door would not move. For a moment I panicked and began to thrash around wildly, but some instinct stilled me, and through the waves of fear and bilious retching I somehow managed to focus my concentration more calmly on my predicament. I was finding it increasingly difficult to breathe the foul air, and the ever deepening water was making it more difficult to move around.

I stopped pushing frantically with my hands and turned myself around so that my feet were against the door. I felt around for something to brace myself against and at first I could find nothing. I could feel the panic rising in me again, but then my flailing hands hit something solid. The same beam on which I had so painfully banged my head. I lifted myself up until I could get one shoulder behind it and I pushed my feet against the door.

The action sent an agonising pain into my shoulder as the sharp edge of the wood cut into my flesh, and still the door, which I knew opened outwards, would not budge. I rested for a few seconds until I realised that the water was now rushing in, and there was perhaps only a foot or so of air left in the cabin. I braced myself against the beam again, steeled myself to ignore the pain, and pushed again desperately with my feet. I almost sobbed with relief when I heard a cracking sound as the plywood of the door began to give way. I heaved again and one of my feet went through a panel in the door. I changed position, and kicked desperately against the next panel, which gave way more easily. The third I removed with my hands and then I half swam, half crawled through the small opening, out onto the deck of the boat, where I stood gulping air and trying desperately to clear my fuzzy mind.

I looked around. It was dark. There was no sign of Eve Dupont, or anyone else for that matter. I looked up at the sky and saw stars. There was a pale half moon low down near the horizon, but it was casting enough light for me to see the faint outlines of the *pinasse* which was wallowing sickeningly in the water. I forced myself to be calm and in that moment I heard the sound of an engine. Peering into the dark in the direction of the sound I saw a red light which, I deduced from its movement, must be attached to the mast of some boat. For a moment I felt relief, assuming that it must be coming towards me, but it took only a few more seconds for the realisation to dawn that both the light and the sound of the engine were receding. The boat was going in the opposite direction.

There was a stiff breeze blowing and, being soaked, I began to shiver violently from the cold. I forced myself to concentrate. Where the hell was I? The boat was definitely moving, slewing sluggishly around in a strong current, but I had no idea where in the bay I was. I squinted out into the blackness. There. On the right a bright light flashed briefly and was gone. Three or four seconds later it flashed again, and I realised it was the lighthouse at Cap Ferret. I looked in the opposite direction, and saw strings of lights and illuminated buildings in the distance. That had to be Arcachon. And if I was between Cap Ferret and Arcachon, then I had to be in the turbulent channel that was the entrance to the bay!

I focused for a moment on establishing the direction of the boat's movement relative to the lights I could see, and another bolt of fear went through me. The boat was clearly moving south. The tide must have turned again, and I was being swept by the powerful current towards the open sea.

But things were even worse than that. The water in which I was standing was getting deeper at a perceptible rate, and there was no doubt that the boat was sinking. In my frightened and confused state, there was no attempt to wonder about what had happened. The closest I got to analysing the cause of my predicament was a vague, almost unconscious presumption that something terrible had happened, that the boat must have hit something and that Eve must have been knocked, or washed, overboard. There wasn't time for much thinking. I knew that I was in desperate trouble and that I had to find a life-belt, a life-raft or at least something buoyant to hold onto when the boat went down. Shaking with cold, I began to search the deck, feeling under the bench seats for anything loose that I could use to keep myself afloat. There was nothing at all.

Within a few minutes the water had risen to my knees and the movement of the boat had become more sluggish as it settled. Then the water was around my thighs and little waves began lapping over the sides. The sea poured in. The boat was still for a tiny moment and then it began to disappear. I felt the deck lower itself beneath me, and I was deposited with an ominous gentleness on the surface of the sea. The *pinasse* had gone, without a trace and without a sound.

My first sensation was one of comparative comfort, since the water felt relatively warm after the biting cold of standing, drenched, in the stiff breeze, but I knew that I was in a desperate position. I was being carried out to sea by the vicious current which was draining the unimaginable volume of water from the hundreds of square miles of the Arcachon Basin, and I knew without having to think about it that the chances of rescue were non existent. Even had there been any boats about, the darkness was almost complete, and no-one would have been able to see me in the choppy water.

Despite my fear and confusion, I knew that any attempt to swim to shore would be fatal. I was being swept along by a powerful current, and any lateral headway I could have made would have been cruelly outweighed by the exhaustion that would have set in within minutes. I am an averagely good swimmer, but even the strongest long-distance swimmer would have been defeated by a current of this magnitude. I knew that my only hope of survival lay in staying afloat until daylight, until the tide changed, or until I could somehow attract the attention of one of the fishing boats that would be setting out for the sea in the early morning. I concentrated on preserving my energy, treading water slowly while trying to float on my back.

It was depressingly more difficult than it sounds. I was being buffeted about in the water, and in the darkness I could not really see more than a few yards in any direction, and I was frequently caught unawares by small waves which washed over me, leaving me spluttering and gulping for air. I couldn't decide whether to drag off my shirt and trousers; being naked would have made it slightly easier to tread water, but the clothing didn't seem to be affecting my buoyancy and, thinking ahead optimistically, I decided that I might need them later on. It was a decision that probably saved my scrawny neck.

I have no real idea of how long I struggled in the water. Seconds of conserved effort merged into minutes and then, agonisingly, into hours, and as each unspecified unit of time passed I could feel myself getting weaker and weaker. The water which had at first felt warm compared to the cold wind, was now feeling icier by the minute. My arm and leg muscles

71

were beginning to ache with the effort of staying afloat, and I was regularly swallowing too much water as I was swamped by waves. My eyes and lungs were burning from the sea water, and I was still occasionally wracked by moments of acute nausea.

At some stage in that icy blackness I began to believe that I would soon drown, and the waves, nausea and fatigue were supplemented by an acute depression. Where were my millions now that I needed them? Of what use was all that money when all the riches in the world couldn't buy me a piece of driftwood to cling on to? When I died, the money would all go to the Edwina Llewellyn Memorial Trust. The newspaper, restaurant and hotel would go to other trusts. They would all survive; only I was the superfluous factor in it all.

At times I raged against the threat to my existence; then I would fall into a kind of resignation towards my fate when I began to wonder whether it would ultimately be easier, and kinder, to myself, just to let the water take me now. In one of these periods I actually allowed myself to start sinking, perhaps merely to see what my reaction would be, and as the water closed over my head, fleeting images began crashing through my mind. They were insubstantial, half-formed memories and pictures of my life, but then one solidified and became dominant. I saw little Wheezy Wallis handcuffed in his car, struggling frantically as the toxic exhaust ate away at his life, and my rage returned. I struggled to the surface, whooping for air, a new determination pumping blood to my screaming legs and arms.

Then I brushed against something slippery but solid and invisible in the darkness just below the surface of the water, and what felt like long strings of seaweed briefly caressed the right side of my body before it was gone again. A second later my right foot and the whole of my right arm were engulfed by fire; by a pain so total and intense that my body was, for a moment, shocked rigid. Air rushed from my lungs as I gasped and shrieked unashamedly with the agony. Bright flashes of fear passed through me and I was suddenly certain that I would soon be dead. And then, just as quickly as it came, the pain subsided. My shocked mind had only an instant in which to experience relief, before I realised that my right arm was completely numb, and also partially paralysed. I could not feel my right foot at all. I surmised that I had brushed against some kind of large jellyfish whose tendrils, laced with poison, had dragged across my exposed skin. Had I not still been wearing my shirt and trousers the area affected would have been vastly greater and I would no doubt have drowned instantly. As it was I was really floundering now, swimming only with my left arm and leg, rolling disastrously and taking in even more water through my nose and mouth as I struggled to breathe. I could feel the last reserves of my strength ebbing fast, and a final resignation began to steal over me like a dark curtain descending.

Then my left foot touched sand.

I kicked down again. More sand. I tried frantically to dig my toes in as the water pulled me along, and then I could feel the sand with my left hand too. I found some purchase, and then a little more, and with a final scrabbling motion I managed to stop moving, the water still rushing quickly past me and threatening at any moment to wash me off my fragile perch. One large wave would have done it. I inched, literally inched, myself into shallower and shallower water until finally I was lying with my shoulders and chest on soft wet sand, the rest of me still dragging in the water. I stopped moving, concentrated on breathing deeply, and let tiny amounts of energy begin recouping in utterly expended muscles. I can't remember how long I lay there like that. I desperately wanted to put my head down on the sand and close my eyes, but I knew that I couldn't. Not yet. Then, millimetre by millimetre I pushed myself higher and higher out of the water, my right arm and leg completely useless, managing to move somehow with pathetic pushes with my left leg and arm. Until all of me was out of the water.

I was back in the icy wind, shaking feebly with the cold, but I let my head drop to the sand and I was taken instantly back into black oblivion.

Chapter Twelve

A gull was screaming at me to wake up but I couldn't open my eyes. It screamed louder and flapped its wings until I forced myself to look. The bird was actually perched on my hip, and as I moved my head it took flight with a mighty beating of wings and screech of alarm.

I sat up and looked around me, my head swimming with dizziness, my muscles trembling with fatigue. But at least I wasn't so cold now; the wind had dropped and there was a weakly warming sun flooding across the bay. I was on a large, bare sandbank somewhere between the point of the peninsula and the looming sand dune of the Arcachon coast. The next few minutes were spent removing sand from my mouth, nose, ears and eyes. I inspected my right arm and foot, both of which were horribly swollen, with vivid red weals slowly oozing tiny trickles of blood. I shuddered to think what my fate might have been had I been washed out to sea leaking blood like that.

There were still throbbing pains in the affected limbs, but the paralysis appeared to be wearing off. I shuddered again. And again. I was shaking generally, not only from cold now but also from desperate weakness and, I realised, hunger. I had vomited what food I had eaten in the boat with Eve, and my exertions in the water throughout the night had drained my body of energy.

I had a monster headache, I felt ill from the sea water that I must have swallowed, I needed food and medical treatment for the jellyfish poisoning, I was suffering from exposure and total exhaustion, there was an unhealthy rasping sound coming

74

from my lungs, but there was a kernel of triumph in my soul. I had thought I was going to die, and I had survived.

I couldn't quite focus well enough to see how far the sandbank stretched or whether it connected with the mainland or not. In any case I could not have stood up, let alone walked some miles. But I considered that I was safe enough for some hours at least. The tide appeared to have gone right out and I looked down at relatively still, placid water where only a few hours before a swirling current had so nearly dragged me to my death.

The sun was growing stronger by the minute and the warmth alone was a tonic. Sitting trembling on the sand, I began to be aware that the pockets of my trousers, which had been empty the last time I had been aware of them, now contained unfamiliar objects. I was surprised to find my wallet in my back pocket. I could not imagine how it had got into my trousers, since it had been in the inside pocket of my jacket, which I presumed had gone down with the boat. It was soaked by the seawater but a brief inspection revealed that all my money, credit cards and my press card were still there.

I inspected the right-hand pocket next, and drew out a black plastic package tightly wrapped with adhesive tape. My shaking fingers took ages to open the package, and then a fat wad of cash fell onto the sand. I was astonished. I picked it up and found that it consisted of crisp, brand-new five hundred franc notes. Blinking in disbelief I counted two hundred notes, a hundred thousand francs, well over ten thousand pounds.

Now I was intrigued by the contents of my left hand pocket, which yielded a similar black plastic package. Expecting to find another wodge of dosh, I was bewildered when a series of little clear plastic bags fell out. I shook my head to clear my fuddled brain, but then I knew what they were. The little bags each contained small amounts of fine white powder. I held one up to the light and squinted at it; tiny crystals glinted in the sun. Cocaine. I managed to open the bag with my teeth, pinched a tiny quantity of the powder between my fingers and sniffed it up one nostril. Nothing happened. I took a slightly larger pinch and repeated the sniff. Then I did it again with the other nostril. It was just what the doctor ordered. Seconds later warmth began to steal through my body, my shaking all but stopped, and I felt renewed energy flooding my limbs. I

75

was suffused by a feeling of well-being and my mind, which until then had been tired, confused and sluggish, suddenly began to sparkle with intense clarity. Now I knew, or thought I knew, the explanation for all these confusing events. I lay back on the sand, feeling almost good despite my physical distress, and nearly laughed aloud at the simplicity and sheer devilment of the attempt on my life.

There could be no question that the lovely Eve had been sent to pick me up, perhaps by the driver of the Renault 25 who had seen me turn off to the beach at La Vigne. While I slept they would have had time to make their plans. She would have been told to pick me up, get me onto the boat and drug me somehow. She must have put something in my wine; I had been so intoxicated by her presence that I probably wouldn't have noticed if she'd given me drain cleaner.

After I passed out she would have signalled to her accomplices, one or more of whom would have come aboard. They drove the boat to the entrance of the tidal channel, waited until it was dark and the tide was running strongly towards the sea, locked me – still unconscious – in the cabin, and then holed the boat or pulled out its plug or whatever one does to make something like that sink. They must have been in the boat I saw nearby when I escaped from the cabin. Their mistake had been one of over-confidence; they should have hung around until the thing actually sank, but perhaps they were anxious to get as far away from the area as possible.

The most cunning part of the plot had been to plant incriminating evidence on me. My wallet had been placed in my back pocket to ensure that I would immediately be identified when my body was found in the cabin of the sunken boat. The police would then also find the cocaine and the money, and assume that I had been involved in a drug deal which had obviously gone wrong. It was all so clever it made me angry.

I sniffed another generous pinch into each nostril, aware now why people are so easily seduced by the drug, and then opened each little bag, one by one, pouring the priceless crystals onto the sand. Then I buried the bags.

The money I kept. It could not possibly compensate me for the ordeal I had endured, but it would serve, for the time being, as a tiny down-payment.

Chapter Thirteen

I sat on my sandbank, weak as a kitten but high as a kite, for another half an hour or so before I saw the first boat heading for the channel and the open sea. It was a fishing boat and I waved at the men on board as they passed about fifty yards away. My heart sank as they stared at me blankly, no doubt wondering what on earth I was doing there at that time in the morning. One of the fishermen waved back, but the boat continued chugging out to sea. It was the same with the next two boats, and I realised that I was not managing to get my message across to them.

The fourth which hove into view was a yacht, its sails still furled and using its motor to take it through the channel. I struggled shakily to my feet, waved until I got their attention, and then simply collapsed into a heap on the ground. It was not difficult, I assure you. Just getting to my feet had taken some of my last reserves of strength. For a moment the yacht continued on its way, its crew, which included a woman, perhaps wondering whether I was playing some sort of practical joke. But as I continued lying there without moving, I saw to my relief that the yacht was coming round and heading in my direction.

Until that moment I had been relatively in control of my mind and body, but as soon as I saw assistance very clearly on the way, I must have allowed myself to let go to some extent.

I have no clear memory of my rescue. I vaguely remember people jabbering at me in French, covering me with blankets, forcing hot, sweet coffee down my throat, and I remember too the crackling sound of radio communication.

At one stage I saw a man's face looking down at me, his lips mouthing words. I forced myself to concentrate on what he was saying. It sounded like 'cop'. I looked at him blankly. He smiled, began waving his hand around above his head and tried again. 'Helicop', I heard at last. There was a helicopter on its way.

I remember the deafening sound of the helicopter arriving, and the strong hands which lifted me onto some sort of stretcher, but I have no memory of the flight or of my arrival in hospital in Arcachon. Perhaps they had started giving me drugs immediately, or perhaps it was just that once I was certain that I was in safe hands, I surrendered my exhausted body to oblivion.

I awoke slowly, wondering why I was in pain and why every inch of my body ached fiercely. I opened my eyes and thought I saw God. It was not God. It was Ambrose Pendleton, looking down on me with an anxious expression on his face.

'You're not God,' I said.

'And you're not dead,' he replied.

'You sure?'

'Well, if you are, we have all just wasted a great deal of your money on some very expensive medical care and have been woefully misled about your condition by some very greedy French doctors.'

I smiled, and split my lip. 'How am I?' I asked him.

'Apparently, better than you were three days ago.'

'*Three days*?'

'Three and a half, if you count this morning.'

'What's today?'

'Wednesday.'

I closed my eyes and began to realise that a whole series of floating dreams about tubes and pinpricks and respirators and drips had not been dreams at all but brief moments of very uncomfortable lucidity.

'They tell me that you were suffering from a very serious combination of hypothermia, advanced fatigue and a rare form of blood poisoning from a highly toxic marine invertebrate; each not terribly serious on its own, but together extremely life threatening. They've been pumping you full of antibiotics, feeding you intravenously, and keeping you heavily sedated.'

'I don't feel too well,' I admitted.

Ambrose brought his head lower and spoke quietly. 'They also found traces of cocaine and other narcotics in your blood! What on earth have you been up to, Horatio? I hope you're not going off the rails and getting hooked on drugs! And what on earth were you doing on a sandbank in the middle of the Arcachon channel for heaven's sake?'

I risked a further split in my lip, and smiled at him. 'Don't worry, Ambrose, I'm not a junkie. It's quite simple really – someone tried to kill me.' He went pale.

I told him the story, in abbreviated form, but with enough detail to allay his fears about the drugs – although he didn't look too reassured when I was finished. His lined face was drawn and anxious.

'I don't know why you have to get involved in such intrigues,' he said. 'These are things best left to the police, surely?'

'There are things that the police can't do. They can't fly off to France at the drop of a hat like I can, and they can't talk to the kind of people who talk to me,' I said.

'They also don't tend to be kidnapped by Mata Haris who leave them to drown in sinking boats,' he snapped.

'OK, OK.' I changed the subject. 'How did you get here, anyway?'

'They had your identification, and they contacted the *Explorer*. Bloch telephoned me for authorisation to fly out, but I told him I would go myself.'

'He probably wanted to come and gloat,' I said, 'or fire me for not coming to work.'

'Nonsense! He was very concerned about you. Anyway, I was here by lunchtime; I chartered a plane.'

'Which I paid for, no doubt.'

'Of course. You are also paying dearly for the best private medical care available in the west of France. It's not cheap, I can assure you, but I think you can afford it.'

That's when a fierce looking woman walked into the room. She looked at me and said. 'Ah, ze patient is awake.'

'Yes,' I said, 'and I'm in a lot of pain. I have a terrible headache, my whole body hurts, and I'm also very hungry.'

79

She said nothing, just held my wrist and took my pulse. She plunged a thermometer into my mouth, waited half a minute during which she glared at me, and then took it out and looked at it. 'You are much better. Please not to complain all ze time.' And she swept out of the room.

'This is the best private medical care available in the west of France?' I asked Ambrose. 'I think I'd do better with Rosa Klebb.'

'Who?'

'You know, the woman in the James Bond film who had poisoned blades in the tips of her shoes.'

'I haven't the faintest idea what you are talking about,' Ambrose said wearily. It was only then that I noticed how tired the elderly gentleman looked, and I realised that he must have spent a great deal of time at the hospital with me, probably sitting at my bedside. I wondered how much sleep he had had since Sunday.

'Ambrose,' I said, with as much strength as I could muster, 'that nurse really is right, you know. I really am feeling much better and I think you should go back to your hotel or wherever you are staying and get some rest. We can talk again tomorrow.'

He didn't need much persuasion. 'I'm not going to argue with you, I confess.' He got up. 'I'll telephone later to see how you are, and I'll see you in the morning.' He was halfway to the door when he stopped suddenly. 'Oh, I should warn you that the French police are anxious to interview you. They also want to know what you were doing on that sandbank pumped full of drugs and with a large amount of cash in your pockets. You might want to give some thought to what you are going to tell them.'

'Thanks for the warning,' I grinned, and split my lip again. 'I shall tell them the truth, of course. My heart is pure and my conscience is clear. Mind you, perhaps I'll leave out the bit about the cocaine. They might have some difficulty swallowing that.'

'You didn't appear to,' he said archly.

'Ambrose, you don't swallow cocaine! Don't you know anything about the late twentieth century?'

'Thankfully, no,' he said, and he was gone.

*

Actually, the fierce nurse wasn't so bad – as long as I pretended I was feeling fine and was in no pain. She brought me a tasty onion soup and a baguette for lunch, and only scowled when I asked where the garlic croutons were.

'Croutons are too rich,' she said. 'Otherwise you will throw up on my bed.' How strange; I had thought it was my bed.

I felt even better after the food, and when she'd taken the tray away, I decided to take a walk and explore my surroundings. I pulled the covers away, swung my feet round to the floor and stood up.

Well, that's what I meant to do. But I just crumpled instantly, my legs feeling as weak as rubber matchsticks. I must have grabbed at something as I fell, because when I hit the floor I was followed by a variety of kidney dishes and small bottles which made the whole experience resemble the sound effects from an old Goon Show. Rosa Klebb came rushing in, and the next few minutes were quite embarrassing.

Eventually, however, I was put back to bed. Klebb gave me some tablets, and the rest of the day was all darkness and peace.

The next time I woke there was a very tall policeman with a big nose sitting where Ambrose had sat, and smoking a foul-smelling French cigarette. Only in France, I thought. The sun was coming in through the window, and I realised that another night had passed, and it was now Thursday morning. Poor Wheezy had been dead for a week.

'You're not the angel Gabriel, are you?' I asked.

'M'sieur?'

'Never mind. Something tells me that you want to speak to me.'

'I do, M'sieur Parker. I am Captain Jules Aristède of the Arcachon police.' He paused, looking at me thoughtfully. 'The doctors have said that you are well enough to talk now, and there are some questions I must ask you.'

'My French is terrible,' I said.

'My English is very good, if I say so myself. Which is why I am here and not some sergeant from the station.'

'Tell you what, I'll make a deal with you.'

'A deal?' He was looking at me suspiciously.

'Yes, a deal. You throw that cigarette out of the window, and then I'll tell you what happened to me. And then, when I've finished, if there are still some questions you want to ask, I'll do my best to answer them.'

'That sounds like a fair deal,' he said with a smile, getting up and heading for the window with his foul weed.

'Oh, one other thing,' I said. 'I don't say anything before I have had breakfast. Perhaps you would be kind enough to ask the nurse to bring us' (I stressed the 'us') 'some coffee and croissants. Her name is Miss Klebb.'

He obviously thought that was a very good idea and, after a little confusion about Miss Klebb's name, we were brought the breakfast we desired. Captain Aristède immediately endeared himself to me by plunging his croissant into the hot coffee and then, throwing his head back, he stuffed more than half the soggy item into his mouth. I could see this was not going to be a very formal occasion.

Then we talked. Or rather I talked. I told him that I was a journalist, and explained that I had visited Professor Beaumanoir to learn more about François Bretton (although I didn't tell him why). I told him of my lunch at Chez Hortense (when I mentioned the mussels he wrote down the name of the restaurant in his notebook), of my drive up the coast of the bay, about the green Renault I had thought might have been following me, about the beach at La Vigne, and about the beautiful girl I had met there. I said nothing about breathing in a nose-full of sand. I told him about the *pinasse*, about the picnic, about the wine and about falling asleep. I somehow forgot to mention my nude swimming and the massage session.

I told him the dramatic story of my awakening in the cabin of the sinking boat, of the boat I saw receding, my struggles in the water, the encounter with the jellyfish and the timely meeting with the sandbank. The little bags of cocaine quite slipped my mind. He listened carefully, his eyes glued to mine, and when I had finished, he was silent for a good few minutes.

'I have only a few questions,' he said finally. 'The first is: why were you carrying a hundred thousand francs in cash?'

'I always carry a lot of money with me. It's in case I need

to buy something.' He said nothing, but his eyes invited me to explain further. 'You know, like a painting perhaps, or a boat, or maybe even a car ...'

'Or drugs?' he said quietly.

'No,' I said equally quietly, 'I have never bought drugs in my life.'

'In normal circumstances I would not believe you. You are, I understand, an employee of a small newspaper, and yet you drive a rented Porsche and carry large amounts of money. However, Mr Pendleton, who is obviously an honourable man, vouches for you. He tells me you have a small private income. He also referred me to a policeman in London, an Inspector Bernstein, who also vouches for you.'

'Theo said nice things about me?' I was amazed.

'No, he said that although you are honest you are an extremely irritating person, and that I should lock you up.' Good ol' Theo.

'Ha ha,' I laughed weakly. The policeman did not join in my mirth.

'I should also tell you that we have recovered the *pinasse* from the basin, and what you have told me matches what we have found. The boat was deliberately holed, and we also found a still-corked bottle in the locker which contained a small amount of wine heavily contaminated with a narcotic drug.'

'That's good to hear,' I said.

'One more question. Why did all this happen?'

'Good Lord, I haven't the faintest idea!' I said.

'Bullshit. The people who did this to you did not do it for fun. They did not do it to rob you. They did it to stop you from doing something, or to take revenge for something. Which?'

It was the former, obviously, but I said: 'I truly don't know.'

'More bullshit. You are lying, I know.' There was an uncomfortable silence before he added: 'However, you do not appear to have broken any French laws, and you are therefore not under any restrictions as far as the police are concerned.' He got up, presumably to go.

'I have a question,' I said. 'Do you have any idea who these

83

people are? The girl said it was her father's boat; have you checked that out?'

He looked at me for a moment. 'We will speak again tomorrow, when you are stronger. *Au revoir.*' He left the room.

A little while later Ambrose visited, clearly relieved to see me obviously recovering, and the rest of the day was spent with doctors and nurses. My relationship with Rosa Klebb improved dramatically, to the extent that by the end of the afternoon she had me walking, albeit unsteadily, around my room and the corridor outside. I was slightly unnerved to discover that her real name was Rosalie.

On the Friday morning I really was feeling very much better, and I was in my dressing gown pacing around my room when Aristède arrived.

'Ah, you are walking,' he observed.

'Yes, quite well, actually.'

'So, please come with me.'

I followed the policeman out into the corridor and down towards a bank of elevators. We went up two floors and he led me along a corridor until we reached a door with a policeman standing outside it. He saluted my escort, opened the door for us, and we went inside.

We were in a room very similar to mine except that the bed and sparse furnishings suggested that this was being paid for out of the public purse. In the bed was a woman, apparently asleep, whose face was horribly bruised and swollen.

I looked at her uncomprehendingly. Only when the policeman said to me: 'Is this the woman who took you on the boat?' did I realised that it was, indeed, Eve Dupont.

Chapter Fourteen

She was in a very sorry state. The area around her left eye was so swollen that the eye itself could not be seen at all. Her left cheekbone was a mass of multicoloured bruising and small cuts covered by transparent pieces of sticking plaster, and her lips were swollen to at least double their original size. When she moved her head I saw that the other side of her face was relatively unscathed, and it was most certainly my delectable picnic companion.

'Is this the woman?' Aristède repeated.

'Yes,' I answered.

She was awake now, and when I spoke her good eye seemed to come into focus on me, and when she recognised me it filled with tears. Was this to be the story of my life? Beautiful women with eyes full of salt water? For a moment, no-one said anything, and the tears continued to well up and then splash onto her pillow.

'I thought you were dead!' she rasped hoarsely and desperately through cracked and puffy lips.

'Ah! It speaks. Until now she has refused to speak a single word,' the policeman said triumphantly.

'What happened to her?' I demanded.

'We do not know. She was found, the same morning that you were found, clinging to one of those pieces of wood which mark the oyster beds in the basin. She was discovered by one of the oyster workers who brought her to the hospital. But until now she has refused to speak.

'The doctors say that she has been hit on the head. She was in deep shock, with concussion, and it was a miracle, firstly,

85

that she did not drown in the water and, secondly, that she did not die from hypothermia. Lucky for her, she is young and healthy.'

'God! They must have tried to kill her too! She had done her stuff for them, and they didn't want any witnesses.'

I looked at Eve. The tears were still flowing freely. 'Is that right, Eve? Did they try to kill you?' But she didn't answer.

I sat down on the chair next to her bed and took her hand. Her fingers closed weakly over mine, and the sobbing intensified.

'I did not know they wanted to kill you!' she wailed. 'They told me they wanted to take the car, the Porsche. You were to sleep on the boat, so that they could drive far away before you call the police.' The words came out with difficulty, in a cracked voice, between the sobs. Her accent was even stronger than before.

'Oh God, 'Oratio, I am so sorry! It is all my fault for being so stupid.' I squeezed her hand.

'Never mind that. I'm perfectly OK now, as you can see. Just tell us who they were, and what happened.'

'I do not know their names. Two men. Bad men, from Bordeaux. They telephoned in the morning and they offered me money to do this. I said I would not do it, but they said they would hurt my father if I refused. And me. So I was afraid, and I said yes.'

'You must know who they were!' Aristède barked in French.

Eve ignored him and continued looking at me. She answered in English: 'No. I don't know their names.' She paused, and looked down. 'They are friends of my brother. He lives in Bordeaux, and he is not a good person. He sells drugs. That is how they knew I live in Piraillan, near Le Canon, and that we had a *pinasse*. My brother must have told them.'

'His name?' Aristède demanded.

'Dupont, like me. Bertrand Dupont.'

'We'll try to find him. Go on.'

'So they came in the morning and we followed you.'

'In the green Renault?'

'Yes.'

86

'How did you know I would be at the beach?'

'We didn't. We knew you would stop somewhere, and when you were alone I was to speak to you, you know, make friends, and invite you to come on the *pinasse*. They gave me pills to put in the wine.'

'OK, I remember what happened during the afternoon, but what happened after I fell asleep?'

'The plan was that I would signal to them, and they would steal the car.'

'But what actually happened?'

'When I made the signal, they came to the *pinasse* in another boat. They were horrible! They told me to be quiet. Then they put things in your pockets and put you in the cabin. Then one man broke the bottom of the *pinasse* with a hammer. I tried to stop him, but he hit me.

'They put me in the other boat, but I told them that if they did not go back to save you I would tell the police.' She paused, and fresh tears gushed forth. 'Then one man hit me again, very hard, with a piece of wood, and I fell in the water. I heard them laughing as the boat went away. It was very cold.'

'What happened then?' I asked.

'I remember nothing more. Only when I got here. I thought you were dead!' Her voice broke completely.

'That's enough!' snapped a voice behind us, in French. It came from a very angry-looking man in a white coat whose name tag said he was a doctor. 'This is my patient, and there'll be no more questioning of her until tomorrow at the earliest.' He spoke in a tone of voice that would allow no protest. 'Now, everyone out!'

I pressed Eve's hand softly. 'Don't worry; it's all over. Everything is going to be alright. Believe me.' She squeezed my hand back.

Outside the room I turned to Aristède. 'It's perfectly obvious that whatever she did was done under duress. It's also quite clear that she was not aware of their real intentions, so I hope you're not going to charge her with anything. I certainly don't want to make a complaint, and I will not give evidence against her. I think she's been punished enough already, poor girl.'

He sighed. 'I suspect you are right, but we will have to confirm her story. We must get descriptions of the men tomorrow and we will try to locate her brother in Bordeaux. But even if we do track him down, I doubt if we'll ever find those men.'

'I hope you do, because until they are caught, her life could be in grave danger,' I said sharply.

He glared at me. 'Perhaps your life will also be in danger if we don't find them.' He looked as if he relished that thought. 'What was it, I wonder, that those men put in your pockets? The money, perhaps, and something else? I am not stupid, you know.'

'Yes, I wonder what it was?,' I said innocently. 'The money was mine and whatever else they put in my pockets must have fallen into the water.'

'But not the money?'

'I must have been lucky,' I said sweetly. 'But at least we know now why they did this to me,' I added.

'And why is that?'

'As the girl says, they wanted to steal the Porsche, and the bastards didn't want me around afterwards to report it to the police. It's logical,' I said, hoping it would get him off my back.

'So why didn't they steal the Porsche, then?' he asked.

'They didn't?'

'No, it was still parked peacefully in Le Canon when we found it. No-one had touched it.'

'Ah,' I said.

'Ah, indeed.'

'Where is it now?' I asked.

'In the hospital car park. That's where Monsieur Pendleton said you would want it.' Good old Ambrose.

'Also,' Aristède continued, 'there is no sign of Professor Beaumanoir. One of my men went round there this morning, and his housekeeper said the Professor had gone on holiday. She did not know where, and knew only that he had left hurriedly a few days ago. I suppose you have no idea where he is?'

'No idea at all,' I replied honestly. Aristède gave me one more long, skeptical look, and then departed.

I found my way to the office of the director of the hospital. Within the hour Eve was moved to a private room with individual nursing care, and one of the top plastic surgeons in the country was on his way from Bordeaux by helicopter to look at the cuts on her face.

And by the afternoon I had sent poor old Ambrose down to the harbour to start making inquiries about how much it would cost to repair the Dupont *pinasse* and restore it completely. Probably not more than a hundred thousand francs, I thought.

Chapter Fifteen

After lunch I summoned up what rusted iron was left in my soul and telephoned Arnie Bloch to see if I still had a job.

'They tell me you were nearly dead,' he said delicately.

'That's what they tell me too, but I'm OK now. Fully recovering,' I said brightly.

'So when are you coming back to work?'

'Uh, Arnie, I thought I might take some time off, you know. The doctors say that I should rest for a while, and a fortnight will do it. It will come off my holiday time.' I waited for the eruption, but explosion came there none.

'Rubbish! If you're sick you're sick and you get sick leave. You don't have to take your holiday time.'

'You're a card, Arnie, thanks.'

'Well, never mind the cards, just make sure we get a good story out of this. You know, "How I survived my night of horror in the sea", that sort of thing. Man, I can see the head-line:

SHARK BAIT!
Explorer reporter Horatio Parker
tells of his death-defying ...'

'OK, Arnie,' I interrupted. 'In the meantime, do you know if the police have got anywhere on the Wheezy Wallis case?'

'No, they haven't. I spoke to Bernstein yesterday, and it sounds like they've got sweet bugger all. Incidentally, Bernstein wanted to know what you are doing in France, and why he has been getting strange phone calls from French policemen asking about you.'

'What did you tell him?'

'I told him it was none of his bleddy business, of course,' Bloch said, and he put down the telephone.

My next call was to Ambrose at his hotel in Arcachon, and it took me nearly half an hour to convince him that since I was well out of danger, well along the road to recovery, and well able to take care of myself, he should return to London. Eventually he agreed and said he would arrange to fly back later that afternoon.

Then I went to my room. I did two knee bends and one push-up and lapsed into exhausted slumber until I was awoken by hunger pangs.

I managed to persuade Rosalie, who was turning out to be much less dangerous than I had thought, to bring me a bottle of wine with my dinner, and she even agreed to have a glass with me. I explained that I wanted to go somewhere for a fortnight's holiday and asked if she could recommend a place.

'You should go to a spa,' she said. 'For ze mud baths, for ze massage, for ze swimming, for ze tennis. It's good for you.' I was unconvinced.

'Oh yes, zere is a very good one in Landes, not far from Bordeaux, in Eugénie-les-Bains, with a five-star hotel. Ze owner is ze famous chef, Michel Guerard, and ze restaurant has three rosettes in ze *Guide Michelin*.' Now she was talking! Ze food. Ze massage. That was exactly the therapy I needed.

On Saturday morning the doctor watched me working out in the hospital gym. I did three knee-bends, four push-ups and more than 60 metres on the exercise bicycle.

'See?' I told him breathlessly. 'I'm perfectly OK now. All I need is some rest, some decent food, a mud bath or two and a couple of massages. Oh, and a bit of tennis, perhaps.' I had weighed myself and discovered that I had lost seventeen pounds during my little adventure in the water.

'I have seen healthier people,' he said with a grin, 'but if you feel well, there is no reason to stay in hospital.'

'What about Eve Dupont?' I asked.

'She also is weak and needs rest, but there is little more in the way of treatment that we can offer her. If she wishes to leave, I can give her some tablets that she should take for the next few weeks. You too, for that matter.'

Then I went to see Eve. Her face was still horribly swollen, and there were a few new pieces of sticking plaster covering cuts on which the plastic surgeon had done some repair work, but her mood had improved. She was sitting up in bed reading a magazine, and she gave me what approximated to a smile when I walked in. The withdrawal, distress and guilt so apparent the previous morning were clearly lifting.

Not only had she had discovered that I was alive, but Aristède had also told her that, pending corroboration of parts of her story, and ongoing inquiries in Bordeaux, the police were not at present considering any proceedings against her, particularly as I had refused to make any complaint against her.

I accelerated the healing process even more by quietly telling her about the hundred thousand francs that had been planted on me, and about Ambrose's inquiries at the docks – where he had established that the cost of repairing and restoring the *pinasse* would be around eighty thousand francs.

'You will pay for ze work?' she said, her good eye wide with astonishment.

'It won't be me paying. This is not my money. Think of it as compensation from those two men.'

'But after what I did; putting drugs in your wine ...?'

'Never mind about that. You were as much a victim as I was. Anyway, there's still twenty thousand francs left over, and I want to offer you a job.'

'A job?'

'Yes, just for two weeks. I urgently need an interpreter. Will you do it?'

'Yes, of course, but why ... when ...?

'Starting now. You need to get dressed, and we'll stop by at your flat to pick up some clothing. I will have to do some shopping ...'

'But ...' she tried to interrupt, but I cut her short.

'No buts. Everything is arranged. The doctor agrees that you can leave and he'll give you tablets to take with you. We're going to a spa for a fortnight, both of us, to recover, and the cost will be covered by the twenty thousand francs.' It wouldn't be, of course, not by a long shot if I knew French five-star hotels. 'Please say yes. I need you.' Nothing like a

92

little blackmail on an already guilty conscience.

'Yes,' she said. I felt so good I could have done maybe three knee-bends then and there.

It didn't take more than a couple of hours to complete all the formalities and get discharged from the hospital, but then we had to drive all the way around the bay to pick up Eve's things from her flat in Piraillan, on the peninsula, and buy some clothing for me. So it was early afternoon before we got on to the N10 route nationale south of Bordeaux, heading in the direction of Biarritz. We turned off onto the N134 and drove along the deserted road, through forests and vineyards, past the town of Mont-de-Marsan and, finally after about a hundred and twenty miles, to Eugénie-les-Bains.

Michel Guerard's hotel was perfectly set in a little valley, and we were welcomed by staff who wafted dreamily around in flowing pink robes and turned not a hair at our rather battered appearance, as if dealing with the walking wounded was a daily occurrence, especially if they arrived in Porsches. The adjacent rooms were sumptuous, and when you opened a window there was just a trace of sulphur in the air to remind you of the mud baths and other torture chambers elsewhere in the hotel.

We both rested and bathed and then met hungrily – not having had lunch – on the restaurant terrace where we were served Campari-based aperitifs by more staff in pink robes. Then finally to the restaurant where I put Eve to work immediately, translating the incredible menu.

About the food all I can say is that I finally understood why it is that only the very best get three Michelin stars. It was superb, tastes exploding with originality and brilliance in the mouth, but with subtlety too and with great understanding of the essential nature of each ingredient and its contribution to the dish. It was a meal that brought recuperative powers flooding back into my limbs, although when I got back to my room, I slept as if felled by a falling log.

The next day teams of vicious fascists pummelled us within an inch of our lives in a sulphurous dungeon, nearly drowned us in mud, softened us with more massages, cleansed us with steam, wrapped us in towels and then deposited us gently on shaded recliners next to the swimming pool with jugs of cool orange juice. The last thing I remember hearing was the pok pok pok sound of tennis balls being batted around, and then I slept. And thus was the pattern of our stay established, during which I felt strength flowing back into me. It was a regime in which Eve blossomed, every day seeing the facial swelling diminishing, the tension disappearing and the glow returning to her skin.

One evening I dialled Professor Beaumanoir's telephone number from my room. The ringing went on for a long time until, eventually, a woman's voice answered in French. I asked in English whether the Professor was available.

'No,' was the reply.

'When will he be back?'

'Ze professor 'as gone on ze 'oliday. I do not know when 'e will return.' Then she hung up.

We had been there four nights, spending our days together in soft and intimate conversation, which also aided the recovery programme. After our meal on the Wednesday night we had parted as usual in the corridor outside our rooms. A few minutes later there was a tap on my door.

Eve stood there, stunning in just a negligée, an intense expression on her beautiful face.

'What is it?' I asked, slightly alarmed. She said nothing, but lifted her face and kissed me, gently and languidly, her lips so soft and sweet that I got lost in rolling clouds of sensation that began to move the blood around in my body in quite the most alarming way.

'Hang on,' I said breathlessly.

'I want to make love with you,' she whispered. And kissed me again.

Ardour fought a thrilling battle with anxiety inside me, trying to persuade me to sweep her into my arms. But anxiety has an uncanny way of having the final word.

'Wait!' I said, more insistently.

'Don't you want me?' Said with candour, not coquettishly.

'Of course I want you! ' I told her.

'So? I am here.'

'Yes, but this is not right. I am paying you for being here with me; you are an employee.' Perhaps I could have composed the thought more carefully and presented it more subtly. But at that kind of notice, this is all I could manage.

She looked at me squarely, disappointment on her face, the rejection masked by a sudden smile. 'Of course. I understand. I am sorry.' And she was gone.

I sat on my bed, my heart pounding, beginning to feel like an absolute ass, and wondering if I was turning into a ponderous, pompous prick in my old age. Then there was another tap on the door.

Eve again. With a wicked grin.

'I resign my job. Now will you make love to me?'

'Yes.'

What else could I say?

Chapter Sixteen

Ms Dupont and I arrived in London on a rainy June Sunday afternoon, in bouncing good humour and sporting wide smiles and glowing suntans that brought a flash of irritation to the face of the immigration officer at Heathrow who glanced perfunctorily at our passports.

We were met by an equally cheerful Frankie Price, his cheer the result of nearly doubling his income while I was away by plying for hire while still on my payroll. And he clearly approved of Eve.

'Lovely bit of stuff,' he remarked sotto voce to me after she had entered the cab and he and I were putting things in the boot.

'You are an incorrigible sexist pig, despite your degree in psychology,' I told him. 'Miss Dupont is somewhat more than a "bit of stuff".'

'Yeah, well she's still lovely,' he said.

'Yeah,' I agreed, and we headed for London.

We had returned from Eugénie-les-Bains to discover that Eve had been fired from her job at the holiday lettings agency in Cap Ferret. One could not, of course, take that sort of thing lying down, and I instructed Ambrose Pendleton to make immediate arrangements to buy the agency and dispense with the services of the person who had sacked her. My intention was to install Eve as managing director – with her under the impression that it was Ambrose who was her boss, of course.

I had been told that the transaction would take some weeks to arrange and, since we were getting on like hot croissants and coffee, it had seemed natural that she should come back to

England with me for the time being.

'To practice your English,' I had suggested.

'Of course.'

'And some other things.'

'Yes.'

'Practice makes perfect,' I said.

'Aah, practice, zis I like.'

'Try to say this, not zis.'

She took a breath, frowned, pouted her perfect lips and said: 'Zis. 'Ow was zat?'

'Wonderful,' and I kissed her.

There was still some very faint bruising on the side of her face, and still some sign of the cuts and abrasions which, I had been assured, would disappear without trace. But the fear and worry had mostly gone out of her eyes. Her father's *pinasse* was being repaired at the expense of the people who had tried to kill me, and she was fairly sure now that I had forgiven her for her part in the affair.

As for me, I was still a few pounds under my fighting weight but otherwise fully recovered. It was amazing what six days in hospital and then a fortnight at a health spa could do for an exhausted body. My psychological health was another matter, however, and I still burned with an anger and resentment that kept me awake at night and seething during the day.

That what had happened to me in France was connected to my inquiries at the Rupert Cornwell Gallery, with Professor Beaumanoir and the murder of Wheezy Wallis, I had no doubt. I had no direct evidence to that effect, but I trusted my instincts. It was an innate knowledge which trampled underfoot all reason and sense. I knew, too, that the attempt to remove me from the face of the earth had been highly organised, and by someone who had been willing to spend a great deal of money. Ergo, an even greater deal of money had to be at stake.

Another thought that concerned me was that whoever it was who had ordered me killed would certainly also be aware that I was still very much alive and kicking. Would they try again?

When we arrived at the hotel in Chalk Farm I had another brief word with Frankie. 'I think I might need a bodyguard for a while. Do you have any idea where I should look?'

'I think I know just the sort of geezer you need. I'll get back to you,' Frankie said. He didn't ask why I wanted a body-guard. He had long since stopped questioning my odd behaviour and strange activities. I suspect that Frankie knew a lot more about me and my affairs than he let on.

On Monday morning Frankie took Eve shopping in the West End after dropping me at the office.

'Yew OK?' Arnie Bloch snapped at me by way of fond greeting.

'Sort of,' I lied. 'The doctors say I shouldn't be put under any stress.' I saw Arnie take in a sharp breath, as if about to say what he thought about doctors, but then he thought better of it, and slowly exhaled.

'OK. Take it easy.' Then he added: 'That doesn't mean you don't do any work, hear?'

'Of course not, Arnie. You know me.'

'Yes, that's the trouble.'

I told him that I wanted to devote my time to the Wheezy Wallis case, and why. I told him the whole story, and felt his beady eyes unwavering on my face as we spoke. Arnie may have missed out when they were handing out the social graces, but he had grabbed more than his fair share of journalistic acumen.

'You have no evidence of anything,' he said when I'd finished.

'I know.'

'And without cast-iron evidence, we can't publish a word of this,' he added.

'I know.'

'So we'll have to find some evidence.'

'That's what I think.'

'Well, don't just stand there thinking, man, get on with it!' he barked. I was on my way out of his office when he added: 'And just watch the stress, hey?'

'Yes, Arnie.'

An hour later I was in Theo Bernstein's office at Hampstead nick, being told how every avenue of enquiry in the Wallis case had proved fruitless. Apart from confirming the patholo-

98

gist's hypothesis, the forensic examination of the car had yielded no other information. A few unidentified hairs and fibres, but no fingerprints other than Wheezy's and those of other members of his family.

Police had interviewed scores of villains, mainly drug dealers, who might have wanted to put Wheezy down, but all had had alibis – especially the ones still in prison – or had otherwise convinced the officers that they had not been involved.

No-one had seen anything, and no-one had been able to suggest any possible motive for the murder. 'Frankly, it's like it didn't happen. Except that we know it did,' Theo said.

'Have you checked out the Rupert Cornwell Gallery?' I asked.

Theo's eyes narrowed. 'What about the Cornwell Gallery?'

'Did you find out what Wheezy's connection with the gallery was?'

'How do you know about the Cornwell Gallery?'

'What did you find?'

'What are you up to, Parker?'

We could go on like this for hours, Theo and I, asking each other questions which we each refused to answer. The trouble was that Theo was bigger than I, and a policeman to boot, and there was always this hint of a threat that he could fling me into a dungeon any time he wanted, on the pretext that I was obstructing an investigation or withholding pertinent evidence. I knew I would have to answer first. I always did.

'I saw a piece of paper with the gallery's name on it with Wheezy's stuff. You know, that bag of things that was given to you at the morgue,' I explained.

'And what did you do about it?'

So I told him. The whole story, including my visits to the gallery and Professor Beaumanoir. I described with admirable modesty my ordeal in the sea and my dramatic rescue. I failed to mention the cocaine that had been planted on me, and I also said nothing about my discovery that Wheezy had had a copy of the painting hanging on his wall at home. A guy has to have some secrets.

Theo sighed deeply when I had finished. 'That explains the strange telephone calls from the police in Bordeaux and

Arcachon,' he said. 'It also explains the reception I had at the Rupert Cornwell Gallery where I had the distinct impression that my visit was expected and very well prepared for.'

'What did Cornwell tell you?' I asked.

'Nothing. He was welcoming and charming, and when I mentioned Wheezy's name he cocked his head politely and said he'd never heard of him. He even looked through his data base to see if he had a Wheezy or Albert Wallis on his mailing list for exhibitions and auctions, but there was nothing.'

'What did you make of that?' I asked.

'Nothing. What puzzles me is why you think someone like Cornwell and Wheezy were connected in some way.'

'Only the piece of paper that Wheezy had. He wasn't the sort of person who naturally frequented art galleries.'

'Except perhaps to steal something,' Theo said.

'Stealing paintings wasn't Wheezy's style,' I said. 'He knew nothing about art, and wouldn't have known what to steal or where to sell it. Anyway, did Cornwell say they'd had a burglary?'

'No. But what makes you think that the Bretton painting is relevant to all this?'

'Instinct,' I said, 'together with the fact that someone tried to consign me to the deep as soon as I started making serious inquiries about it, someone wealthy and powerful enough to have connections in France prepared to do something like that at short notice.'

Theo looked thoughtful. 'What happened to you in France is bizarre, I admit, but there is just no evidence at all that it was connected with Wheezy's death. For all we know it could have been down to someone like Eduardo Adolfini, for example. There are many people who don't like you, Parker.'

I shuddered. Eduardo Adolfini was a particularly nasty mobster currently serving a long prison sentence for murder, attempted murder and conspiracy to cause grievous bodily harm – a conviction directly due to my efforts during a nasty caper two years before.

'No, I think Adolfini's much too busy running his empire from his prison cell to worry about someone like me,' I said.

'The main thing is,' Theo said with a warning sound in his voice, 'that this is yet another example of you getting involved, uninvited, in a police investigation, blundering around wildly and dangerously without authority or remit. It's got to stop, Parker, or you are going to be in serious trouble with the police.'

'That's gratitude for you,' I retorted. 'Without my blunderings, as you call them, you would never have cracked the Karabekian case, and you would certainly not have found the people who had Murdoch Finnegan killed last year. Without me they would probably still be calling you Sergeant. How about co-operating with me for a change?'

But Theo went into his philosopher mode. 'I am reminded of the words of Nittai the Arbelite, one of the rabbis whose deliberations comprise the Talmud, who said: "Do not associate with the wicked, lest you carry away some impact by him."'

What could I say to that? You can't argue with the Talmud.

Shortly after I got back to the office I received a call from Frankie on the car phone I had installed in his taxi. 'I've found you a bodyguard. Highly recommended by people who know about these things. Very highly recommended,' he said.

'Good, where is he?'

'Buy me lunch at Ed's Diner first and then I'll take you to see him.'

'OK, come past and pick me up.'

Ed's Diner, in Hampstead High Street, is Frankie's favourite restaurant. He loves the pastiche American '50s decor, the old fashioned bottles of coke, the plates of French fries with ketchup and the well-anointed hamburgers so big you have to stretch your lips like rubber bands to get a proper bite. But most of all he loves the jukebox loaded with American '50s and '60s rock and roll and country hits with the volume set high enough to compete with the already animated noise level in the restaurant. Frankie fed in 5p coins and we listened to Dion's 'Runaround Sue' and Little Eva's 'Locomotion' five times each. Then, with my ears still ringing, he took me down to a gym behind a pub on Haverstock Hill and introduced me to a large water barrel.

'Meet Thumper,' he said.

I swallowed nervously as the water barrel stretched out a hand like a baseball glove which engulfed mine as if I was a small child. Until that moment, the name Thumper had conjured up images of the fluffy rabbit from the Bambi film. Never again.

'Pleased to meet you ... er, Mr Thumper. Or is that your first name?'

'No names, no pack drill, Mr P,' Frankie butted in. 'He's just called Thumper, for reasons which will be obvious to many. He comes at three hundred quid a day plus expenses. In cash, payable weekly. But he's very good.'

'Thumper,' said Thumper, shaking my hand with a gentleness quite at odds with the rough and calloused feel of his gigantic hand.

'What sort of expenses?' I asked.

It was Frankie who replied: 'You know, travel, meals, equipment, any legal bills. That sort of thing.'

Something told me I might be getting in beyond my depth.

Frankie continued: 'You're lucky, Mr P. Thumper doesn't work for just anybody. I had to tell 'im all about you, to convince him, like, that your body is worth guarding, ha ha.'

'And are you convinced?' I asked Thumper. But answer came there none; only a genial smile which worked its way across the extraordinary features of his face. He really was a remarkable figure and, all in all, precisely the sort of person you would dearly like to have at your elbow if you had, for example, inadvertently blundered into a den of thieves or one of those pubs in King's Cross with sawdust, spit and blood on the floor.

He was about six feet four inches in his socks, but didn't look very tall at first because he was ... well, very round. My initial image of him as a water barrel was not that inaccurate. But despite the enormous bulk of the man, there was no indication that much of it was fat; there was a solidity to him that made one think in terms of locomotives and combine harvesters. And at the top of it all was his shaven head, with huge jug-like ears on either side, and ... well, equally jug-like features in front. Only his eyes appeared to be of normal size, and they twinkled with good humour.

'He's a bit shy, and a man of few words until he gets to know you, Mr P,' Frankie explained helpfully. I knew that already, having so far heard only one. 'P'raps you'll under-

102

stand if I say that he was a friend of Wheezy's. That's why 'e decided to take the job.'

For the first time I began to feel a pang of sympathy for Wheezy's murderer, but not for long.

'OK, I accept the terms. What arrangements do we have to make?'

'It's all arranged. When we're in the cab he comes with us. At other times he'll be around, looking after you, even if you don't see him,' Frankie said.

'He's hard to miss,' I remarked.

'I told you, Mr P, he's good. He came highly recommended by some people who really ought to know.'

'Right, come on then, we've got things to do,' I said.

When Thumper got into the cab it rocked violently, and I had a momentary panic that it might tip over completely. Even Frankie looked around in alarm. The man mountain gave me another of his genial grins, and took up most of the back seat. I moved to one of the fold-down seats behind the driver, and we set off.

Chapter Seventeen

I asked Frankie to head for the Wallis home in Kentish Town. Thumper sat immobile in his seat, with that genial grin playing over his face. I was beginning to suspect it was a permanent feature of his expression. He didn't seem to be paying much attention to what went on around him until, at the traffic lights in Malden Road, another cab drew up alongside, just slightly closer to us than would be normal. It's not that he tensed exactly, but a certain stillness descended through his body. His small twinkling eyes stopped their amiable roving and one of his colossal hands idly moved to the door handle, while the other went to the seat next to him, as if to brace himself for sudden action. In the event, the other cab drew off smoothly when the lights changed, and the process went into reverse. The hands returned quietly to his lap, and the eyes resumed their easy roving. Perhaps there was more to Thumper's bodyguarding than sheer bulk.

When we got to Wheezy's house, I asked Thumper to wait next to the cab. 'I'll be in no danger inside,' I explained. 'I just want you out here on the pavement.'

'OK,' he said, and the cab rocked violently again as he got out. I'd now heard him say two words.

I rang the doorbell and Uncle Herbert came to the door. ''Ullo, Mr Parker.' He looked at me with some concern. 'I'm afraid Maisie's out at the moment. She's found herself a job at the Sainsbury superstore in Camden Town. The baby's at her sister's and I'll be fetching the other kids from school in a mo.' He looked at his watch.

'Actually, I came to see you,' I told him.

He seemed genuinely surprised. 'Me?'

'Yes, you, if you've got a few minutes.'

He looked at his watch again. 'Oh yeah, sure. I only got to pick 'em up at half three. Come in.' He led the way.

Walking behind him I tried to recall what Wheezy had told me over the years about his Uncle Herbert, his late father's brother. One thing I remembered straight off was that my late burglar friend had once confided that he had learned everything he knew about B-ing & E-ing from his uncle.

'Not from your old man?' I had asked.

Wheezy had replied: 'Nah, he was always in the joint, wasn't he? 'Erbert, on the other hand, never spent a day behind bars. Never got nicked even once.'

When we got to the front room, Herbert waved his hand in the direction of a liquor cabinet and then towards the kitchen, the actions accompanied by the words: 'Drink? A cuppa?'

'No thanks, Herbert. Just had lunch.' We sat down. 'Sorry I couldn't make it to the funeral. I would have liked to have been there.'

'No, that's awright, Mr Parker. We 'eard you'd had a spot of bother 'cross the Channel, like.'

'You heard about that?' I asked.

'Yeah, well, Frankie told us.'

'Did he tell you what it was about?'

'Nah, just that you'd had a spot of bother.'

'Were there a lot of people at the funeral?' I asked.

'Oh yeah, hundreds. All the family and friends from the manor, and there was even some Old Bill there an' all. That Inspector Bernstein and another one. Family liked that, they did. Nice of 'em to come, we thought. Look, you sure I can't get you a beer or something? Wouldn't mind one meself.'

'Go ahead, but not for me, thanks.'

He went into the kitchen, and I took advantage of his absence to look carefully around the room. No picture. I waited for him to come back with a bottle, settle down on the couch opposite me and take a long swig.

I estimated that he was between sixty five and seventy, but alert and fit for his age, with a flat stomach and strong-looking hands. Like all the Wallis family, he had high cheekbones and widely spaced eyes, but not much hair to speak of.

105

'What happened to the picture, Herbert?'

I said it quietly, but clearly, and he went rigid for about half a second. Then he put the bottle down, looked at me guilelessly, and said: 'Wot picture?'

'The one that hung there, over the fireplace, where there is an unfaded patch of wallpaper.' I nodded in the direction. 'That picture.'

'Oh, that picture. I dunno. Maybe Maisie sold it or something. She's a bit short of bread right now, you know.'

'Maisie didn't sell it.'

'How do you know?'

'Because,' I said, still speaking quietly, 'Maisie wouldn't have bought or sold anything without Wheezy's say-so, and I know it was already gone from that wall on the day after he was killed. So Wheezy must have done something with it before that, and I think you know all about it.'

There was total silence in the room, and I could hear the kitchen clock ticking loudly next door. After a while the silence became uncomfortable, but I sat tight. This is an old journalistic trick; when faced with someone who doesn't want to speak, shut up. English people find silences embarrassing and unbearable and sooner or later they feel they have to fill the verbal space.

'Just assuming,' he said eventually, 'just assuming, mind, that I did know something about that bleeding picture, what's it to you? What business is it of yours?'

'You say you heard about my bit of bother in France?' He nodded. 'Well, what would you say if I told you that someone tried to kill me, to drown me on a sinking boat in the middle of the bloody ocean with a pocketful of cocaine, and all because I went to speak to a little old professor about the original of that painting and the man who painted it?'

He was silent for a moment. Then: 'Why did you want to ask him about the painting?'

'Because I found a piece of paper among Wheezy's things with the name of a West End art gallery on it. I went to the gallery, saw the painting, and remembered that Wheezy had a copy of it hanging in this room. When I saw that this one had disappeared, I put two and two together and assumed that it had something to do with Wheezy's murder. What I wanted to establish in France was that the painting in the gallery was the genuine one.'

'And was it?' said Herbert.

'I spoke to the world's greatest expert on the work of the artist, and he confirmed that it was.'

There was another short silence, and then he spoke. 'Well, sorry, Mr Parker. I can see why you're interested in the painting, but I ain't got a clue what Wheezy done with it, honest. I didn't even know it was by this Breeton geezer. So I can't help you.'

That was interesting. I hadn't mentioned the artist's name.

'OK, Herbert, I'm sorry I bothered you with this. I thought you might want to help find out who killed your nephew. It's OK, I'll see myself out.' He shrugged, and I left.

I was feeling thoroughly pissed off, convinced that Herbert knew exactly what I was talking about, but unsure about how to go about persuading him to trust me. Then I saw my new employee leaning against Frankie's taxi and I had an idea.

'I'd like you to do me a favour, Thumper. It's not strictly bodyguarding, but it might help me find out who killed Wheezy.'

'Sure,' said Thumper. Three words.

'I need you to explain to Herbert Wallis, in there, just how important it is for him to talk to me about what he knows. Could you do that? Without hurting him, I mean,' I added hastily.

Thumper smiled at me, and headed for the house. For such a large man he moved extraordinarily gracefully, covering the ground quickly and smoothly. He rang the doorbell. Herbert answered again, and even from my vantage point some thirty metres away I saw him go pale when he saw Thumper. The door closed behind them.

Frankie and I stood on the pavement while I told him what was going on. At any moment I expected to hear the sound of breaking glass, screams and general mayhem, but all was quiet. We waited with bated breath and then, about five minutes later, Thumper emerged, grinning happily as always.

He left the door open behind him and when he reached us, he simply made a hand gesture inviting me to go back inside. Then he got into the cab.

I went back into the house and found Herbert still sitting on the couch, but now as white as a sheet and with a sheen of sweat on his face.

'Jesus, Mr Parker, where did you find that bloke?'

'He's my bodyguard,' I explained pleasantly. 'He also knew Wheezy, and he seems as anxious as I am to find out who killed your nephew. He didn't threaten you, I hope.'

'Christ, he didn't have to. He just stood there and said: "I think you should speak nicely to Mr Parker".'

'And that convinced you?'

'Yeah, well, then he took the poker out of the holder there by the fireplace and he bent it like it was putty.'

I looked at the said poker, lying on the hearth, twisted into a perfect reef-knot.

Herbert continued: 'Then he said: "Should I ask Mr Parker to come back?' and I said yes.'

'Does that mean you've decided to trust me after all?'

'I don't see as how I have much choice. If I don't you'll send that monster back in here and he'll break me in half.'

'No, that's not true. If you decide not to speak to me, I'll leave immediately and you can keep it all to yourself. But if you do tell me what you know, and I think you know quite a lot, I want it to be because you trust me, and because I was a friend of Wheezy's, and because he trusted me, on one occasion with his life.'

I could see the indecision in his eyes; he was wondering whether I really would go away if he decided to say nothing. Then he seemed to make up his mind.

'OK, we'll do it your way. But, straight up, Mr Parker, I can't talk to you now – I have to fetch the kids from school and have them back here by the time Maisie gets home. There'll be hell to pay otherwise. Any road, I don't want Maisie to know about any of this. Not yet anyhow.'

He looked more worried about Maisie's wrath than the threat of Thumper outside.

'OK then, when?'

'I'll meet you down the pub tonight after dinner, about

108

half eight or nine.'

'OK. Which one?'

'It's in Grafton Road, near Prince of Wales Road. It's called the Cock and Bull.'

Which seemed as good a place as any to hear a story.

Chapter Eighteen

It was only half past three, but I didn't feel like going back to the office. God and Arnie had ways to occupy idle hands, and I wasn't in the mood for any more news editor training. So I took my life in my hands and telephoned him from the cab.

'I'm not feeling well,' I announced weakly.

'Oh yeah?'

'Feeling some stress, actually.'

'Oh yeah?'

'Yeah. I mean yes.'

'Well then you better go home right away. We can't have you fainting all over the orifice, can we?'

'OK, I'm on my way.' Did he say 'orifice'? Presumably he meant 'office'. Either way, I was off the hook for the rest of the day.

Frankie dropped me off at the hotel. 'Take the rest of the day off, my good man,' I told him magnanimously. I could see the pound signs click into his eyes, and his arm twitched with the urgency of wanting to turn on his 'For Hire' light. Then I remembered my bodyguard sitting in the back of the cab, still with that benign look of goodwill to all men on his face.

'What about Mr ... er, Thumper?' I asked.

'He'll be around,' Frankie said.

'Around where?'

'Just around.'

'Oh.'

Thumper got out and just stood there. Then some guests came out of the hotel and climbed into the taxi. 'Heathrow airport,' said one in a rich Texan drawl, and I heard Frankie sigh with utter contentment. When I turned around again, Thumper was nowhere to be seen.

I went upstairs to find Eve beginning to unwrap the first of maybe fifteen parcels, most of them packed in tissue paper inside expensive-looking designer carrier bags with the words Whistles, Harvey Nichols, Joseph, Harrods, Janet Reger and Marian Foale printed thereon. My friend at Rothschilds had arranged for a credit card to be issued to her in record time.

'I had a very busy day,' she purred radiantly, with that post-orgasmic look of pure ecstasy that professional shoppers have after a really special spending frenzy. 'I have bought many things.'

'So I see. Show me,' I said politely.

'Ah ... ' she hesitated. 'Much of it is underwear. You know, for the ladies.'

'So show me,' I said, trying to keep my growing enthusiasm in check.

There were urgent flurries of discarded tissue paper, and then a succession of flimsy garments were being held out for my inspection.

'Sorry,' I said, the most beatific look of innocence on my face. 'This means nothing to me. I think you are going to have to model them for me.'

'Ah, Horatio,' she said huskily, sounding the guttural 'r' in my name in a way that made my blood run hot despite the icicles of delicious anticipation that ran down my spine. 'You arrre verrry wicked.'

'Yes,' I admitted.

I think we got through to the fourth or fifth parcel before I was overwhelmed by a pair of pale mint green silk French knickers which, as she bent to open the next tissue-wrapped bundle, revealed the swelling curve of one of the most perfectly formed buttocks between here and Ursa Minor, and maybe even the Andromeda cluster.

I lunged. Eve lunged back. Within a few minutes there was a snowstorm of bits of tissue paper.

We were both very hungry by dinner-time and my chef, Claude – pilfered if you remember, from a restaurant in Reims

111

– outdid himself. This may have had something to do with the fact that Eve had insisted on going into the kitchen and introducing herself as a fellow country-person. She had generated such an approving gleam in Claude's eye that I would have been worried had she not been simultaneously clinging to my hand like a limpet.

After coffee I explained to her that I had to go out, to meet a man in a pub.

'Ooh, a purb. I have never been to the Eenglish purb.'

'Ah, well this is not a typical pub. This is a very rough place. I'll take you to a very nice one tomorrow.'

'So? I have been in many rough bars in Bordeaux and Marseille. I am not afraid.'

'Eve, this is a confidential meeting.'

She pouted. The full Bardot-type pout, her lower lip sticking out angrily, and her eyes sparking with determination. 'So, I will sit at another table while you speak.'

'Eve ...'

'If you don't take me, I will ask Claude to take me.' That was a clincher, and she knew it.

'Come on then,' I said, 'but if you get beaten up in a pub fight, don't blame me.'

I got the doorman to call a cab and I asked the driver to take us to the Cock and Bull.

'The one in Grafton Road?' he said to me, although he was looking at Eve in the mirror.

'The very one.'

'You sure?'

'I'm sure.' He shrugged and we drove off. A minute later he half turned his head as cab drivers do and said through the glass partition: 'You ever been there before?'

'No,' I replied truthfully.

Silence again for a few blocks. Then: 'Sorry, guv. I know it's none of my business, but I have been to the Cock and Bull, and well, straight up, I don't think it's the kind of place you would want to take a young lady to. Especially such an attractive young lady as your companion, sir, if you don't mind me saying so.'

My courage wavered, but to show weakness at this stage

would have been unthinkable. 'I understand your concern, but I have to meet someone there, and this young lady tells me she is more than able to look after herself.'

'Well, it's your funeral. In a manner of speaking,' he said, rather ominously.

I tipped him handsomely for his concern for our welfare and then turned to look at the building outside which we had been deposited. Dirty late-Victorian bricks, filthy windows, door and window frames chipped, stained and desperate for a dollop of paint, and a forlorn and rusty pub sign hanging from one hinge; the cock thus appeared to be impaled on the horns of the bull. Even from the outside I could smell the sawdust, spit and beer on the floor. If Uncle Herbert was trying to test my resolve, he was succeeding.

Eve looked at me nervously, and I grinned at her grimly. She took my arm, I took a deep breath, and we went in.

Had there been swing doors and a man in a cowboy hat playing a honky-tonk piano, the effect could not have been more predictable. What had been a boisterous cacophony of conversation died as if a switch had been turned, and we faced a blank wall of hard, still faces, men and women, who scrutinised us without overt hostility but with unrepentant interest. I remember scores of coils of cigarette smoke curling towards the general fug of pollution that hung visibly about two feet below the ceiling. I was wearing my favourite brown corduroy suit, which always fitted in perfectly in pubs in Hampstead, and Eve was wearing an attractive light blue frock with shoelace shoulder straps, which, in this company, made her look as if she had just stepped naked from her bath. We could have been tourists from Jupiter.

I scanned the faces anxiously until I saw one I recognised. Uncle Herbert, looking a little dismayed that we had actually come and were heading in his direction. The crowd melted before us and, as we neared Herbert's table, three or four men vacated their chairs, leaving Herbert alone. We sat down. A couple of conversations had restarted, but the silence was still oppressive.

'You came then,' he said. It seemed the kind of pointless observation one might make in an establishment of this kind.

'Yes,' I answered, truthful as ever. But the silence was still

113

unnerving me. 'Look here, do you think this bunch might relax a little if I bought a round or something?' I said quietly.

'It would go down a treat,' Herbert replied. 'But you gotta put the money down on the bar up front; they don't run a slate here.'

I went over to the bar where a tightly packed crowd made way for me like the parting of the Red Sea. I said to the barman, a large man with greasy hair and filthy apron, 'I would like to buy a round of drinks for everyone here,' and I put two fifty pound notes on the counter. My words carried to the farthest reaches of the room, and were greeted with a general murmur of approval. There was also a general movement towards the bar, and by the time I got back to Herbert's table people were cheerfully calling out their orders, lifting their glasses to me in thanks and returning to their interrupted conversations.

'What about her?' Herbert asked, nodding at Eve.

Good point. I looked around the room and had an idea. 'This is Eve, a friend of mine from France. She wants to learn how to play darts.'

Herbert nodded and then beckoned to a group of young men. 'Oi, Bill, Jimmie, this nice French girl wants you to teach her to play darts.'

Not only Bill and Jimmie but half the men in the room responded to the call, and Eve was quickly led away to the far corner. She looked pleased at all the sudden attention.

'What'll you 'ave to drink, love?' I heard one ask.

'Pernod,' I heard her say.

'You what, love?'

I didn't hear the rest of the exchange.

Alone at last, and sealed in that unique privacy afforded by a noisy room, I looked at Herbert steadily. 'OK then, what have you got to tell me?'

'First off, tell me what you think is going on,' he said.

I paused for a few seconds. 'Fair enough. I think Wheezy saw all that stuff in the papers about the François Bretton painting being discovered by the Rupert Cornwell Gallery, recognised it as the same one as his copy at home, and somehow saw the opportunity to make a few quid.

'I don't know what he did, or what he had in mind, but I

suspect he approached the gallery with some sort of scam or proposition or something. But it must have gone wrong or turned sour in some way, and he ended up making someone angry or nervous enough to have him very professionally murdered.

'I have no evidence for this, or theories about what Wheezy was up to. All I know is that when I started asking questions about Wheezy and the painting at the gallery and in France, someone saw me as a big enough threat to justify mounting a sophisticated, and expensive, attempt to kill me too. How am I doing so far?'

'Not too good,' he said.

'OK then, let me ask you a few questions. What happened to Wheezy's copy of the Bretton painting?'

Herbert looked me steadily in the eye. 'What makes you think it was a copy?'

'Wasn't it?'

'No, it was a proper painting. The real thing.'

'Well, alright then, a similar one.'

'You're not listening to me,' Herbert said slowly. 'I said it was the real thing.'

There was a pause during which his eyes bored into mine and my heartbeat quickened with sudden understanding which had been a long time coming.

'It was the original fucking painting,' he said.

Chapter Nineteen

'The original? You're telling me that Wheezy had the original painting? The genuine one?' My questions were breathless. Herbert nodded seriously, no twinkle of mirth in his eyes.

'Hanging over his fireplace in Kentish Town? A painting worth millions of pounds?'

'Well, he didn't know that, did he?'

It was an impossible idea – an idea, I began to realise, that should have occurred to me weeks ago. 'Hang on a minute, how do you know it was the original?'

Herbert looked shifty. 'Come on, Mr P. Think about it.'

I thought about it. The undisputed original had been stolen from Munro Forbes in 1966. Stolen by burglars.

'It was you lot that nicked it from Forbes!'

'Now you're getting somewhere, Sherlock.'

'But in 1966 Wheezy was just a kid; he couldn't have been more than eight or nine years old.'

'Yeah, it was his first job,' Herbert said proudly, a dreamy quality in his voice. He finished his pint and tapped his glass. I went off to get him another, the crowd at the bar again opening up to let me through. I got myself a double Scotch.

I put his drink down in front of him and said, 'Come on, you'd better let me have the whole story.'

It took him a few seconds while he lit a fag and settled down. Then he began:

'There was this burglar alarm fitter out of Somers Town, guy by the name of Merv Woodhouse. Guys used to call him Woodlice on account of how he didn't bath and shave too often. Any road, he worked on the burglar alarms on this

116

Munro Forbes geezer's house out in Suffolk. We met him one night in a boozer down in King's Cross ...'

'Hang on a second,' I interrupted, 'who's "we"?'

'Me and Phil, my brother, Wheezy's dad.' I nodded, and he continued. 'Well, this Woodlice had had a few, and we bought him a few more, and of course he starts telling us what an ace burglar alarm "technician" he is and about all the amazing houses he's worked in, whereas we figure him for the kind of guy who carries the toolbox and occasionally hands the guv'nor a screwdriver. Or maybe scratches the boss's arse for him when his hands are full. Anyway, he also tells us about his latest job, this Munro Forbes's house in the country, about this geezer who spends thousands on burglar proofing and alarms but who's too tight with money to do the job properly, like.

'"Oh yeah?" says Phil, "tell us about it then, mate. I'll get another round in." So he tells us that there's this little window at the back of the house, for a scullery or pantry or something, about twelve inches by twelve inches, which this Forbes won't pay to have alarmed on account of how it's too small for any burglar to get through. Says 'e's got piles of silverware and antiques, and is spending thousands on the burglar proofing, but he still won't spring for the extra fifty quid for the wiring and electrical contacts on the little window. He's shaking his head and saying how he doesn't understand how some people's minds work and stuff like that, and we're agreeing with him.

'Later on Phil says to me: "Little Albert could get through a twelve-inch window, no problem," and from then on the job is on. Finding Forbes's place in the country is no problem, and there's even a cosy little hut on a hillside next to the house where we can watch the place from. It only takes a week or two before we can see that nobody actually lives in the house during the week. They live in London and only come up at weekends, and then not even every weekend.

'I also chatted up one of the girls in the village, whose mum turned out to be one of the few people who actually worked in the house any more, and she told me that the staff were only there on weekends an' all. We could see it was going to be a pushover. Bring in a van, drive it right up to the bleedin' front door in the middle of the night and bloody clean the place out. Easy. So that's what we done.' He picked up his glass and took a sip.

'Just like that? No problems?' I asked.

'No problems. Little Wheezy was a star; no nerves that I could see; went through that little window like a bleedin' ferret, found the alarm control box and switched the whole lot off. Then he opened the front door for us like he'd been doing it all his life. A natural,' Herbert sighed.

'Go on.'

'Yeah. Anyway, we took a lot of stuff that night. One of the very best jobs we ever did. Lots of time to pick and choose, you see. Nice collection of jewellery, antique silver, a fair amount of cash, even a few small bits of furniture. I remember one little carved stool which we ended up getting eight hundred quid for, and this was in the sixties, mind you.'

'And paintings, of course,' I prompted.

'Nah, well that's the funny thing. We wasn't going to take any paintings at all. Neither Phil nor me knew anything about paintings and we always felt that they was much too difficult to get rid of, so we never took paintings as a rule.'

'But this time . . ?'

'Well, this time we took one, because little Albert wanted it. Said he liked it and wanted to keep it. We told him we couldn't sell it but he said he didn't want to flog it; just wanted to have it in his room. A souvenir, like. So we let him take it.' Herbert grinned. 'He was a funny kid. Very quick, very bright, but he had some strange ideas, and he knew what he wanted.'

'And then?' I was getting a little impatient, and I could see that the darts game across the room was attracting an unusual amount of spectators.

'Then we kind of kept a very low profile for a while. We did the job on a Monday night, and that stuff was fenced and out of the country by the time anyone missed it the next weekend.'

'Except for the painting.'

'As you say, except for the painting.' He finished his pint.

'Another?' I said, pointing to his glass.

'That's OK, Mr P, I've had my three, and that's about

enough for an old fart like me.'

'Carry on then. You must have realised you had a valuable painting from the press coverage after the burglary?'

'No. First off, as I said, we went to ground for a bit. Spent a fortnight down at a cousin's place near Bognor on the South Coast, keeping indoors a lot and very quiet. So maybe we missed some of the newspaper reports. But we did see some, and I don't remember any mention of a missing painting.

'I been thinking about that recently, and I guess it was one of those times when the Old Bill held back on something, you know? Hoping the villains would get rash with such a well-known painting and try and get rid of it too quickly. Catch them that way. But we didn't even know it was worth more than a few hundred quid at the most, and we'd already made a big score on the job. Maybe it was mentioned later in the papers, but if it was, none of us saw it. After a while we just forgot about it. It was Wheezy's picture and that was that.

'We made a packet on that job, and that's a fact. Cleared nearly nine grand, which was a hell of a lot of money in those days. Organised it well, too. Just sat on it for ages. Didn't go out buying drinks for the whole of Kentish Town and buying motors and the like. Waited about a year at least, and then took a taxi back from the races one day, waving the bread like we'd won it in a big triple on the geegees. That's when we bought the house in Kelly Street, cash down, free and clear. No mortgage.'

'And then?' I prompted. The darts game was getting raucous, and I didn't want to leave Eve alone there for too long.

'And then nothing. Phil died a few years later and Wheezy and I sort of carried on. I don't think any of us gave a second thought to the painting ... until a few months ago.'

'What happened then?'

'It was a Sunday morning, and we was sitting in the front room drinking coffee and reading the papers. And then I hear Wheezy give a kind of a snort and I look up and he's staring at the painting, and his face has gone white. There it was, all over the bleedin' papers, and we'd never even known who the artist was in the first place.

'All that cobblers about the painting being found wrapped

119

up in a cupboard after the old man bought it back from the burglars! We knew that was bullshit right off. That painting had never left our house for twenty-eight years. But I must say, finding out how much it was worth came as a right shock. At first he was kind of stunned, but then he got all excited and it was like this was the Big One, the one that was going to take us all off to Spain to live in luxury in the sun for ever.

'Wheezy didn't tell Maisie or no-one. It was just the two of us knew. And what we also knew was that either this Rupert Cornwell or this daughter of Forbes's, who's supposed to have found the painting in a cupboard, were obviously up to a bit of no good. We didn't know much about paintings, but we did know there couldn't be two genuine versions of the same picture, and we were pretty sure that we had the real one. So much for the big expert from France who said theirs was the genuine article!'

The same thought had occurred to me, and it opened up a number of avenues for careful pondering.

'What did Wheezy do?' I asked.

'Ah, well, here's where I run out of steam, Mr P. I just don't know what he did. Kept everything close to his chest Wheezy did, and when I asked him what was going on, he just smiled and told me to start choosing what kind of swimming pool I wanted for my villa on the Costa del Sol. Straight up, I really dunno what happened.'

'What do you *think* happened?'

'What I think is that he must have contacted this Cornwell geezer and told him that he was onto his game. Maybe he even told Cornwell that he had the real painting. P'rhaps he demanded money to be quiet; or maybe he offered to sell Cornwell the painting for a couple of mill, I dunno. All I know is that he looked tense and excited the day before he died; wouldn't talk to me about it. But it was only after the Old Bill phoned early in the morning to say he'd been found dead that I even realised that the painting had gone.

'I dunno what happened that night, but it's got to have something to do with Cornwell. If I was a few years younger I'd go round there and clobber it out of him myself.'

'How old are you?' I asked.

'Seventy-one last month.'

He was as thin as a rake and slightly shaky, and the thought of him going somewhere and beating the truth out of someone was almost funny. Almost. I thought for a few moments.

'You never had any dealings with Cornwell, did you? He never saw you or spoke to you or anything like that?'

'No, like I said, Wheezy done it all.'

'Would you recognise the painting if you saw it again? I mean the one you had as opposed to Cornwell's?'

'Yeah, I reckon I could,' Herbert said.

'How come? You said you know nothing about paintings.'

He hesitated. 'I took it off the wall once, when we were decorating, and I noticed that Wheezy had scratched his initials on the wooden frame at the back. Well, I assumed it was Wheezy, because the initials was AW, for Albert Wallis.'

A nasty idea had begun to form in my mind, and I was desperately trying to ignore it.

'I want you to do something,' I told him. 'Tomorrow morning, I want you to go to the Rupert Cornwell Gallery. Dress as smartly as you can, try not to say anything to anyone, and just act like you're a punter come to look at the painting. You'll see it's on an easel in the middle of the room, inside a glass case. I think you'll be able to see the frame at the back. Try and see if they've got Wheezy's picture ... I mean the one Wheezy had, the original. I just hope they haven't re-framed it. When you've finished, telephone me.' I also handed him a twenty pound note. 'That's for a taxi there and back.'

'OK,' he said, taking the money entirely without protest.

It was time to go. I had had a busy day for someone supposedly delicate and trying to avoid stress, and I was exhausted. I walked over to the darts area where Eve was surrounded by about a dozen admirers. I tried to catch her eye, but was blocked by a large man in a dark blue shell suit.

'What you want?' he said, deliberately standing in front of me.

'I've come to get Ms Dupont,' I said politely. 'We have to go now.'

'Well she's not ready to go yet, so sod off.'

If he hadn't been a foot taller than me and two feet broader I would have smashed his face in without hesitation, but under the circumstances I was forced to continue the polite approach. I smiled, showing that I could take a joke.

'Ha ha. Sorry to break up the game, but we really do have to go.'

'Ha ha yourself. I said sod off!' He put a finger on my chest and pushed. I only moved back two or three feet. Not much. The bruise would heal.

By this stage the darts game had halted, and another deathly hush had fallen over the pub. Eve was looking at me anxiously, and I was regretting the fact that I had bought drinks for all these ungrateful bastards.

'Come on, Eve, let's go,' I said to her. She made a move towards me, but one of the men grabbed hold of her wrist.

'Oi!' my persecutor snarled. 'You deaf or something? I said sod off!'

The last four words were said loudly and deliberately, each accompanied by a separate jab from stiff fingers in the solar plexus. For an abject coward I must say I kept my head. All I could think of at that moment was whether I would be able to get in a punch or two before they squashed me through the cracks between the floorboards. I took a deep breath and prepared to die bravely. Then a deep voice boomed from behind me.

'Good evening, Mr Parker.' I turned round and almost wept with joy to see the massive bulk of Thumper blocking my view of the rest of the world. 'Do you need any assistance?' That was more than I'd ever heard him say before, and I was surprised to find that his voice, though deep, was quite cultured. Heaven knows where he had sprung from.

The effect of his arrival on my persecutor, however, was electric. The man's mouth had gone sort of slack, and the colour had drained from his face as visibly as if it had been squeezed. His Adam's apple was bobbing nervously.

'You,' Thumper said to him with a deceptively benign smile, 'what are you up to?'

'Nothing,' he gulped hoarsely.

'May I suggest, then, that you make yourself useful. Mr Parker here has told you that he and the lady have to go, so why don't you go outside and find him a taxi?'

The man hesitated for about seven microseconds before he

headed for the door. Thumper then turned to the other darts players and, looking pointedly at the man who had grabbed Eve's wrist, added: 'I really do think that you should buy your guests a drink while they wait. A Scotch, was it?' I nodded. 'And a glass of dry white wine for the young lady. We'll wait at this table here,' he said, indicating a table around which seven or eight of them were seated. Not for long. Within a few seconds the chairs had been vacated, the table wiped and our drinks placed on clean beer mats.

'Where on earth did you spring from?' I asked Thumper after we had sat down. 'Not that I'm complaining, you understand.'

'I was around,' he said enigmatically.

We didn't have much time to wait. A minute or two later the first man was back, hovering respectfully at the table, as if unwilling to interrupt.

'Yes?' Thumper said.

'Taxi's outside.'

'Ah, well why don't you go outside, open the door and wait for us? We won't be long.' Instant obedience. When we had finished our drinks we sauntered out and got into the cab. Thumper shut the door and waved happily at us as we drove off.

'Phew!' I said to Eve, 'Sorry about that, but I did warn you.'

'No, eet was my fault,' she said, with a strange grin, her French accent blossoming with all the alcohol she had drunk. 'I don't blame zose men.'

'What do you mean?' I protested. 'They virtually kidnapped you.'

'No – zey were angry wiz me because I took all zere money.' She delved into her handbag and brought out a fat wad of banknotes which she waved happily in front of me. I gaped. There must have been well over two hundred pounds in her hand.

'I 'ave been playing ze darts since I was four years old ... Zey wanted to try to win ze money back.'

When we got back to the hotel I telephoned Professor Beaumanoir again. but there was no reply.

Chapter Twenty

That night we slept like logs, and I had a satisfying dream in which Eve was throwing darts at a nude Rupert Cornwell pegged out spread-eagled on a huge dart board, with the missiles thudding home uncomfortably close to his naughty bits.

But I woke with my head buzzing with thoughts about Wheezy Wallis. The first thing to do, I thought to myself while shaving and bathing, was to establish which painting was now being exhibited in the gallery. If it was 'Wheezy's' then we knew that Cornwell had to be involved in the murder. If not, we had to find out what had happened to the real one.

Then there was the question of Munro Forbes's mysterious daughter who claimed to have discovered an apparently non-existent painting among her late father's effects. Some digging could profitably be done in that direction, I decided, and I knew a very beautiful *Observer* reporter with amazing green eyes who would be able to assist me in that direction.

And what about the kindly and scholarly Professor Beaumanoir? He who had fed me coffee and delicious croissants along with some whopping lies about the painting in Cornwell's gallery, which he must certainly have known was a fake. Why had he disappeared?

I also needed to know when Cornwell was planning to auction the painting, since the nasty thought which had occurred to me the day before, and which I was still trying diligently to ignore, was taking stronger and stronger shape by the hour.

I also needed to talk to my friend Mohan Mistry, who had a

small but specialised electronics supply shop in one of those little streets near Tottenham Court Road. Mohan knew everything there was to know about practical electronics, and I assumed the subject of modern burglar alarms could be classified under that heading.

All in all, I had a hefty agenda that Tuesday morning. I was therefore dismayed when Arnie Bloch blustered into my office within minutes of my arrival and announced: 'Phillips is sick. You're in the hot seat. Get to it, news editor.' Then he turned on his heel and went out.

My heart sank. This was exactly what I had been afraid of: having to run the news-gathering operation and oversee the work of all the reporters – a full-time job, when all I wanted to do was get on with my own work. But he didn't even give me time to argue, and I knew better than to go in and try to talk him out of a decision like that.

Drastic action was called for.

I wandered disconsolately over to the newsdesk and spent a few minutes looking through the mail, the news agency reports and the various events already listed in the news diary.

After a while, a thought occurred to me. It was high-risk, dangerous even, but I had no alternative.

I summoned all eight reporters and spent ten minutes giving them a detailed briefing on what I wanted done. All were puzzled, some were suspicious and some were downright worried. But I was clear and firm and when I said: 'Right, get on with it, on the double!' they moved obediently towards the door. Some of them had that look on their faces which read: 'It's your funeral, mate.'

'Hey, hey, hey! And let's be careful out there!' I added. No-one laughed.

It was nice and peaceful in the office without any reporters around, so I took the opportunity to make some telephone calls.

'Funnily enough,' Theo Bernstein told me tetchily from Hampstead police station, 'nothing at all has happened in the twenty-four hours since I last told you that nothing has happened.'

I couldn't help winding him up. 'That's what you think,' I told him cryptically.

'What are you up to, Parker?'

'Nothing. Well, nothing that I can tell you about. All you need to know is that I am on the case, and as soon as I need someone arrested, I'll let you know.'

'If I find that you are withholding evidence that I should know about I'll have you arrested for obstructing the course of justice so fast that it will make your head spin.' He sounded angry.

'Trust me, Theo. As soon as I have something you can use, I'll tell you immediately.'

'"Woe unto them that seek deep to hide their counsel from the Lord, and their works in the dark",' he quoted.

My next call was to Nigel Regan, arts correspondent on the *Telegraph*. 'You owe me lunch,' he complained.

'You'll get it.'

'I'll believe it when I taste it. What do you want, anyway?'

'When is that François Bretton painting going to be auctioned?'

'What is it with you and that painting, Parker? I've never known you to show the slightest interest in art, and suddenly you're on the phone to me about Bretton every two minutes.'

'Come on, Nigel, two phone calls in four weeks is not exactly every two minutes.'

'In terms of your interest in art, it is. Come on, I know you. What's up? I smell a story here.'

'All I can promise is that I'll let you interview me when the whole thing breaks, but it's my story and I'm not letting you in on it. Take it or leave it. I can get the information elsewhere, you know.'

'You're full of shit, Parker. But it just so happens that the auction is going to be on Wednesday next week, nine days from now. It was going to be next month, but the gallery has brought it forward by three weeks. I got the press release about it this morning, as a matter of fact.'

That was interesting. Was Cornwell getting nervous?

'Any reason given for the change of date?' I asked.

'Hang on ... here it is. "Due to unprecedented international interest", it says here.'

'What time will it start?'

'At eleven o'clock in the morning our time. That'll make it

very early in the morning for the Americans, but Cornwell is far more interested in the big money he expects to attract from Europe and the Far East, especially Hong Kong and Japan.'

That suited me fine. That time on a Wednesday was early enough to get something into that week's *Hampstead Explorer*, should anything interesting occur, that is.

I was just about to make another call when my phone rang. Herbert.

'It's Wheezy's!' he hissed excitedly.

'Where are you calling from?' I said urgently. I had visions of him having asked to use the telephone at the gallery.

'Call box. I'm not daft.'

'Sorry. Look, you're sure about the painting?'

'One hundred per cent. No question. You can see the initials on the wood.'

So, Cornwell was involved. There was no doubt about that now.

And the only evidence we had could put Herbert in prison.

We had to find another way to bring the suave, handsome, murdering bastard down. The nasty idea in my mind climbed another notch towards implementation, and I couldn't ignore it any more.

'OK, Herbert, jump in a cab and come here, to my office. We need a council of war.'

When I put the phone down I became aware that three or four of the reporters' phones were ringing, and there was no-one around to answer them. Furthermore, Arnie was standing in the doorway of his office with a bemused look on his face.

'Where's everyone?' he asked me. I steeled myself, knowing that brown stuff was about to be dispersed by the air circulation system.

'Out on a job,' I explained.

'All of them on jobs, at the same time?' He was puzzled. My heart rate went up to around 160 a minute.

'Er, not jobs, Arnie. One job.'

'One job?'

'Yes.'

'All eight of them?'

'Yep.'

127

'Must be some important job,' he said. There was a terrifying stillness in his voice. He looked calm, but I knew that he could kill at any time without warning.

'Very important,' I agreed. I was treading a delicate path indeed.

'What job is it, exactly?'

'The industrial tribunal. That teacher claiming she was wrongfully dismissed by Camden Council's Education Department because she was always coming to work late. It's going to last two days.'

I saw muscles in Arnie's jaw begin to twitch. He came closer and I knew my life depended on my ability to appear sincere. He even adopted a kind of grin, which made me think of a saying from the Talmud that Theo had quoted to me: 'Do not think that the lion is smiling when he bares his teeth.'

'Explain,' he said.

'Explain what, Arnie?'

'Explain why you thought an industrial tribunal was important enough to send eight reporters out of the office for two days to cover it.' There was a very strained edge to his voice. I could see that he was forcing himself to stay calm and only just managing it.

'OK. It's just that I see a lot of angles to this story,' I said earnestly. 'There's the political side – the implications for Camden Council – and Paul is onto that. I've got Amanda talking to women's groups about the feminist issues. Roger's talking to the unions about the benefits of flexitime. Linley and Malcolm are covering the actual tribunal hearing itself, taking it in relays so that we don't miss any of it. Then I've got Mike trying to find out if this teacher had children of her own, you know, who could have been behind her poor time-keeping. Then there's Lara checking out the school where she worked, trying to find out if there was a vendetta against her. Oh, and Jo is at the Tavistock Clinic, talking to a psychoanalyst about the unconscious reasons for persistent lateness.

'It's a great human interest story, Arnie, and it's going to make a great spread on page three.'

The twitching had spread now to the little muscles around his eyes, and I could see that he was gripping the edge of a desk unduly tightly. He cleared his throat.

128

'Er, what about the rest of the newspaper? Who's going to write the stuff that's supposed to be on page one and page two, or on page four, five, six and seven, for that matter, not forgetting, of course, the back page and pages eight to sixteen?'

I looked totally perplexed. 'I hadn't thought of that!'

'Didn't think of that, eh?'

'Gosh, no. I'm afraid it didn't occur to me. But now that you mention it, I can see that it poses something of a problem. Perhaps I can get a couple of them back.'

Arnie didn't say anything. His face was as immobile as a plaster-of-Paris mask. He turned slowly and walked back into his office, although there was a strange stiffness to his gait that I didn't recognise. He shut the door quietly.

My heart was hammering against my ribs, and I took four long, deep breaths before there was the sound of an almighty crash in his office. I didn't know what had happened, but what it sounded like was the large blue vase that usually stood on his filing cabinet hitting the wall with considerable force. I continued my deep breathing, and about a minute later the phone on my desk rang. It was Arnie.

'Parker, can you come in here a minute, please?'

'Sure, Arnie.'

When I went in, the first thing I saw was a lot of water, flowers and broken bits of blue vase on the floor. And there was a big wet mark on the wall. Arnie was sitting in his chair behind his desk. He waved me to a chair.

'I dunno how I'm gonna tell you this,' he said. 'But I have to say that I think I made a mistake. I had thought that you could take over from Phillips, but ... how can I put this ... I just don't think it's going to work out. No, don't interrupt. It's not that you are not a good journalist; you are, and you've had some great stories in the past, the best, but you just don't have the right instincts for newsdesk work.'

I let my face show the intense disappointment I was supposed to feel. Inside, my heart was singing.

'This industrial tribunal spread; not a good idea, huh?' I said.

'No,' he said in a very controlled manner, although he was breathing heavily, as if under some great strain.

I sighed. 'OK, Arnie, I accept your decision, and I'm sure you're right. Come to think of it, I'm best working on my own, and on one thing at a time.'

'Yes,' he agreed. Then he added: 'Look, Parker, I think you should take the rest of the day off. I don't think it would be a good idea for you to be around the office for the next few hours. I don't know what might happen otherwise.'

'Sure, Arnie. The doctors did say that I should sort of ease back into things. I'll be off then.' The muscles around his eyes were still twitching dangerously, and his ham-like fists were clenched tightly in front of him on the desk.

It was all I could do not to leap in the air as I left the office. I felt as if a great threat had been lifted from my life.

Frankie was, as usual, waiting unmolested on the double yellow line outside. Thumper, who had risen incalculably in my estimation since his perfectly balanced piece of body-guarding the night before, was sitting quietly in the back of the cab reading a book called *Jigsaw – A History of the Balkans Since 1848*. I had seriously underestimated his brain-power, too.

'You been sacked again?' Frankie asked. I didn't deign to answer.

We waited about twenty minutes before Herbert arrived in a taxi, and I waved him over. He got in looking flushed and agitated.

'I been thinking,' he blurted. 'If that bastard's got Wheezy's painting he must have topped Wheezy!'

'Calm down, Herbert. That thought had already occurred to me.'

'Then why don't we go straight round to that Bernstein copper and tell him about it?'

'Well, for one thing, how do you propose to explain to Inspector Bernstein how you and Wheezy acquired the painting?' I enquired. 'I don't think there's a statute of limitations on multi-million pound art thefts.' Herbert didn't reply, but he calmed down a little. 'No,' I continued, 'we are going to have to find a way of exposing Cornwell and his scam in some other way. I don't suppose you happened to notice the security arrangements at the gallery when you were there?'

'Come on, Mr P, I am a professional!'

'Does that mean you did or you didn't?'

'Of course I did. It's a matter of habit.'

'And?'

'And what?'

'Let me put it this way: assuming someone wanted to gain access to the gallery late one night – without attracting attention, of course – could it be done?'

'We going to break in there?' There was a certain eagerness in his tone.

'First things first. Answer the question.'

'Well, getting in would be a piece of cake. There's a flimsy little door lock. Also there's a loo window at the back which could be jemmied in three seconds flat. But it would have to be a very quick in and out cos the alarm would go off.'

'Ah. That's no good. This nasty idea that I have in my mind demands an undetected entry and exit.'

'It's not on,' Herbert said. 'They got one of those bleedin' new electronic alarm systems; you know, no moving parts. All magnetic sensors and laser beams, and it's connected direct to the Old Bill.'

'Can't it be by-passed?'

'No. As soon as you try to do anything at all it goes off and the Bill come running.'

He seemed very sure of himself, but I wanted a second opinion. I used the car phone to call Mohan Mistry and asked him to pay a discreet visit to the gallery to have a look at the system and see whether it was possible to take it temporarily out of service. Mohan and I were old friends, and I had done him some significant favours, and he agreed gracefully.

'Now,' I said to Herbert, 'I assume you and Wheezy have some place where you stash your loot.'

He looked shifty. 'What d'you mean?'

'Don't play games, Herbert. You and he must have some lock-up garage or something where you store the valuables that you liberate from other people's premises.'

'What of it?'

'It's possible the other version of the Bretton painting is there; maybe Wheezy swapped it with Cornwell before he was murdered.'

131

'No, it's not there, I've looked.'

'You sure?'

'Positive.'

'Right, then I think we can safely assume that Cornwell still has it somewhere. He wouldn't have wanted to risk disposing ot it, and it might be difficult to burn. We need to find it.'

'Why?'

'Never mind why at this stage.' I thought for a few moments. 'My guess is that he won't have the fake at the gallery where there would be a chance of his staff coming across it. Perhaps he took it home. Come on, Frankie, let's go and have a look at Cornwell's house. It's in that little road behind the Old Bull and Bush in North End Way.'

We set off up Fitzjohn's Avenue towards the Heath. I looked at Herbert. 'You game for a spot of breaking and entering in a good cause?'

'If it's got anything to do with finding Wheezy's killer, I'm in,' he said.

'But are you up to it?' He was seventy one years old, after all.

'Bloody 'ell, Mr P! I'm as fit as a bloody fiddle. Only last week I ...'

'Don't tell me!' I interrupted hastily. I turned to Thumper. 'What about you?'

He looked up from his book as if he had not been listening to the conversation, but I suspected he had heard every word. I waited, and he smiled. 'As I understand it, my engagement is for the duration of this affair. That means I am at your disposal when and where I am required.'

'Thank you. What about you, Frankie?' I said.

'Will I be on overtime?' my devoted driver asked.

On the way I telephoned Ambrose Pendleton to give him the good news that the threat of my promotion at the *Explorer* had been withdrawn due to my extreme incompetence.

'Congratulations,' he said.

'Thank you.'

It took about ten minutes to get up to Cornwell's home, a sumptuous seventeenth-century farmhouse-style homestead on

132

the edge of Hampstead Heath Extension. We were looking at the front but I was sure that the windows and terraces at the back had wonderful views over the Heath. Why was it, I wondered, that those who were most privileged were also very often most corrupt? Then I remembered that there was usually a correlation between corruption and their privilege in the first place.

'Well, go on, case the joint,' I said to Herbert. He slipped out of the cab, which Frankie had parked across the road, and miraculously melted into the heavy foliage in the garden.

I was left in the cab with Thumper who, as always, was smiling benignly.

'Why do they call you Thumper?' I asked him.

'My real name is Jerome José Manuel Furtwangler. My mother was Spanish, my father German, both refugees from the Nazis and fascists. I was born in Hartlepool where I occasionally felt the need to express my disapproval to those of my more spirited Geordie contemporaries at school who found my name more than reasonably amusing.' No further explanation was necessary.

Herbert was back a few minutes later, grinning broadly. 'Piece of cake. Ancient burglar alarm, must be at least five or six years old, and endless ways to get in.'

'Good. Now we need to think up a way of ensuring that the house is empty tonight when we go in.' I remembered with a shudder the occasion a year before when, having broken into a flat with Wheezy, we had been disturbed by two very large adversaries and forced to hide ignominiously under a bed. It was an experience I did not want to repeat. To ensure that Cornwell was out of the house, we had to make him an offer no sane person would refuse. I had an idea.

I picked up the phone, dialled the Cornwell Gallery, announced that it was the Bluebelle Restaurant calling and asked to speak to Rupert Cornwell. I disguised my voice with a faint French accent – and by sticking bits of tissue paper up my nose.

When he came on the line, he said charmingly: 'What can I do for the famous Bluebelle Restaurant?'

I said nasally: 'It is more a question of what we can do for you, sir. This is the marketing and publicity department of the

133

Bluebelle, and we are currently engaged in a customer expansion programme in which every night we invite selected London celebrities to dine, as our guests, in our restaurant. Are you perhaps free this evening?'

'Goodness me, that's very flattering. Actually I did have an engagement, but nothing that can't be cancelled.'

'You are welcome to bring your whole family. We are offering a full choice from the à la carte menu, together with Champagne and wines.'

He chuckled. 'Well, that is an attractive offer, I must say. I don't have a family, but I shall be bringing a woman friend with me, if that's acceptable.' I suspected he might bring the lovely Erica.

'But of course! I will reserve you a table for two for, shall we say nine o'clock tonight?'

'Nine is fine.'

'There is one other service we offer, Mr Cornwell. You will be collected from your home by taxi, at our expense, and then taken home again afterwards, so you will not have to limit yourself on alcohol because of having to drive home.'

'That's excellent!' said Cornwell, who then proceeded to give me the address of his home, outside which we were still parked.

I then made a call to Ambrose Pendleton, to get him to warn the staff at the Bluebelle to give Cornwell a royal reception when he arrived. The taxi, of course, would be Frankie's; what better way of ensuring that he didn't arrive home unexpectedly early?

We were just about to drive off when a shiny black Range Rover came up the road, turned into the driveway of Cornwell's house and parked. A striking woman with long dark hair got out and then let herself into the house with her own key. So this was Cornwell's woman friend, and it certainly wasn't the lovely Erica.

Chapter Twenty-One

The last time I had gone burgling I had dressed myself completely in black clothes so as to be able to flit unseen from shadow to shadow, and Wheezy had looked at me in horror.

'You look just like a bleedin' burglar!' he had complained.

Now, as a more experienced criminal, I knew the drill and I had dressed as I imagined the average young punter at the Old Bull and Bush might turn out – designer jeans, expensive trainers, T-shirt and blouson jacket.

'Oh Gawd,' Uncle Herbert said when he saw me, 'you look like a bleedin' plain clothes copper!' You just can't win, and I decided to ignore the comment.

Everything had gone exactly to plan, except for my leave-taking of Eve. It had taken her exactly three minutes of very determined interrogation to find out where I was going, and another four minutes of equally insistent argument before I wearily agreed that she could come along. If we all got caught and went to jail, why shouldn't she share our fate?

Frankie stopped the cab just before we got to Cornwell's house, and Thumper, Eve, Herbert and I got out. He then drove into the drive, as if dispatched by the restaurant, and rang the doorbell. We ducked out of sight. A few minutes later we saw him drive past with Cornwell and the dark-haired woman in the back.

It was just after half past eight and, it being mid-summer, it was still broad daylight.

'Shouldn't we wait until it gets dark?' I said to Herbert.

'No, this is the best time. Lots of people around; everyone busy with what they're doing, and lots of background noise to cover any noise we have to make,' he said. 'It's when you start skulking around the streets late at night carrying heavy objects that you attract attention.'

Herbert was clearly in charge now, and gave us our orders. Thumper would hang about inconspicuously outside to deal with any exterior threat. Eve and I would secrete ourselves behind a large rhododendron bush while Herbert did a basic recce and checked that there was no-one left in the house. He did the latter by going up to the front door and ringing the bell long and hard. No-one answered, and he disappeared around the side of the house. After a few minutes he was back.

'Right, come on,' he said, and we followed him round to the back, which was really the front of the house and which, as I had suspected, looked out over a particularly attractive part of Hampstead Heath. There were no neighbouring houses with windows behind which Neighbourhood Watch members could be lurking.

I will not, out of public duty, describe the process used by Herbert to by-pass the alarm system or to open the French doors on the back patio, except to say that the whole operation took about thirty seconds. So much for expensive security services. Once inside he went straight to the cupboard under the stairs and switched off the whole alarm system.

'It's always in the cupboard under the stairs,' he whispered to me.

'Right,' I said to Herbert and Eve, 'we're looking for the painting. But no damage, and leave things exactly as you find them. We don't want anyone to know we've been here.'

Then we started looking. Thoroughly and methodically, starting at the top of the house where Herbert also checked the attics and roof spaces, through the bedrooms and living rooms and down through reception rooms, kitchen and basement, where we found a large cellar full of wine. As it got dark we started using small torches. It took us nearly three hours to do it properly, with me checking periodically with Frankie by mobile phone on the progress of Cornwell's meal. But, apart from the ones on the walls, and we didn't want any of those, we found nary a painting.

There was one moment of high excitement when Herbert discovered a large safe at the back of a cupboard in one of the bedrooms. Huge anti-climax to discover that not only was it empty, but it wasn't even locked.

It was just before midnight when I checked with Frankie again. 'I've just been summoned by the head waiter to take them home, and traffic's very light, so I think we'll be there in twenty minutes. Better get out now.'

Herbert and I spent ten minutes going through the rooms one final time and checking that everything was as we found it, and then we prepared to leave.

'Where's that gel?' Herbert said. I looked round, but could not see Eve.

There followed two or three minutes of acute tension while I rushed round the house looking for her. I found her coming out of the kitchen carrying a heavy box.

'What are you doing?' I said urgently.

'I have found a very wonderful wine down there, a '78 Pomerol. It's too good for this horrible man, so I have taken one case. There are still four cases, so he will not know.'

My feeling was that anyone would miss a case of '78 Pomerol, but I literally did not have time to argue with her. Even Herbert was beginning to look anxious, so we left after switching the alarm system back on and locking the French door behind us.

I couldn't see Thumper anywhere, but when we reached the road he suddenly materialised out of nowhere. It was astonishing how easily he managed to hide his considerable bulk.

'Nice case of loot you have here,' he noted, relieving Eve of the case of wine and tucking it under his arm as if it was no bigger than a rolled up umbrella. We secreted ourselves in some dark shadows and waited for Frankie to arrive.

He was there in less than ten minutes and a few minutes after that he had dropped Cornwell and his lady friend at the house – much the worse for alcohol it appeared – and the four of us were in the cab and being ferried back to Hampstead.

'The head waiter said he ordered two of the most expensive wines on the list,' Frankie told me, and immediately I felt better about the case of wine we had nicked.

I felt even better about it when we opened a couple of bottles back in the hotel room and tasted it. It was smooth and full of flavour, and at the peak of its maturity, and it went a long way towards helping us relax after a busy night's burgling. It also dulled the disappointment of three hours of fruitless searching.

Chapter Twenty-Two

My entrance to the *Hampstead Explorer* office that Wednesday morning was a careful one. The first thing I noticed was that Ed Phillips was back in his place at the newsdesk, with a pale face, red eyes and equally red nose. I assumed Arnie had summoned him from his sick-bed. I felt bad, but not as bad as I would have felt had I been sitting in his place.

Most of the other reporters were in their places too, and some of them gave me dirty looks. They knew I had sent them off on wild goose chases the day before, and they had borne some of the brunt of Bloch's wrath on their return, I was sure. I resolved to make it up to them somehow.

Right now, however, I had to find a way of getting out of the office with Bloch's blessing, since I had nothing to write for that week's edition, and much to do in tracking down the fake painting.

I took a deep breath and went into Arnie's office. He didn't look up.

'Uh, Arnie?' I said hesitantly.

'I don't wanna hear about it.'

'I have to go ...'

'Go then,' he snapped, 'and don't come back today.' Perhaps he was still experiencing an element of disappointment in me.

I stood not on the order of going, but went, as per Polonius's advice to Laertes, and got an irritated scowl from Frankie as I climbed back into the cab.

'How'm I supposed to do any work if you never do any?' he grumbled, packing away his Open University papers and text books. I ignored his bleating.

'Mohan's shop, please,' I ordered.

Thumper was deep in another book, this one called *The Scramble for Africa, 1800 – 1900*. He appeared not to be listening to or looking at anything, but if I watched him closely I could see that every few seconds his eyes would flit quickly around, and I also knew that he heard every word, and more.

Mohan Mistry had been a devoted friend ever since I had discovered that the person who had been making his life a misery by daubing racist graffiti on the front of his shop, ringing up suppliers and cancelling orders and occasionally tossing bricks through the glass window was not a member of the National Front, or any other fascist group, but another Asian, a disgruntled competitor with a similar shop around the corner.

Mohan's shop window was crammed full of odd-looking doodahs, switches, wires, capacitors, transistors, connectors and a million other things that meant nothing to me. The inside of the shop was crammed full of enthusiasts buying this kind of stuff by the handful, and there was a healthy roar of money changing hands.

When he saw me, Mohan handed over to his assistant and waved me through into his office cum workshop at the back and put on the kettle for some cardamom tea.

Once niceties had been exchanged, I asked him: 'Did you manage to get to the art gallery?'

'Yes,' he said. 'Very interesting collection of paintings, I must say.'

'Never mind the paintings, what about the alarm?'

'Ah yes, also a work of art, I'm afraid. Some of the very latest equipment, and very impressive it is.'

'Can it be by-passed?'

'No. Without getting technical, let me explain. It is a system that relies on a series of laser beams and movement sensors. If any of the doors, windows or plate-glass windows are disturbed, or if movement is sensed in the gallery, there is a ten-second delay before all hell breaks loose – unless you punch in a five-digit code number at the control panel within that time.'

'No way of switching it off during those ten seconds?' I asked.

'No, any attempt to interfere with any part of the system or do anything at all without first entering the code number, and that includes entering the wrong code number, will set the alarm off.'

'Bells ring, sirens wail, that sort of thing?'

'Not at all. It's completely silent, and you would only know if you'd set off the alarm when the boys in blue came running in with the handcuffs. It's connected via digital British Telecom telephone lines directly to a central control office manned twenty four hours a day and, if that wasn't enough, directly also to the nearest police station.'

'Damn! So I can't get in there without being detected.' My disappointment was strong.

'Hey, I didn't say that. What I said was that the system cannot be disabled nor by-passed.' He had a wicked grin on his face.

'Come on, Mohan, spit it out.'

'I have a secret weapon.'

'What's that?'

'My cousin, Pravin, who just happens to be the night supervisor at BT's Marylebone exchange. Should you require it, Pravin could very easily disconnect those two telephone lines for a given period, during which someone could blunder about in there to their heart's content. And, before you ask, I can assure you that he can be trusted.'

'That's brilliant!'

'Yes, of course,' he said modestly. 'The alarms will still be triggered, of course, so that when Pravin reconnects the lines, the control room and police will be alerted. But, as long as you are out of the gallery by then, they will arrive to find everything in order, and they will assume it was a false alarm. The owner of the gallery will have to be summoned from his bed to enter the release code, but I am sure that will not cause you undue heartache.'

'None whatever. I think the bastard killed Wheezy Wallis.'

When I got back to the taxi I had the feeling that the tide had turned, and that things had definitely started flowing in the right direction

It had been a good morning so far and I was getting hungry, so I telephoned the *Observer* and asked to speak to the woman with the loveliest green eyes in the whole of England. Actually I asked for Andrea Ferris, who had once worked for the *Explorer* and had been my close (very close) friend during the period when I received my inheritance and tracked down the murderer of film star Monique Karabekian. She had, quite understandably, found the complexities of living with a secretive multi-millionaire – who was also, covertly, her boss – and (at the same time) being my news editor at the office, a bit too confusing, and she had removed herself from my life.

When she came on the line, I said: 'Name your lunch. Any lunch.'

It took her two or three seconds to work out who was calling, but then she said: 'I'm in an expensive mood. Signor Carluccio's Neal Street Restaurant, and you'll have to pick me up from my office. I assume you're still hiring that ginger runt's taxi?'

'Yes,' I said, wondering how Frankie would react to being called a ginger runt.

'I assume, too, that I will have to sing for my lunch, since the only time I ever hear from you is when you want to delve into the *Observer's* files,' Andy said.

'Correct again,' I admitted.

'Right, pick me up at half past twelve.'

My heart always gave a distinct flutter when I saw Andy Ferris, and this time was no different. When the cab drew up outside her office, she was ready, waiting and looking stunning. She got in and gaped at Thumper.

I introduced them, and explained that Thumper was my bodyguard.

'Don't tell me any more,' she demanded. 'You are involved in another of your hare-brained investigations, and all kinds of nefarious people are probably trying to measure you for concrete shoes. For all I know my life is in danger just being here with you.'

'I assure you, Miss Ferris, that you are perfectly safe,' Thumper said quietly. 'I will make your safety my first priority.'

How do you like that? This from someone I was paying an exorbitant daily rate, plus expenses, to protect *my* body. But, since Andy had calmed down considerably, I said nothing.

Carluccio's was, as always, absolutely brilliant and seriously over-priced. We had mixed plates of sautéed funghi, all said to be collected in person by Mr Carluccio at secret places around London, followed by excellent, tender, mouthwatering medallions of beef in a rich cep sauce.

We were both admirably abstinent and declined amazing puddings, and after coffee we managed to be back at her office by half past two.

She took me into the newspaper's library, sat me down at a table and said: 'Right, Parker, what files do you want?'

'Anything on Rupert Cornwell, the art dealer, and on a guy by the name of Munro Forbes.'

She came back a few minutes later with two files, one bulky, one quite thin. 'You're in luck. These are still on paper. The whole library is being computerised, and in future we'll have to scan through files on screen.' She shuddered, gave me a peck on the cheek and left me to go back to her work.

The bulky file was the Rupert Cornwell one, and I looked through that first. There was a lot of stuff about the gallery – acquisitions, sales, auctions and exhibitions – and I realised that he had always gone out of his way to provide good copy for the newspapers. He thrived on publicity, personally and professionally, and there were countless photographs of his superbly handsome face and of him meeting artists, royalty and celebrities of all kinds. He also seemed to have had at least two wives and quite a large number of girlfriends.

There were a few profiles and interviews but they were depressingly similar, as if they had all been based on the same personal background handouts probably provided by Cornwell himself.

Only one appeared to be a genuine objective look at the man, and from that I gleaned that he had come from a middle-class, artistically Philistine home in suburban Edgware. He had been to a local grammar school, after which he had taken himself to the Hornsey School of Art – his parents having virtually disowned him after his refusal to follow his father into chartered accountancy.

His career at Hornsey was undistinguished to say the least, the journalist quoting a number of tutors who were distinctly uncomplimentary about his drawing, painting and artistic skills generally.

It was not clear whether he had ever tried to make it as an artist himself, but what was clear was that he had a natural flair for wheeling and dealing in art. Small beginnings had taken him up the ladder in the art world, and when he finally opened his smart gallery some years later, most opinion seemed to be that it was, and would be, a great success.

I was just about to close the file when a small piece of pink paper caught my eye. It was a three-month-old cutting from the *Financial Times*, part of a gossip column in which the journalist revealed, in fairly guarded terms of course, that Cornwell had been scouting City sources for much needed funds, and that perhaps his gallery wasn't the vast success everyone had assumed it was.

The Munro Forbes file was very thin. It held a few cuttings from society pages and magazines which reinforced the picture of a once very grand family that had fallen on economic hard times and therefore out of high society. The only news clippings were about the celebrated burglary in 1966 and, more recently, cross referenced clippings about the so-called 'discovery' of the Bretton painting.

The last item in the file was a photograph, taken at the Cornwell gallery, of a woman with long dark hair, posing with the painting. She was described as Margaret Forbes, daughter of the late Munro Forbes.

She was the woman currently living with Cornwell in Hampstead, the one we'd seen arriving in the Range Rover, whom he had taken to the Bluebelle.

The stench of conspiracy filled my nose.

Chapter Twenty-Three

That afternoon I gathered my team for a council of war in the back of Frankie's cab, and told them who Cornwell's girlfriend was. A few seconds of intrigued silence, then Frankie spoke: 'So?'

'So, it could be that the fake painting is at her house,' I said.

'You mean the place in Suffolk?' asked Herbert.

'Yes. I mean, think about it. If the two of them are an item, which certainly looks to be the case, the chances are that they concocted this whole thing between them. Who knows where they got that fake from? They may have stumbled across it somewhere and realised its potential for a scam, or they may have actually had it done to order. And if we're right, Cornwell stands to take a fat share of the actual sale price, and not just the auctioneer's commission as I had been assuming. That in turn would explain the dramatic – and very expensive – action taken against me when I started asking awkward questions. Millions of pounds are at stake, and we know that his gallery is in financial trouble.

'When they thought up their scam, the real painting had been missing for nearly thirty years, and after all this time they never dreamed that it would show up again. All they had to do was think up a story to explain the sudden reappearance of their painting, and then bribe or blackmail someone like Professor Beaumanoir to declare it genuine. They knew that no-one would argue with Beaumanoir on the subject of Bretton.

'But, no sooner had they announced the amazing discovery of their painting, than along comes Wheezy to tell them, firstly, that he's onto their scam and knows for a fact that their painting is a fake and, secondly, he has the real one.

'It must have been a terrible shock. But then, when they thought about it, it was like a dream come true. Wheezy may have tried to blackmail them, but I think it's much more likely that he offered to sell them the real one. The newspapers had reported that the painting would probably sell at auction for between five and seven million pounds, and I wouldn't be surprised if Wheezy asked them for around two million for it.

'They could have bought it at that price, and then everyone would have been rolling in dough, and the Wallis clan would be preparing to move to the Costa del Sol, but Cornwell was too greedy for that, wasn't he?

'He didn't like the idea of having to part with millions of pounds, and decided it would be much more cost effective to kill Wheezy, take the painting, and who would be the wiser? All they had to do then was hide or get rid of their own fake, and they were left with the painting they had claimed to have in the first place. Neat and diabolical.'

There was another silence while they digested the plot.

'Zey are devils!' Eve exclaimed.

'Yes.'

'So you think the fake might be hidden at this Forbes woman's house, then?' Herbert asked.

'Well, we know it's not at Cornwell's house, and I doubt if he would have it at the gallery where his staff might stumble over it, and I also doubt that he would have destroyed it. Who knows, there might have been another opportunity at some stage in the future to sell it to some sucker as the original. I think there's a good chance they've got it stashed away in Suffolk.'

'Let's go and get it then,' said Thumper, in his mild voice.

'Just what I was thinking,' I replied.

'Bet you a tenner that they never did get round to wiring that little window at the back – especially since the loot had already been nicked and it would have been like closing the door after the horse had bolted,' Herbert contributed.

'Do we know anyone small enough to go through a twelve-inch window?' I asked. I was certainly too big, and so was Herbert. And the idea of Thumper going through it was in the

146

camel-and-eye-of-needle range of possibility. All eyes turned to the ginger runt that drove the cab.

'Oi! No. I'm the getaway man, the driver. I don't go through windows. No way. No. There's no way I'm going in that window. For all we know there's starving Rottweilers in there. I'm a family man with two expensive kids to support. I've never been in trouble with the law. I'm certainly not ...' His voice trailed away under the unrelenting stares of four pairs of eyes.

We drove up to Suffolk later that afternoon and stopped in charming Lavenham where I bought everyone dinner at the famous Swan Hotel with its ancient Tudor beams and reproduction English bar. The restaurant was pretty good, though, and we all tested it thoroughly; Thumper having two main courses before he even looked at the gateaux on the sweets trolley.

We also kept the wine waiter busy, drinking to keep stomach butterflies inebriated, while Frankie morosely sipped Perrier, muttering every now and then about how easy it was for everyone else and how he was the one who was likely to be impaled by booby traps, torn limb from limb by savage guard dogs or accosted by instant armed response guards with nervous trigger fingers. He didn't enjoy his dinner, Herbert having warned him at the menu stage that he might get stuck in the window if he ate too much.

The house, we had established from the local telephone directory, was on the outskirts of Lavenham, and we found it easily with the aid of an Ordnance Survey map and Herbert's memory, secluded in its own little estate and nicely screened from adjoining properties by rows of trees in full foliage. It was a large and brooding house, built around the turn of the century I estimated, and looking decidedly down at heel, even in the moonlight. We parked a little way down the lane and I got busy with the car telephone. First I rang the house. No answering machine and no answer, even though I let it ring for five minutes. No-one at home.

Then I rang Cornwell's home number in London. After three rings a woman answered.

'Miss Fibs please,' I said.

'This is Margaret Forbes,' she said, stressing the surname.

147

'Oh, sorry, I wanted Caroline Fibs.'

'You have the wrong number.'

'Sorry.' Click. We were in the clear, it seemed.

By this stage it was quite dark, and Frankie drove into the Forbes property with his headlights off, parking in a clump of trees at the top of the driveway.

'Wait here. I'll go and have a look around,' Herbert said, and slipped off into the darkness. It was very quiet, and I thought I could hear Frankie's heart beating in the front of the cab. Or maybe it was my own. Or Eve's. Thumper, however, seemed to be asleep, although I knew he was not.

Herbert returned after five minutes with a big grin. 'Told you!' he said triumphantly. 'Same little window and still no alarm wires. Same alarm system as before and ordinary Yale lock on the door. No mortise. Piece of cake, as long as our hero here can get in.' Even in the darkness, I could see Frankie's face lighten a shade.

'You lot stay in the cab,' Herbert said, indicating me, Eve and Thumper. 'Frankie, come with me.' Herbert had taken charge, and since he was an expert in matters of this kind, that was OK by me. Our heroic driver complied, but as if weighed down by heavy weights, and trudged off behind the elderly team leader.

Then we waited about fifteen minutes, which felt like fifteen hours, the tension mounting with the passing of each agonising minute, and Eve clutching my hand more and more strongly.

Suddenly Frankie was back, limping slightly, but with a huge grin on his face. 'All clear, Mr P! Nothing to it, really.'

'Why are you limping?'

'Tripped over something in the dark. Twisted me ankle a bit. Not serious.'

Then Herbert arrived. 'Let's go. Frankie done well. Was a bit of a squeeze but he got in and opened the front door no problem.'

He sent Eve down to the entrance to the drive with the mobile phone, with instructions to keep an eye on neighbours' houses. Any movement, or any unexpected arrivals at the Forbes house, and she was to dial the house's telephone, let it ring twice and then hang up.

Frankie stayed with the cab, ready to crank her up and drive like the clappers if anything went wrong, and Thumper, Herbert and I went into the house.

'Once again, don't take anything and don't disturb anything. We don't want anyone to know we've even been here. All we want is the painting, if it's here.'

We started at the top of the house – which looked, and smelled, as if no-one really lived in it at all. There was dust everywhere and an odour of must and mould. There wasn't much furniture to speak of, no paintings on the walls and almost no clothing in the cupboards and wardrobes in the bedrooms. That made it easy to search, though, and within an hour we had been through all the upper floors thoroughly.

The ground-floor reception rooms were equally musty and sparsely furnished. I could imagine how a half-share of a six or seven million sale price could be used to turn the house back into an elegant and comfortable country residence. But no painting here.

That left the large kitchen, pantry area and one or two small utility rooms. Nothing.

Then Herbert whispered: 'Over here, Mr P.'

The beam from his small torch fell on a massive wooden door with metal bands and studs, which looked as if it led down to a cellar. But it was locked shut with a large bolt secured in position by a serious-looking padlock.

'Can you open that?'

He looked at it closely, and frowned. 'Maybe. But it could take a long time. It's a Swedish lock; very difficult.'

'There's another possibility,' said Thumper quietly. 'I might be able to lift the door off its hinges.'

I looked again at the door which, I realised, was not one of the original fixtures of the house. It was much older, and looked as if it could easily have come from some monstrous dungeon somewhere. It was not set into the opening, but across it. The hinges were two large rings, set deep into the brick-work, which were penetrated by two long spikes emanating from the edge of the door. From the length of the spikes, I could see that Thumper would have somehow to lift that side of the door nearly a foot to free them from the rings and, given the size and probable weight of the door, I didn't think any human being could do it. Another problem was that apart from

149

the old iron bands running across it, which were only about half an inch proud of the wood, there was nothing to get a grip on.

'I don't think so,' I said.

'Let me try,' he replied.

'Is there enough play on the bolt side?' I asked. 'If we bend it, it'll be obvious someone has opened the door.'

He looked at the bolt in the light of Herbert's torch, and then looked at me. 'I think so. It's quite loose really, and if I can lift it off the hinges, there'll be enough space for one of you two to squeeze through.'

'OK, have a go,' I said simply.

He didn't throw himself at the door, but first stood looking at it for a full minute or so, as if sizing up the weight and capabilities of a respected adversary. Then he knelt down at the hinge end of the door, his cheek and chest pressed against the wood, put his left hand underneath it, and his right on the horizontal edge about a third of the way up from the lower hinge, and began to breathe deeply. He spent another minute or so in that position, as if feeling the door and whatever message it might contain. He made minute adjustments to his posture, as if improving his balance, and was very still.

I expected him to heave at the door, but he didn't. I only realised that he had started lifting when his breathing stopped. His eyes were tight shut, his body as rigid as stone and, incredibly, that side of the door was rising slowly, millimetre by millimetre. After what felt like an age the spikes had cleared the rings in the wall and Thumper, his face purple with effort, slowly lowered the door to the floor. We waited a minute or two for him to recover with some very measured breathing and loosening-up movements of his arms and legs.

Then he grasped the door again and pulled it outwards about a foot before Herbert whispered: 'That's it. Any more and the bolt will bend.'

In the light of the torch we could see stone steps going down into total blackness. I tried to squeeze through the gap, but being a biggish sort of chap, I couldn't make it. Herbert was much scrawnier and didn't have any trouble, and we watched him and his torchlight disappear down the stairs.

It didn't take long. There was a scratchy little whoop of

triumph and seconds later he was back with us carrying a heavily wrapped parcel. I tore off the black plastic and protective bubble wrap and there she was: Silvie with her enigmatic smile. Perhaps not as enigmatic as the Mona Lisa's, but at that moment I preferred her to the Mona Lisa. We turned it over and looked at the frame.

'That's the fake. See, no initials,' Herbert said, indicating an area of the wood on which the canvas had been stretched.

'We're in business,' I said happily. The nasty idea in my mind that I had resisted for days was now becoming a reality. 'Now all we have to do is move the door back.'

Thumper smiled, positioned himself carefully again, went through his breathing routine, and repeated his astonishing feat, a little more slowly this time. The effort was immense and when he had finished he was looking quite drawn.

'Let's get out of here,' I said, and within minutes we were back in the cab, much to Frankie's relief. We picked Eve up at the end of the drive and a couple of hours later we were all back home in London and tucked up in bed.

I lay in bed, listening to Eve snoring quietly, my mind buzzing from all the adrenaline flowing around my veins. I imagined Cornwell and Margaret Forbes asleep in their bed, dreaming about how they would spend their millions. I thought, too, about Wheezy and how he'd probably lain awake at night, imagining how he would spend the money. A picture of Wheezy came into my mind; he was grinning, and gave me the thumbs-up sign. Then I finally slept.

Chapter Twenty-Four

My burgeoning career as a burglar was temporarily interrupted when, in a telephone conversation with Mohan Mistry that Thursday morning, I learned that his cousin Pravin would not be on duty at the Marylebone telephone exchange until Monday night.

That left things uncomfortably close to Cornwell's auction, which was due to take place two days later, but there was no way round that particular problem.

On the other hand, I could think of a few ways to fill the time.

The first was to see Arnie Bloch and bring him fully up to date on the Wheezy Wallis murder investigation.

I went into work very early that morning, which I knew was always a very good ploy with the editor. He himself was at his desk by seven, and frequently let it be known how disappointed he was that most people came in at around nine, only half an hour before they were due to start work. I got there at about quarter to eight that morning, cleverly bearing a freshly-baked jam doughnut from the Rumbolds bakery in South End Green. This, I knew, was about as close as I could get to bringing a peace offering.

'No hard feelings, hey?' he said through a mouthful of doughnut, the caster sugar forming a kind of minstrel ring around his mouth.

'None whatever,' I said sincerely. I assumed he was referring to my short and abbreviated career as trainee news editor.

'I've decided to promote Amanda Popplewell instead.'

'Excellent choice.'

'So, what's this bribe for?' he asked, indicating the last small morsel of doughnut before it met its terrible fate.

'I need to tell you what's been going on with the Wallis story, and I wanted to be sure you were in a good mood.'

'Hey, I'm always in a good mood.'

I let that one pass, and began to tell him the story. Arnie listened carefully to my tale, his piercing eyes never leaving my face as I laid out the whole tale as I had pieced it together, including the accounts of the original theft of the painting and how we had broken into Cornwell's Hampstead home and Margaret Forbes's country house to liberate the fake Bretton.

I would have liked to have told the same story to Theo Bernstein, but I couldn't imagine him condoning the felonies and misdemeanours we still had in mind, not to mention the ones we had already committed.

I also told Arnie what I intended to do during the coming week, and when I had finished there was a period of relative silence during which all I could hear was the sound of him slurping his tea, something I will not attempt to describe other than to suggest that the disappearance of Atlantis must have sounded something like that.

'I think there's an eighty-five per cent chance that you'll end up in jail,' he said encouragingly, 'and if you do, I will deny all knowledge of this whole business.' It was great to know one could rely on one's employer to stand by one through thick and thin.

'Hell, there's even a chance that I could end up in jail with you.' He paused; and then: 'On the other hand, this all stinks of a helluva good story if we can pull it off!' Suddenly it was 'we', I noticed, if everything went well.

'Your problem is that the only evidence we have for this whole conspiracy has been obtained absolutely illegally, and we are going to have to find a way round that.'

'I fully intend to,' I assured him.

Back in the cubby-hole they call my office I spent ten minutes on the telephone speaking to politely and eagerly unhelpful people at the National Gallery in Trafalgar Square before I finally found one who knew what I, and he, was talking about.

153

'Who are the world's experts on François Bretton?' I wanted to know.

'The most obvious one is Professor Robert Beaumanoir,' the deputy curator told me. 'He's generally acknowledged as the authority.'

'Is there another?'

'Why, yes. There's Professor Berndt Perrsen, of course.'

'Ha ha, does he smoke?'

'Pardon?'

'Never mind. Is he in Sweden or Norway?' I said.

'No, California. He's the head of art history at the University of California in San Francisco. He's written books and numerous articles on Bretton, but he and Beaumanoir don't get on very well. They've frequently disagreed, loudly, and sometimes in public.'

'Sounds like just the man I want. You wouldn't happen to have his telephone number, would you?'

He didn't, but he did have an address, and international directory inquiries supplied the number. I dialled it immediately.

It was only when an extremely irascible voice picked up the phone after fifteen rings and snapped: 'Who the almighty hell is this?' that I realised that it was three o'clock in the morning in California. I decided to get right to the point.

'Professor Perrsen, I'm terribly sorry to have woken you up, but I'm calling from London and I forgot about the time difference.'

'Who are you and what do you want?' he barked.

'My name is Parker, I'm a newspaper reporter, and I'm authorised to offer you a first-class return air ticket with all hotel expenses paid to come to London and inspect a François Bretton painting which is to be sold at auction next Wednesday.'

There was a short silence during which we could hear the distant high-pitched squeaking of thousands of other conversations, but I knew I had his attention.

'That would be the one at the Cornwell Gallery? The Portrait of Silvie?'

'Correct.'

'So what makes you think I'm interested in looking at it? I'm not flying halfway round the bloody world to look at a

154

painting I know like the back of my hand.'

I sprung the trap: 'It's been authenticated by Professor Beaumanoir,' I said mildly.

'Then it's probably a fake!' he snapped. 'Beaumanoir is an idiot.'

'That's exactly why we want you to look at it,' I said. No reply. 'I'll have the air ticket delivered to you in San Francisco, to fly on Monday night, and I'll book you in for five nights at the Savoy, a suite of course, from Tuesday morning. Do you think you can make it?'

'If you're on the level and the ticket arrives, I'll be there.'

'Excellent. I'll meet you at the hotel on Tuesday morning, and in the meantime, please don't say anything about this to anyone, and especially no-one in the art world.'

'If you're paying the bills, I won't even tell my wife where I'm going,' he said.

Then I rang British Airways to organise the ticket, and the Savoy to book his suite. I nearly asked for a room with an extra fire extinguisher. Having a name like Berndt Perrsen was tempting fate a little, I thought.

I was just about to leave the office when the telephone rang and I heard Theo's voice. 'What are you up to, Parker?'

'What makes you think I'm up to anything?' I said indignantly.

'You haven't pestered me for days, and that makes me anxious.'

'I can't win with you, Theo! If I contact you you complain that I am wasting your time, and if I don't, you ring up to harass me.'

'I'm not harassing you!'

'Then what's this phone call all about?'

'Nothing. My nose is itchy, and when my nose gets itchy I know you are up to no good.'

'Just scratch it, Theo.'

That was all I needed. So many things to plan and worry about, and now I also had to watch out for Theo Bernstein's disturbingly accurate nose.

The next time the telephone rang it was Jules Aristède, the police captain from Arcachon.

After polite inquiries about my health he said: 'We have found your Professor.'

'Beaumanoir?'

'The very one.'

'Where is he?'

'In a hospital in Périgueux.'

'What's wrong with him?'

'He is suffering from gunshot wounds,' the policeman said.

'Wounds, plural?'

'Yes, more than one. But he is lucky. He was shot three times, once in the abdomen and twice in the chest. At close range. Miraculously, however, nothing vital was damaged, although his attacker must have thought he was dead. He's had some surgery, but will make a full recovery, I am told. He is already quite healthy and will be discharged in the next day or two.'

'Who shot him?'

'Ah, that's another thing. Beaumanoir claims to have lost his memory. He says he does not know who he is, who his would-be assassin was, or why he might have been shot. Very convenient for him, really. He was only identified because I had sent out a missing persons report to all hospitals in the South West of France. His doctors, however, believe he is faking the amnesia. In any case, he is under police guard, and we are continuing to interrogate him. It is a delicate situation, though, because we have no evidence that he has broken the law in any way. Getting shot is not, in itself, a crime. Anyway, I thought you would be interested.'

Aristède was right. I was very interested. He also gave me the name of the hospital, and I telephoned British Airways again to book three seats on the first flight to Bordeaux the next morning. Then I went in to see Arnie. When I said I needed a few days off work to go to France, there was a short and difficult silence.

'Why?'

'I need to speak to Professor Beaumanoir again.'

'I'm not paying expenses for any trip to France.'

'I didn't ask you to.'

'Well, OK then, but the time comes out of your holidays.'

Chapter Twenty-Five

Eve, Thumper and I flew to Bordeaux early that Friday morning. On arrival at Heathrow, the amiable figure of my bodyguard drew many anxious glances in our direction, particularly from the security men, some of whom seemed to be wondering which country we would be hijacking the plane to. The people who add up the weight of passengers and baggage might also have been upset, but the plane turned out to be half empty, and it seemed to take off OK even though Thumper was sitting in it.

It landed OK too, and we took a large Renault estate from the airport car hire desk. I didn't think Thumper would have fitted into a Porsche.

The drive to Périgueux was a pleasant one, and was made even more memorable by the little detour we made to a small village and a patisserie owned by a relative of Eve's who served us freshly ground coffee and the most heavenly pain au chocolat ever to see the inside of a stomach. My bodyguard ate seven.

Aristède had warned the police bodyguard at the hospital that we were coming, and there were no problems getting into Beaumanoir's room.

The professor went pale as the three of us, including Thumper, filed in to the room, and I had no doubt that he recognised me instantly. Then some of his composure returned and sparked off some indignation.

'Who are you, and what is the meaning of this outrage? How dare you force your way into my room? If you do not leave immediately I will telephone the police!'

157

No-one answered him, but Thumper put a hand on his shoulder and gently pressed him down onto the bed.

'Nice of you to visit me in hospital in Arcachon,' I said to him sarcastically.

'I don't know who you are ...'

'Of course you do. And you know what happened to me. It was all over the newspapers and television in this area. And you knew I had been hijacked on my way back from seeing you.' He was silent now.

'The game is up,' I told him. I thought of some more clichés: 'You've come to the end of the road, the show is over, your goose is cooked, your race has been run and the reckoning is nigh. We have, in fact, got you bang to rights and it is certainly a fair cop guv'nor.' He looked at me with staring eyes.

'In a moment, Mr Thumper here is going to remove his hand and then, if you wish, you may telephone the police. Indeed, you won't even have to telephone since, as you know, there is a policeman standing outside the door. But be advised that we too will have some very interesting things to tell them.'

We didn't, of course, but the professor didn't know that. And, when Thumper lifted his hand, he just sat frozen in his bed.

'OK, first I'm going to tell you what I know, and then you are going to tell me what you know. I show you mine, you show me yours. That's fair, isn't it?' I suggested. No reply.

'I know, for example, that you lied to me, to the newspapers and to the British art world. I know that the François Bretton painting that was at the Cornwell Gallery a few months ago was a fake, that you knew it to be a fake, but that you nevertheless declared it to be genuine. What I don't know is, why?'

But answer came there none. Beaumanoir was sitting stricken in his bed, as if his worst nightmare had just come true. And so, I supposed, it had. There was a long pause while we all listened to the sound of the professor's laboured breathing and the steady beeping of a heart monitor in one of the adjacent rooms.

'It seems to me that you have two ways out of this,' I told him eventually. 'The first is that you are exposed as a fraud and a liar and your entire professional and academic reputation

158

goes down the toilet for ever and you spend the rest of your life in disgrace, living like a hermit. And that's just assuming, of course, that you are not extradited and prosecuted by the British police for conspiracy to defraud.' His face seemed even more stricken.

'The other possibility is that you talk to us. And, if you do, we may be able to limit the damage to your reputation. Anyone can make a mistake, and most people will forget it in time. Think about it for a while.'

He thought about it for a while. 'What is it you want me to do?' Beaumanoir said eventually in a small voice. He looked completely crushed.

'First tell us what happened,' I said.

He took a deep breath and, after another long pause, started speaking shakily: 'About four months ago, Rupert Cornwell came to see me at my house. He brought that painting and asked me if it was genuine. I told him immediately it was a forgery; a very good one but a forgery nonetheless. But I do not think that news came as a surprise to him.'

'Was he alone?'

'Yes.'

'Go on.'

'You must understand that I am not a wealthy man. I have a small pension, a few savings, a small stipend as an emeritus professor.'

'Get to the point, please.'

'The point is that Mr Cornwell pointed out that if the painting had been genuine, it could have been sold for many millions of dollars. He also argued that if someone generally regarded as the foremost expert on Bretton were to authenticate it, that certification would not be challenged. It took him some time, of course, and we spoke for a very long time, you understand, but in the end it became clear what he wanted me to do, and he offered me five per cent of the eventual sale price.'

I started trying to work out in my head what five per cent of seven million pounds was.

'Three hundred and fifty thousand pounds,' Thumper said helpfully. 'Or, to put it another way, more than three million francs.'

159

'That is a great deal of money, and I succumbed to the temptation. I have not slept properly since then,' the professor said weakly.

'What did you do?' I tried to feel some sympathy for him but couldn't.

'I wrote him a letter, stating that in my considered opinion there was no doubt whatsoever that the painting was the long lost Portrait of Silvie by François Bretton, which was known to have been stolen from Munro Forbes. I thought that would be the end of it, and that whatever millionaire bought it would be happy forever, thinking that he had bought the real thing. I thought that I would have no further role to play.'

'But you did, didn't you, when I started asking questions?'

'Yes, unfortunately. Cornwell telephoned me to warn me about you.'

'Just to warn you?'

Beaumanoir looked stricken with guilt. 'No, he also said that I was to call a particular telephone number when you left, and tell them what car you were driving. I didn't like this, but by that time I was trapped in this business and I could not refuse.'

'What telephone number?' I said.

'I can give it to you. It is at home.'

'Go on,' I said.

'I knew nothing of their plans, and when I read about you being rescued from the Arcachon channel, I felt terrible.'

'But still you did nothing.'

'To my shame, that is correct. But when you were rescued, I was telephoned and told to disappear for a while. It was terrible. This is not the sort of life I am used to.'

'Who shot you?'

'I don't know them, but perhaps they are the same men who attacked you on the boat. I never saw them. I was walking in the street in Périgueux when I was shot from behind. I thought I was dead until I woke up in this bed. Now I am afraid that they will discover that I am not dead …' His voice had become a wail.

'Have you ever heard the name Wheezy Wallis, or Albert Wallis?' I asked him, staring intently at his face.

He looked puzzled. 'No, I have never heard this name. Who

160

is he?' I could see that he was not lying.

'Was, not is. He's dead. He was in possession of the genuine Silvie portrait, and when he tried to sell it to Cornwell, he was murdered.'

'*Mon dieu!*' He looked absolutely horrified. 'Mr Parker, you must believe that I knew nothing about this, nothing at all! I have never heard that name before.'

'I believe you,' I said, 'but I wonder if the police will.' I didn't think his face could go any paler, but it did.

'What can I do?' he wailed, close to hysteria.

I told him.

We decided to spend the night in Périgueux. It is, after all, in the heart of the district which produces such delights as foie gras, truffles and confit, not to mention cassoulet and rillettes, and none of us could think of a good reason for rushing back to London late on a Friday night when one could spend a weekend in Périgord.

We checked into the nicest hotel we could find and then spent the rest of the afternoon shopping. In the evening Thumper announced that he would be going to listen to some jazz in one of the city's many squares. Eve and I had dinner in a charming little establishment in one of the lovingly restored streets in the old section of the town, after which we perambulated, hand in hand, through the narrow alleys and had a discussion about why it was that English shops couldn't have windows with the same style and aplomb as in France.

Thus engaged, we were oblivious to the rest of the world, let alone the two men coming towards us in the poorly-lit narrow street. The first indication of trouble was a gasp of dismay from Eve. Had I been the hero in an American film, I would have dropped into a defensive crouch, reached for my Magnum revolver or given everyone in sight a lethal karate chop to the neck. As it was, by the time I looked up and realised what was going on, it had all happened already.

All I could see in the gloom was that there was a man holding Eve from behind, a large forearm across her neck. I could not see his features clearly, but I could see that he was, as they say, a big mother, but clearest of all was the shiny knife blade he was holding delicately in the fingers of his right hand, the tip of which was pressed to the side of Eve's neck. The other man was shorter, with fair hair, and he was now leaning against the wall, a relaxed grin on his face.

'Do nothing,' he advised me quietly in heavily accented English. I did nothing. Apart from the fact that I couldn't think of anything to do, I am also a natural coward.

Eve, however, had no intention of doing nothing. My French is very poor, but even I could recognise that the torrent of words emanating from her mouth comprised the very choicest selection of Gallic four-letter words and abuse, casting many aspersions on the chastity and morality of the men's mothers, wives and sisters, not to mention the doubtful issue of their own sexual orientation and their distinct resemblance – in both smell, intelligence and consistency – to a pile of pig shit.

I don't think the men took the insults too seriously, but they were clearly worried about the amount of noise she was making. My fear was that the one with his arm around her neck would stab her, but I realised that the knife was there to keep *me* quiet, not Eve. What he did was increase the pressure of his arm on her throat, and her torrent of words was cut off in mid-stream. I could see that she couldn't breathe, and that her efforts to remove his arm from her neck were useless.

Even natural cowards have limits. I leaped at him, intent on first pulling the knife blade away and then beating the bastard to a bloody pulp. Unfortunately, my journalistic training had not prepared me for this kind of activity, and as I lunged I forgot entirely about the other man. This was a rather serious mistake, because he took his time, came up behind me, and hit me smartly behind the ear with something which felt like a cannon ball. I remember experiencing a flash of light in my brain, feeling my knees turning to water and seeing the dark pavement coming up to meet me, and then I took a little nap.

Consciousness returned painfully. The world was dark, noisy, distinctly unstable and there was something wrong with my arms, which seemed to be stuck together behind me. When I moved my head hurt, and then there was a stinging sensation on my cheek, and I realised I had been slapped.

A voice I recognised said: 'Don't move!' It was the same voice that had earlier told me to do nothing. I decided to take his advice for the time being. After a few moments my head began to clear and I realised that I was lying in the dark in the back of a moving van, and that my hands were either tied or handcuffed behind my back.

Another voice I recognised said: 'Horatio, are you OK?' It was Eve, and my spirits rose another notch or two.

'I'm OK. Where are we?' I said.

'Be quiet!' our tormentor shouted. I assumed that the other one was doing the driving.

Another torrent of abuse in French was directed at him by Eve, and then she said to me: 'These are the bastards who tried to kill you on the Arcachon basin, the ones who hit me and threw me in the water.'

'Shut up!' the voice bellowed, and I heard the sound of a blow. Eve was silent for a moment and then spat out a single insulting epithet. A hand grabbed my shirt and foul-smelling breath wafted over me. 'Tell her to shut up, or I will cut her.'

I said nothing, and Eve was quiet, too. Perhaps she realised that if she pushed too hard he really would use the knife. I was, not to put too fine a point on it, terrified. I could think of no reasons why these two men might want our company other than extremely depressing ones.

The vehicle we were in suddenly made a turn onto a very bumpy road and after another minute it stopped. I heard the doors open, and another wave of Gallic swear words as they pulled Eve out. Then hands grabbed my ankles and I was pulled from the back of the van, my head banging painfully on the floor of the vehicle and on the soggy wet ground.

What I saw put an icy grip on my spine. We were in the middle of nowhere. There were no houses, no lights and no other people. In the dingy moonlight I could see the dirty little van we had been travelling in, a rough farm track which petered out where we had stopped, and two men facing us, one holding the knife. Not too far away I could hear traffic passing on the road we had turned off, and otherwise there was silence – except for the heavy breathing of the men. They were both nervous and excited, their emotions pumped up by what I knew they meant to do with us. It is only in books that men kill in cold blood without feeling.

I struggled to my feet, my hands still bound behind me, and

moved over to where Eve was lying on the ground. Her hands were not tied and I had a sudden surge of hope that I might be able to occupy their attention while she made a run for it, but then I saw that her feet were tied tightly together. For a few moments I had felt frightened. I mean really frightened – the kind of fear that loosens the bowels and interrupts clear thought – but now I just felt cold and depressed. These men intended to kill us, and there appeared to be nothing we could do about it. I could see that Eve, too, had read the situation and understood their intentions, and had gone quiet.

'Why have you brought us here?' I asked, my voice shaky.

There was no answer. The two men stood together, still breathing heavily, until the still life was broken by the fair haired one. '*Allez,*' he said with a hiss, and he nudged his knife-wielding companion hard in the ribs. The man with the knife started forward, going towards Eve. I moved to head him off, determined to inflict whatever damage I could with my feet.

The whole scene felt utterly unreal. Battling for one's life in the middle of the French countryside against a couple of homicidal thugs was just not the kind of thing local newspaper journalists from England got involved in, but there was no doubting that this was actually happening. And, unreal and shocking as it was, there was also no doubting the seriousness of his purpose – or of my determination to try and stop him.

Also utterly unreal was the way the knife man suddenly fell to his knees making bellowing and whimpering sounds like a wounded buffalo, his hands covering the side of his face where he had been struck, almost soundlessly, by a large rock. Despite the dim moonlight, I could see the blood seeping through his fingers. I did not have to turn around to know where that rock had come from, and relief and hope began to flow back into my soul.

'Evenin' all,' said Thumper as he walked into the now suspended tableau of action. Quite casually he cuffed the kneeling man on the side of his neck, and we watched him topple over and lie still on the ground.

I looked at the other man, and felt an almost physical pain as my hope began to drain away again. He did not have a knife in his hand, but a large automatic pistol, which he was in the process of cocking by drawing back the slide. Almost in the same movement the gun was being levelled at Thumper, and I braced myself for the sound of a shot. Instinctively I knew that there would be no threatening gestures, no convenient delay while the hero found a way of talking himself out of trouble. Thumper was an obvious and immediate source of extreme danger, and from the way the man was bracing himself and holding the weapon in both hands, even I could see that he did not intend to do anything but shoot at Thumper who was still moving quickly and smoothly in his direction. I froze in complete panic.

It was Eve who bought Thumper the one-second diversion he needed. Almost as soon as Thumper had appeared, and perhaps even before that, she had scooped up a handful of gravel, and she now flung it wildly in the direction of the man with the gun. His eyes flickered in her direction, and one hand left the gun to protect his eyes from the sand, and that was all Thumper needed. It was incredible how much ground this huge man had covered in the four or five seconds since he had first appeared, and when I dared to look I saw his massive hand close over the wrist holding the gun.

Then there was a shot, shockingly loud, and a flash which briefly lit up the surrounding trees and bushes like the flash from a camera. I held my breath, but no-one fell down.

For a moment there was stillness, apart from the wild beating of my heart and pounding pain in my head. Thumper and the fair-haired man were standing toe-to-toe, the gun now pointing towards the ground, the latter's face contorted with shock and pain.

And then there were two more sounds, the first being the somehow unmistakable crack of a bone breaking, and the second the dull thud of the gun falling onto the soggy ground. The man sank to his knees, his left hand cradling his right, which was now at a rather odd angle to his arm, a desperate whimpering sound coming from his throat.

An icy cold sweat and a wave of nausea washed over me. Whether it was from witnessing this chilling display of raw violence, or from the after affects of the blow to my head I don't know. Whatever the reason, I found myself vomiting enthusiastically into a bush. While I was thus dispensing with my dinner, Thumper executed another of his apparently casual

165

cuffs to the side of the groaning man's head, and he rolled quietly onto his side and lay still.

'Are you alright, Mr Parker?' From the calmness of his voice you would never have been able to tell that he had just prevented two murders, got away with his own life by the skin of his teeth, and knocked two men unconscious after crushing the wrist of one of them. I was trembling like a newborn kitten and felt like shit.

'Fine,' I said. 'How did you manage to get here?' He ignored me.

'Miss Dupont, are you alright?' He turned to where Eve was still lying on the ground and, I noticed now, crying softly.

'I'm OK,' she snuffled, 'just help me untie my feet. I want to kick those bastards.'

And she did, while Thumper was releasing me from the cord which still held my hands behind my back. She pushed the two prone men onto their backs, kicked open their legs, and delivered to each a crushing stomp in the balls. I have previously described the sound of this particular manoeuvre as being something like the crushing of ripe plums, and I have no further refinement to make at this stage. We made no move to stop her, and there was no response from the two eunuchs, but I knew that when they awoke they would have more problems than just headaches and a broken arm. Eve, panting slightly, surveyed her handiwork and then, as if the thought had just occurred to her, kicked them each again, just as hard. In the same place.

I felt no pity at all. All I could remember was the terror and pain I had experienced while floating in the Arcachon channel, the way Eve's face had looked when I first saw her in the hospital. I also thought of the pale stillness of poor Wheezy Wallis's body at the mortuary in St Pancras.

Thumper broke the silence. 'Something told me that it would not be wise to assume that those who shot the professor, and failed, would quietly retire to their picturesque French village to ruminate on their misspent lives.

'I suspected that they might be keeping an eye on the hospital and that, if they saw you two, they might be tempted to complete the job they attempted a few weeks ago. As it happens, I was right, although unfortunately I was not close enough to intervene when they accosted you.

'I did manage to hail a taxi while they were bundling you two into the van, and the cabbie was delighted to follow the vehicle, possibly because I gave him lots of francs. Anyway, when the van turned off the road, I saw that it only travelled a hundred yards or so and then stopped. So I paid off the cabbie and did the rest of the journey on foot.'

'Arriving in the nick of time, I may add,' I remarked.

'As you say. I regret that I wasn't a moment or two earlier.'

'You saved our lives!' Eve gushed.

'Perhaps, but I would like to add that your presence of mind with that handful of sand more than likely saved mine too. So I consider that we are all square on that score.' He smiled at me. 'Are you really alright?'

'Not really, but I'll feel a lot better when these two are chained up in police dungeons and I am in my hotel bed after a hot bath.'

As it happens, none of us got to bed before about 7 am the next morning. While Thumper stood guard over the eunuchs, Eve and I drove the van back into Périgueux where we had an interesting few minutes at police headquarters before they realised that we were not drunk or mad, or both, and decided to send a team of officers – and an ambulance – to the scene. Aristède was raised from his bed in Arcachon and arrived by helicopter two hours later. Lights were set up, photographs taken, measurements made, statements written down and thermos flasks of coffee passed around. A doctor was even summoned to inspect my noggin, which was pronounced bruised but not broken.

Aristède, after initially regarding Thumper with distinct suspicion, finally realised that he had an open and shut case before him. Eve could testify that these were the men who had tried to kill us in Arcachon, and both of us would testify that they had tried again that night. He had the gun which, he felt sure, would turn out to be the one that had fired the bullets extracted from Beaumanoir. All in all a mountain of evidence which would do his reputation and career no harm at all.

His only frown followed my insistence that there should be no publicity about the incident for at least a week. He took some persuading, but in the end I managed to convince him.

The last thing I wanted was to warn Cornwell that his nasty plot was beginning to fall in on him with great force.

167

Chapter Twenty-Six

We burgled the Rupert Cornwell Gallery on the Monday night. I had taken Pravin, Mohan Mistry's cousin, out to lunch and explained what we needed him to do; or rather, he explained to me what it was he was able to do and the times he was able to do it.

If the door of the gallery was opened after two o'clock in the morning, the alarm mechanism would start frantically dialling the police and the control room but, mysteriously, would not be able to get through until half past four, by which time, he fervently hoped, we would have done what we had to do. His fervent hopes were more than matched by my own.

I gathered my team of criminals together in the evening and we held our planning session at The Restaurant, in the West End. I needed to calm their nerves. No, I needed to calm *my* nerves, and what better way than indulging in a truly regal supreme of salmon on a bed of spinach with a herb overcoat and an extremely expensive bottle of Meursault? You will know how expensive the wine was when I reveal that a bottle of fizzy water cost six pounds.

'When you open a bottle of wine like this, you will always remember where you were when you drank it,' said the very pompous sommelier who had, incidentally, greeted Thumper like a long lost brother.

I would certainly remember that night, but not just because of the wine. Herbert tucked into a sirloin steak at least two feet long, apparently entirely unconcerned about the monumental crime we were planning to commit. Thumper tasted the wine like a connoisseur, with a beatific smile which suggested that there was nothing more on the agenda than a splendid meal. Frankie and I picked at our food like skittish sparrows, jumping nervously whenever someone approached the table to arrest us for conspiracy to steal a painting worth at least seven million pounds, even when it turned out to be the waiter. I still had a large bruise on the side of my head, and a fair-sized lump, but was otherwise not worse for wear after our weekend in Périgueux.

'Three times and you're out,' Frankie muttered with that buoyant optimism for which he was so famed. 'Seems to me we're pushing our luck.'

'Don't worry. Piece-a-cake,' said Herbert, his mouth full of prime, well-hung beef.

I attempted to express my fears more articulately. 'On our previous jobs, we were working in the dark, literally, screened from prying eyes by numerous trees, shrubs, hedges and an absence of strong lights. This one, however, is different. We are talking about breaking into a gallery which has lights on all night, in St Christopher's Place, a well-known pedestrian precinct where there are not only endless bright street lights, but bound to be late-night walkers and passers-by, not to mention the interest we might generate in people who happen to live in the flats above the shops on either side of the street. How are we to gain entry unobserved and unarrested?'

'Audacity,' said Herbert, shovelling another piece of cow into his gob.

'What?'

'Audacity, nerve, chutzpah, cheek, daring. Whatever you want to call it. You have to look like you own the place, and then no-one turns a hair.'

'Oh yeah.' I was not convinced.

'Well, it worked at a department store in Oxford Street,' he said.

'What worked?'

'Couple of years ago, six guys in caps and white overalls with trolleys and a lorry outside, walked into the store on a Monday morning. Said good morning, respectful like, to the floor manager, joked with the shopgirls, and then spent two hours clearing four window displays of fridges, freezers, washing machines, dishwashers, televisions, hi-fi sets and video recorders – which they wheeled cheerfully through the store and then loaded in the motor.' He paused to devour another chunk of steak.

'Then they drove off, and it weren't until about four that afternoon, when the floor manager rang the window display department to ask when the new display was going in, that all hell broke loose. By that time, the stuff was already in France.'

'I don't believe it,' I said.

'Straight up, Mr P. I knew one of the blokes who done it.'

'I seem to remember reading something about it in *The Times*,' Thumper added.

It was a good story, but I can't say it totally calmed my nerves, and when we left the restaurant just after midnight my heart was behaving like a ferret chasing a mouse through the maze of essential organs in my chest and abdomen.

We spent another hour and a half sitting anxiously in Frankie's taxi, trying not to think of handcuffs, juries, iron bars, slopping out and exercise yards.

'Look at it this way, guv,' Herbert said, trying to cheer me up, 'If anyone notices us, they'll see people walk into the gallery carrying a painting and walk out again carrying the same painting.' I gave him a wan smile.

And, twenty minutes later, just after two o'clock, there we were, three people jovially walking down St Christopher's Place, one of them with a painting tucked underneath his arm, and the other carrying an odd little box. We had left Frankie parked in Wigmore Street, after trying vainly to persuade him that it was not necessary to leave his engine running.

And in the end it went off like clockwork. While Thumper and I stood quietly chatting, Herbert attacked the lock of the gallery door, partly shielded by the massive bulk of my bodyguard. It only took him about thirty seconds and then we were in. I unwrapped the painting and, praying that all the little winking red lights on the movement sensors all around were not silently summoning the boys in blue, neatly swapped it for the one on the easel in the middle of the gallery. Thumper lifted up the glass case as if it was the top of a cheese cover.

The paintings looked identical to any casual glance. I quickly wrapped the real picture, and within less than five minutes we were out of there. Just before we left, Thumper opened his box and released a rather irritable-looking rat into the gallery.

'Good luck, Ratty,' he said. The rodent jumped up onto a desk and began to chew on a pencil.

Outside, Herbert locked the door and we walked back to the cab. We had to yell at Frankie to slow down, reminding him more than once that he was not being chased by the police, and, by the time Pravin reconnected the alarm telephone lines at four o'clock, all four of us were tucked up in bed, fast asleep. Well, Frankie, Herbert, Eve and I were, at any rate. Thumper had volunteered to hang around in his invisible sort of way, to see what happened.

Not much, as it turned out. Shortly after four o'clock a police car had screeched to a halt at the top of St Christopher's Place and three coppers had come haring down the precinct. They calmed down when they saw no evidence of a break-in, and then just hung around for fifteen minutes or so until Cornwell turned up. He too had run down from his car in Wigmore Street, but had visibly relaxed on seeing that the gallery, and his precious Bretton, were apparently untouched. He unlocked the door and accompanied the three policemen inside.

After a few minutes they had discovered the rat, the discovery being followed by a loud bang consistent with the sound of an instrument such as a cricket bat descending on a small mammal with deadly force.

Then Cornwell, looking grumpy, and the police, looking irritated, had departed.

RIP, Ratty. Rest assured that your sacrifice was not in vain.

Chapter Twenty-Seven

Professor Berndt Perssen was a surprise. I had expected a large, beefy, Nordic type with flaming red hair and a bushy beard, or at least an elegant, beautifully dressed history of art type with long, sensitive fingers and half-moon reading glasses. He was neither, and I walked past him twice in the lobby of the Savoy Hotel the next morning when I was looking for my guest.

Eventually the receptionist became a little impatient and pointed him out to me. 'There, that one,' he said, pointing distastefully, 'the one that looks like a tramp.'

An unkind description, perhaps, but not wholly inaccurate. My expensively imported Bretton expert was slumped in one of the hotel's very plush chairs with his legs sticking out. And, judging by the snorts and snufflings emanating from his nose, he was fast asleep. Mr Perrsen was wearing very creased stone-coloured trousers, blue trainers and a shirt that had once been yellow but now bore the evidence of an encounter with a large portion of steak au poivre – evidently made with green peppercorns.

There was also a rather worrying haze of alcohol around him which was almost visible in its intensity.

'The taxi driver said that he was put into the cab by British Airways staff. He appears to have brought no luggage with him at all.'

'How long has he been asleep?'

'Ever since he arrived, about two hours ago. We tried to get him to go to the suite you had booked for him, but he insisted that he had to wait for you in the lobby.'

I thought it was time to wake our sleeping expert. 'Professor,' I said, nudging one of his trainers with my shoe. The snoring stopped and, after a while, one eye opened blearily.

'Parker?' he grunted.

'That's me.'

He gave a lopsided grin which both the receptionist and I misinterpreted as an expression of wry sobriety, but which quickly turned into a grimace. Then he rolled over, vomited noisily onto a priceless Persian rug, and went back to sleep.

It was the sort of situation that could only be retrieved by the application of money in large quantities. I pressed a satisfyingly fat wad of banknotes into the horrified receptionist's hand.

'Look here,' I said, 'I need someone to take charge of all this, get him cleaned up, sobered up and put into a decent suit of clothes. It's absolutely vital that he's alert and presentable by tomorrow morning. I need him bright eyed, bushy tailed and well dressed at the Phillips auction rooms in New Bond Street at eleven o'clock sharp tomorrow morning. Can you deal with it?'

The man's horrified expression had melted somewhat when he saw how much I had pressed into his hand. 'There's more where that came from,' I added, 'and of course I'll reimburse you for any clothes you buy him, so get him some nice stuff.'

'Leave it all to me, Mr Parker.'

I left it all to him, gratefully.

My next appointment that Tuesday morning was with Ambrose Pendleton and Martin Douglas, the enormously calm and competent man from N.M. Rothschild, assets managers, investment advisers and Mrcnt Bnkrs, who looked after my millions. We met in Ambrose's dusty office in Lincoln's Inn, and I began by assuring both men that I was of sound mind and in full control of all mental faculties.

When they heard what I had in mind they needed a great deal of such assurance, and even then they looked distinctly unhappy about my detailed instructions.

'You are aware that bids made at an auction result in a binding contract, and that you might have to pay the sum bid if anything goes wrong?' Douglas said anxiously.

'Nothing will go wrong,' I assured him. I even half believed that myself.

Then I had to face Arnie Bloch and somehow explain to him what we were going to do – a somewhat more difficult task since he was not aware of my wealth, and saw the scheme as something that could rebound on the *Hampstead Explorer*.

'Trust me, Arnie,' I said.

'Trust you?'

'Yes.'

'That's like putting a fox in charge of baby bunnies.'

'Arnie, have I ever let you down?'

'Yes.'

We sat glaring at each other for a good five minutes before I broke the silence.

'Pendleton's prepared to go along with it. I saw him this morning,' I said. There was another five-minute silence.

'You went over my head to Pendleton?'

'Only because I knew you would be worried and I thought it would be useful for you to have his support.'

'Christ, sometimes you act like you own this bloody paper!' I carefully said nothing. Then: 'Well, if it's OK with Pendleton, it's OK with me, but if it ends in catastrophe don't say I didn't warn you.'

'Good man,' I said. 'Think of it this way, Arnie: it's going to be a bloody good story.'

'Yeah,' he said, and his eyes glinted hungrily. 'What time does the auction start tomorrow?'

'Eleven o'clock. You're going to be there?'

'Wild horses couldn't keep me away.'

Later that afternoon I telephoned my new little helper at the Savoy and asked him how he was getting on. Perssen, he reported, was sober if a little hung over.

'It seems he had never flown first class before, and all that free champagne went to his head, literally,' he said.

'Clothes?'

'Stolen. Said he put his bag down in the concourse while he went looking for a drink, and when he came back, surprise, surprise, it was gone. Anyway, I've bought him some lovely

174

things at the Paul Smith shop in Covent Garden. Also a tooth-brush, razor, things like that.' I winced at the likely bill. 'It's OK, Mr Parker. I'll keep an eye on him tonight, and I'll have him at Phillips in the morning.'

'What's your name?'

'Lloyd Barker.'

'How would you like a job, Lloyd Barker?'

'I've already got a job.'

'I mean a much better one. There's a hotel in Chalk Farm which needs a new manager, and I think the owners would be impressed by an enterprising young man like you.'

'Sounds interesting.'

'I'll have a word with the owners,' I promised.

Chapter Twenty-Eight

Wednesday dawned hot and steamy, one of those days when the air hangs still, there is not a cloud in the sky, and by ten o'clock motorists all over London are punching each other.

Frankie dropped us outside Phillips at about half past ten and we caused quite a stir. It might have been the sight of Thumper, nicely dressed that day in a dark suit, but more likely it was because of Eve, who was wearing one of those summery off-the-shoulder numbers held up by a thread.

Thumper smiled sweetly at the security staff, but they didn't even notice him because their eyes were pasted on Eve, and we proceeded into the air-conditioned interior. I was immediately struck by the size of the building which was concealed by the modest entrance in New Bond Street. There were long, dark corridors with satisfyingly creaky floorboards and helpful, smiling people who directed us to the viewing room where all the old masters in that day's catalogue were hanging.

We didn't stay there long; I noticed Cornwell was floating around the room, greeting people and oozing charm, and I didn't want to have more contact with him than was necessary.

So we went through to the large auction room. On the right as we came in, people were registering with the auctioneers, receiving little cards with numbers on which they would use to make their bids. I bought a catalogue for a mere eighteen pounds and we sat down in the second row of seats, the first row having 'reserved' cards on them. Thumper melted away somewhere. I noticed Herbert Wallis sitting near the back; also wearing a suit and looking faintly ridiculous with his hair plastered down with shiny Brylcreem. Arnie Bloch came in, waved

176

at me and also took a chair at the back.

The atmosphere as the room began to fill up was one of sophisticated excitement; a deep animation under the surface, carefully masked by extremely suave people anxious to give the impression that they did this every day. I noticed, too, that there was a babble of foreign languages all around, from French and German to Japanese, Spanish and Italian. I began to realise that the serious bidders were probably those modest types who were already sitting quietly, paging though their catalogues and reorganising the little slips of paper marking particular pages and paintings which had caught their eyes.

Most people were smartly dressed, many as if they had just stepped off a large yacht, but there were a few odd types, too: a man in blue jeans, long hair and a dramatic black eye patch; a very little man in a T-shirt who had commandeered two chairs so he could put all his papers on one. An enormously fat man came into the room; obviously someone important, who was expected, since a sturdy armchair was instantly brought out to him.

I saw Martin Douglas and Ambrose Pendleton come in separately, and I watched carefully as they registered at the desk and showed their credentials. After they had been given their numbered cards one of the men on the desk whispered discreetly in the ear of the man next to him who in turn got up and walked over to an important looking man near us and whispered in his ear. I caught the word 'Rothschilds' in the exchange. The important man's eyebrows went up and he pursed his lips in an interested sort of way. My back-up team sat on opposite sides of the room from each other, Douglas next to me and Ambrose near the important-looking fat man.

By ten to eleven all the seats were taken, including the reserved ones in front of us. Cornwell was sitting with his female partner in crime in the reserved section, about four or five seats to our left. As far as I could tell, he had not noticed me yet. Much too busy beaming away at everyone and, I thought, wondering how he was going to spend the millions that would shortly be coming his way.

By eleven o'clock the room was full and buzzing loudly with conversation. Along the left hand wall were a bunch of people holding house telephones, and there were also some at the back near a window, with their own mobiles. Three television camera crews had also set up shop and were busy filming the paintings, the audience, the staff and anything else that moved.

There was a ripple of comment as the auctioneer climbed up to his podium, looking immaculate in a blue pinstripe suit and a subtly striped yellow shirt, the cuffs of which protruded from his sleeves by precisely the right amount, and tapped his hammer. Silence fell, except for the ear-splitting beating of my heart. Apart from anything else, I was acutely aware that Professor Perrsen had not arrived yet.

The auctioneer welcomed the audience, reminded everyone of the conditions of sale and pointed out that the television monitor, which would show the current bidding in both sterling and a range of other currencies, was there only as a guide. The hammer price would be that noted by the auctioneer.

Then he began, and I was shocked at how quickly it all took place. The first lot, a painting by the Dutch seventeenth-century artist, Pieter Jansz, was bid up from four thousand and sold for eight thousand eight hundred pounds in about twenty-five seconds flat.

No sign of Berndt Perrsen. My unease began to grow.

Next was a portrait by Giovanni Martinelli, estimated in the catalogue to sell at between five and seven thousand pounds.

'Lot two, portrait by Martinelli,' the auctioneer intoned. 'I'll start at four thousand. Thank you. Five thousand. Six thousand. Seven thousand. With you sir, on the telephone. Thank you, nine thousand. At the back, eleven thousand. Thirteen thousand. Fifteen thousand. Seventeen thousand. Eighteen thousand. With you sir, on the telephone. All done? At eighteen thousand, then [bang went the hammer]. Number 342.'

That's it. Thirty six seconds; that's how long it takes to sell an old master. I was amazed, having imagined that the sale of each painting would be a serious, thoughtful affair.

An hour later the auctioneer had dealt with no less than seventy paintings, including one by Pieter Breughel the Younger which sold for three hundred and sixty thousand, and a Canaletto that was expected to fetch between half a million and eight hundred thousand, but remained unsold after the bidding stalled at three hundred and twenty thousand.

At the end of it, the young men and women with their Phillips badges who had been carrying the pictures in and out looked exhausted. The auctioneer had also become slightly croaky and he stopped for a glass of water while the Bretton was brought in and put on the viewing stand. There was utter silence in the room and Eve gripped my hand tightly. I looked over at Cornwell, and saw him leaning forward in taut expectation, his eyes fixed on the auctioneer, his mouth partly open.

For my part, sweat was beginning to trickle down my forehead, mainly due to the fact that there was still no sign of Berndt Perrsen ...

'Thank you, ladies and gentlemen. We now come to the major item in today's auction, lot number seventy one, the Portrait of Silvie by François Bretton, the property of the Cornwell Gallery in London. As you will see from the catalogue, the estimated sale price is between six million and seven million pounds, and I will therefore start the bidding at five million.'

There was a rustle of noise as people towards the front of the hall turned around in their chairs to try to see who would make the first bid. The camera crews were filming furiously. No-one was looking around more eagerly than Cornwell.

One or two seconds passed, and then the big fat man with his own chair, lifted his card.

'Thank you, the Musée d'Orsay. Five million two hundred thousand.'

A card flickered somewhere else.

'Five million four. Five million six. Five million eight. Thank you, sir, six million.'

After each competing bid the auctioneer looked back at the fat man who confirmed the higher bid with the smallest lift of an eyebrow. At six million Cornwell turned round, looked at Margaret Forbes, and made a little triumphal motion with his fist.

'Six million two.' There was a lull in the bidding. Whoever it was who had been bidding against the fat man had fallen by the wayside at six million. Then another card moved at the left, and we were off again, but this time in only one hundred thousand pound leaps.

Where the hell was that bloody Perrsen? My eyes were half

179

glued to the entrance.

'Six million three. Four. Six million five.' A short pause, and then a new bid from the bank of house telephones.

'Thank you, on the telephone, six million six hundred thousand pounds.' The fat man twitched an eyelid.

'Six million seven. Six million eight. Six million nine.'

The Musée d'Orsay obviously wanted the Bretton very badly indeed.

'Seven million. Seven million. At seven million pounds, then ... Ah, thank you, seven million two.' A mutter of interest in the crowd, because a new bidder had started. Cornwell was slouching back in his chair, the most satisfied smile of contentment on his face that anyone could ever imagine.

The auctioneer looked over at the fat man. 'Against you, sir.' A facial muscle trembled. 'Thank you, seven million three.'

A card flashed. 'The Getty Museum, thank you. Seven million four.'

Back to the fat man.

'Seven million five.'

Back to the Getty Museum man, a bidder whose features were so nondescript he almost didn't have a face at all.

'Seven million six.'

Like spectators at a tennis match, all eyes switched to the face of the fat man. But the fat man's face remained completely still. No sign of irritation, resentment or even disappointment. Just an absolute absence of a bid. The Museé d'Orsay had clearly decided the Bretton was not worth more than seven and a half million.

The auctioneer was scanning the audience. I was frantically scanning the entrance, looking for my wayward Bretton professor, on whom all my plans rested. The only sound was the soft murmur of voices into telephones. 'At seven million six hundred thousand pounds then, with the Getty Museum. At Seven million six ...' The tension was unbearable, and I gave Douglas a sharp dig in the ribs.

'Bid!' I hissed desperately in his ear. He looked at me as if I was mad. 'Bid or I'll kill you,' I threatened.

'Eight million!' Douglas croaked, and there was a buzz of excitement in the room as everyone turned to see the new bidder. Cameras focused in on him relentlessly.

180

The auctioneer tasted blood. 'Eight million five. Thank you.' The Getty Museum was still in. I nudged Douglas again, and he waved his card gaily, with the kind of abandon which comes from knowing you are not bidding your own money.

'Nine million.' Necks craned and everyone focused on the faceless man from the Getty. But there was no bid.

Where the hell was Professor Perrsen?

'At nine million pounds, with you, sir. Rothschilds, I believe, on behalf of a client. At nine million pounds ...' I caught Ambrose's eye and nodded vigorously.

'Ten!' he called out, speaking calmly and clearly from the back of the room, and looking serenely oblivious to the renewed hum of speculation his bid had caused.

'Another new bidder, thank you sir.' He looked at Douglas.

'Keep bidding until that bastard Perrsen gets here!' I commanded.

Douglas waved at the auctioneer. He was beginning to enjoy himself. I wasn't enjoying myself. I was thinking of painful ways of torturing American art history professors who were always late.

'Eleven million.'

Across to Ambrose. 'Twelve million.'

To Douglas. 'Thirteen.'

To Ambrose. 'Fourteen.'

There was by now a loud chatter of excitement. 'Quiet please, ladies and gentlemen. Against you, sir, at fourteen million pounds.' Douglas winked.

'Fifteen million.'

Ambrose waved his card excitedly.

'Sixteen!' Even the auctioneer was getting excited. I sneaked a look at Cornwell and his girlfriend. He was sitting with a stupefied look on his face, unable to believe his ears. She had her head against his shoulder, and there were tears of joy flowing down her cheeks.

I thought of Wheezy Wallis fighting against the handcuffs in his car.

Douglas nodded. 'Seventeen million,' intoned the auctioneer, regaining his poise.

'Against you, sir,' he said, looking at Ambrose. Ambrose looked at me. I looked into my soul and saw disaster there.

181

Perrsen had not turned up, and my carefully composed plan was collapsing like a house of cards. With a feeling of despair I quietly shook my head. The auctioneer was still looking at Ambrose, but he carefully didn't even blink.

'At seventeen million pounds then. At seventeen million. I'm going to sell it at seventeen million.' He raised his hand with the hammer, and I was about a half a second away from paying a very large amount of money to Rupert Cornwell for a fake painting.

Chapter Twenty-Nine

'The picture is a goddamn fake!'

The sharp Californian accent rang out like a cracked bell from the back of the room, and I watched in glee as Berndt Perrsen, wearing what had once been the most gorgeous Paul Smith outfit in subtle greys, emerged into the central aisle like the Seventh Cavalry relieving a fort. Cameras had whipped round and were filming his every step. Or perhaps a better description would be his 'every lurch', since my hired expert was clearly the worse for wear. He looked as if he had been out walking in the rain.

I later learned that although he had been delivered to the auction rooms on time, and had actually managed to inspect the painting in the viewing room, he had decided to nip out for a quick drink, and had had an altercation with a Glaswegian in a pub. A pint of beer had been poured over his head.

'I beg your pardon?' said the auctioneer.

'You heard what I shed,' he slurred. 'The painting is not a Bretton, but a very obvious forgery!' And, attempting to march in a commanding fashion up the aisle, Perrsen then tripped on his own feet and fell flat on his face.

There was an instant scrum by the cameramen trying to film the professor's attempts to stand up again. There was a minute or two of confusion and loud discussion by everyone, until the auctioneer managed to restore order again.

'I'm sorry, the issues of provenance and authentication have already been dealt with to the entire satisfaction of all concerned. These are not matters which can be raised at this stage. If there are no more bids ...' he raised his gavel again.

'Excuse me,' said Mr Douglas, speaking with all the weight of the Rothschild trillions in his voice, 'I consider that I have a very strong interest in what this gentleman appears to be saying. If he is correct, I am being sold a painting under false pretences, and that would surely nullify my contract with you. Let's find out who he is. I insist.'

'Who are you sir?' the auctioneer asked the beer-soaked academic.

'Proffesor Berndt Perrsen, of the art history department at the University of California. I am as some of you may know, an authority on the works of François Bretton, and I can assure you all that this is not one of them. It is a crude forgery!'

Cornwell was on his feet now, his face puce with concern and rage. 'This is outrageous! The painting has been authenticated without hesitation by no less than Professor Robert Beaumanoir, who is generally regarded as the world authority on Bretton. There can be no challenge at this stage.' He turned to the auctioneer and shouted: 'I insist that you continue with the sale!' All cameras were now trained on the gallery owner.

His last words were lost in the general babble of excited comment and conjecture. It was time for me to act. I pulled out of my pocket the letter Beaumanoir had written and signed under my direction in Bordeaux a few days before, and I got up and handed it to the auctioneer. It was then that Cornwell noticed me for the first time, and his face became contorted with fury.

'What are *you* doing here?' he bellowed, oblivious of the cameras which were now all focused on him alone. I ignored him and returned to my seat.

The auctioneer was shouting for silence, and when at last he could be heard, he said into his microphone: 'I have here what purports to be a letter from Professor Beaumanoir, dated four days ago, which I intend to read. It says:

"To whom it may concern. It is with great regret that I must now announce that, following further study and research, I realise that my earlier authentication of the so-called François Bretton in the possession of the Rupert Cornwell Gallery, was a grave error. I am now of the certain opinion that the painting is a forgery, a poor copy of the original Portrait of Silvie. I extend my most profound apologies to anyone who has been inconvenienced by my initial, and inexcusable, mistake."

'It is signed "Robert Beaumanoir",' the auctioneer said.

For a few seconds there was pandemonium, but the noise was silenced by the auctioneer angrily banging his hammer on the side of the podium. But when the room was halfway quiet again, it was Cornwell's voice that filled the space.

'That letter is a forgery!' he screamed.

'No, it's not.' The quiet voice from the back of the room stilled the hubbub faster than any shout could have done. And to my eternal joy, I saw Beaumanoir himself walking with great dignity down the central aisle, a look of grim purpose on his face. Cornwell's eyes nearly popped out of their sockets, and I was sure the man was going to burst a blood vessel.

When he got to the front, Beaumanoir turned and faced the now hushed audience. 'I am Beaumanoir and I wrote that letter on Saturday. It is quite genuine. Now I have come to confess in person to having made a terrible mistake.' He turned to Perrsen who, like almost everyone else, was gaping at him in astonishment. 'This gentleman and I have had our differences in the past, but on this occasion he is right and I was wrong, and I am happy to make that acknowledgment now, without reservation.' The cameras were hoovering up the drama, and they stuck with him as he walked over to his American rival and shook his hand warmly.

'You treacherous bastard! You snivelling ...' Cornwell, incandescent with fury, launched himself at the Frenchman. He managed to grab the professor by the throat before four or five strapping Phillips picture carriers dragged him off and pinned him to the ground.

There was general uproar again, over which some of us heard the auctioneer shout: 'This sale is suspended pending further inquiries!'

I walked over to where Cornwell was being held on the ground, kicking and struggling, his lips curled back in ecstatic fury. His rage was awe-inspiring, and he was practically frothing at the mouth. There was not the faintest trace of the suave, handsome man who had once welcomed me into his office. Then I managed to catch his eye.

I smiled and winked at him, and blew him a kiss. 'Gosh, so

close to seventeen million smackeroos! It nearly worked, didn't it?'

It was as if I had given him something to focus his fury on, and he went berserk. A few more strapping young men had to lend a hand. But then, suddenly, he stopped struggling.

He looked at me with that baleful, pitiless, glazed stare that sharks have just before they come sliding in with rows of razor-sharp teeth to disembowel you. I held his gaze for a few seconds, even though it was turning my backbone to jelly and my bowels to water, and winked at him again. He made a desperate gurgling sound, as if there was no speech that he could summon to express his hatred of me.

I took Eve's hand and we walked out. 'I hope you were up there watching, Wheezy,' I thought. 'You'll have enjoyed that.'

Chapter Thirty

I was at my desk that Wednesday afternoon, tapping my own beautifully observed piece on the morning's exciting happenings into my computer, when the expected telephone call came through just after lunch.

'Parker.'

'This is Rupert Cornwell.' Malice and malignancy hissed along the telephone wires and assailed me.

'You mean the Rupert Cornwell who nearly became a multimillionaire this morning?' I let the sarcasm drip heavily off the words. I could hear him breathing deeply, trying to keep control.

'You have something of mine,' he said, the tension vibrating through the words.

'Well, you're wrong there,' I said cheerfully. 'I can safely say, without threat to my immortal soul or conscience, that I am not in possession of anything that belongs to you.'

'You know what I mean.' Lots of menace, laced with threat.

'Do I?' I chirruped.

'Yes.' Through gritted teeth. 'I don't know how, although I can make a shrewd guess, but I don't doubt that you've got it.'

'This "it" that you refer to; what would that be?' I said innocently.

'Are you recording this call?'

Of course I was. 'Of course not,' I said, slightly wounded.

'I need to speak to you. In private.'

'Go ahead.'

'Not on the telephone.'

'Where, then?'

'Hampstead Heath, in about half an hour?'

'Where, exactly?'

'At the top of Kite Hill.'

'Actually, it's called Parliament Hill. It's a common mistake, but it's not called ...'

'I don't care what it's fucking well called!' he yelled into my ear. I could tell that he was definitely not in a good mood.

'OK, half an hour then,' I said chirpily. 'See you.'

'Come alone,' he said and hung up.

It was about a quarter to three when Frankie dropped me at the end of the road called Parliament Hill and I walked onto the Heath. Cornwell was already there, sitting alone on a bench at the very top of the hill, silhouetted against the sky. He was carrying a pair of field glasses, through which he scrutinised me as I walked towards him. He then did a complete three hundred and sixty degree scan with the glasses. Suspicious bugger didn't trust me to come alone.

'Eschew all thoughts of violence,' I said to him pleasantly as I sat down. 'Even a raised finger will mean that you will never see the Bretton again.'

'So you have got it! I knew it!'

'Of course I have.'

'You stole the copy from Margaret Forbes's house and you switched it with the one in the gallery.'

'An ingenious deduction,' I said.

'How did you get into the gallery?'

'My lips are sealed.'

'The alarm on Monday night. That wasn't the fucking rat, was it?' My thoughts turned to poor Mr Ratty.

'I can neither confirm nor deny your allegation.' People had said that to me as a journalist so often, I had been dying to say it myself for years.

'How did you know there were two paintings?' he demanded. He did not appreciate my flowing sense of humour.

'Sorry, lips sealed and all that.'

'I could kill you.' He said it like he meant it.

'You already tried once,' I answered quietly.

'Pity you didn't drown.' He meant that too.

'You're going to pay for that, and for the real Bretton, if you want it back.'

'How much?'

'Five million pounds.'

'You're mad!' he gasped.

'I don't think so,' I had dropped all hint of humour.

'What makes you think I'll give you five million pounds?'

'Because you need to compensate both me and Ms Dupont for a pretty horrific experience, and because you know that if you can get your hands on the real Bretton, there is a client of Rothschilds who appears to be willing to pay seventeen million pounds for it. You'll still end up making a profit of around ten million pounds.'

He considered the sums for a while, but I could sense that he was really making other plans. 'OK, five million, I agree. Immediately after the sale.'

'Oh come on, Mr Cornwell, you're not dealing with some kind of halfwit here. The day after the sale you'll be saying to me with that charming smile: "Agreement? What agreement?" I want the money now, tonight at the latest.'

'That's impossible!'

'Fine, I'll find another buyer.' I got up.

'I don't have that kind of money, for fuck's sake!'

'Sure you do.'

'I don't!' He paused, decided to show his cards, and continued: 'The gallery is trading insolvently, if you must know, and the banks are beating down my door.' I knew that already, of course.

'Foreign accounts? Switzerland, places like that?'

'Nothing! If I had money abroad I would have left the country years ago, or brought it over here to refinance the gallery.' The words had a ring of truth to them.

'I don't believe you,' I said. 'People like you always have a lot of lolly salted away somewhere very safe in case of a very rainy day or even a hurricane. Probably in cash in a Gucci suitcase.'

There was no answer. Jackpot? I sat down again.

'How much have you got?' I pressed. 'Careful now, don't bullshit me. Because If I even suspect you are holding out I'm going to walk away and find someone much more reliable to do business with. So you get one chance to mention a figure, right now.

'And if you're thinking that there might be some other way of getting that painting, such as by stealing it from me, forget it. It's hidden away so securely that you'll never find it in a million years.' Actually it was hidden under my bed at the hotel. 'It's time to cough up what you've got, Cornwell. You're still going to make a monster profit.'

There was silence for another minute or two while he thought about it and I watched a flock of Canada geese come in to land on one of the Highgate ponds, splashing down like overloaded jumbo jets.

'I do have some cash,' he said eventually.

'Yes?' Almost uninterested.

'I can come up with seven hundred and fifty thousand in cash,' he said.

'Sorry,' I said, getting up again, 'that's over four million short of the target. I'm off elsewhere.'

'Hey! That's it! That's all I have, damn you, I swear!'

I stood there, looking down on him, his upturned face full of desperation – and hatred.

'Make it eight hundred thousand,' I said.

'I don't have eight hundred fucking thousand! I only have seven hundred and fifty!'

I decided that he was telling the truth. He believed that he stood to make a vast pile out of the deal and he was prepared to pay what it took to get the painting. Had he had the extra fifty thousand he would have agreed to give it.

'OK,' I said quietly, sitting down again, 'I'll take the seven hundred and fifty in cash as a deposit, and you give me an IOU for the rest, here and now, and sign and date it.'

'It's a deal,' he said. He pretended to look relieved but I could see the evil gleam in his eye. I pulled out my notebook, tore out a clean page and handed it to him. He started to write.

'What's your name, I mean your first name?'

'Horatio.' He looked at me to see if I was taking the piss. I wish I had been. 'Horatio Thorpe Parker, Thorpe as in Jeremy. That's what's on my birth certificate.'

It only took a few minutes and then he showed me the paper. He had written, under that day's date: 'This is to certify that I owe Horatio Thorpe Parker the sum of four million, two hundred and fifty thousand pounds sterling. Signed, Rupert Cornwell.'

It wouldn't even have been good enough for use as toilet paper in a court of law, but I had no intention of going anywhere near courts of law. For one thing, both of us would find it very difficult explaining to a judge how the debt arose. The point was that Cornwell clearly thought that I believed it was a binding agreement, and I was perfectly happy with that.

'I'll give you that, and the cash, when you hand over the painting.'

'It has to be tonight,' I said firmly.

'How about here?'

'No, it's much too public, and I'm not walking around on Hampstead Heath in the dark carrying a suitcase full of money. There's no telling what kind of thieves, footpads and gallery owners one could run up against.'

He ignored the jibe. 'Where then?'

'That little lay-by in Swain's Lane, next to the gates of the old Highgate Cemetery.'

'Why there?' he asked, a shining razored edge in his voice.

'Why not? It's dark, it's secluded, it's not overlooked by any houses, there's no-one around there at night, and if we meet at about two o'clock there will be very few passing cars.'

'Alright, two o'clock, Swain's Lane. But you come alone, right, with the painting. If there's anyone else around, there's no deal.'

'I'll be accompanied only by the painting. Make sure you're alone too, or you'll never see it again.' He grunted.

'Incidentally,' I added, 'how are you going to explain the sudden reappearance of the genuine Bretton?'

'Easy,' he said, with that brilliant charm flowing back into his face, 'I will produce both paintings, and reveal the sensational news that the owner of the genuine one, a modest private collector, who had bought it in good faith for a few hundred pounds shortly after the original robbery in the belief that it was a good copy, had come forward following the publicity surrounding this morning's auction. I have no doubt that Beaumanoir and Perrsen will have no qualms about authenti-

cating the real one, and the "collector" will be rewarded handsomely for his honesty.'

'It's a good plan,' I admitted. I only hoped my own plan was
that good.

Chapter Thirty-One

The day had begun hot and had got even hotter as the humidity rose and the last vestiges of a breeze disappeared when the sun went down. It was the kind of weather that causes comment on the television and a determined run on pubs, outdoor restaurants and the oxygen facilities of hospitals.

I was in need of a little oxygen myself as I sat in the car I had hired that afternoon in Kentish Town, and I wondered for the fortieth time why I hadn't taken one with air conditioning. I had all the windows open, but the air still hung hot and wet around the skin like some heavy creeper firmly colonising a wall.

I am not superstitious, but there was something about sitting in a parked car, in almost total darkness outside a cemetery, that was a little unnerving. I wasn't afraid of the ghosts and spectres in the graveyard, but of the human variety of ghouls who are attracted by such places. I remembered that someone had been sent to jail in the early '70s for breaking into a mausoleum and putting desiccated bodies into cars parked nearby.

Or perhaps it was because I was sitting, unaccompanied, in a deserted spot, in the middle of the night, with a painting worth millions of pounds on my knee, waiting for a charming villain who was probably also a murderer.

Cornwell's Jaguar purred up a few minutes after two o'clock. I had previously seen the car go up the road, and then down again – presumably looking for possible accomplices of mine in nearby parked cars. Of course he found none.

He parked four or five feet away from my car and his

passenger window slid down silently. He had air conditioning, I noted with some irritation.

'Have you got the painting?' he said.

'Yes. Have you got the money and my IOU?'

'Yes.'

'Show me,' I said.

'Show me the painting.'

'Tell you what,' I said, 'I'll get into your car and while you examine the painting, I'll count the money.'

'Fine,' he said, much too readily, I thought.

And that's what we did. I got into the passenger's seat. I handed him the still wrapped painting and he lifted a sports holdall off the back seat and put it in my lap. By the light of the car's interior light and, in Cornwell's case, a torch, we began to do our stuff. The air conditioning, although blowing strongly, didn't seem to be coping with my level of perspiration, and I wasn't sure whether it was the heat or the fact that I was becoming more and more nervous with each passing second.

What I found in the bag, to my relief, was bundles of fifty pound notes. I counted a few bundles with sweaty, trembling fingers, and found a hundred notes in each. Assuming that all the bundles contained a hundred notes, or five thousand pounds, I expected there to be a hundred and fifty bundles, and there were. Three quarters of a million pounds, in cash, sitting on my lap. It felt about as safe as a bag full of weapons-grade plutonium, and just as evil.

By the time I had finished counting, Cornwell had finished his examination.

'Satisfied?' I said.

'It's the real Bretton.'

'Right'o, then, just give me my IOU and I'll be off.'

Cornwell put his hand into his inside jacket pocket and the next thing I knew I was staring at the black muzzle of a really nasty looking revolver with a very short barrel. It wasn't a dinky little thing like you see in the movies, but a big, ugly, heavy gun which gave the impression that it could make holes in my body the size of manhole covers. I could smell the gun oil, and I could smell the fear on my body and the tension on his.

'Don't do anything sudden and don't do anything stupid,' he said, his voice trembling with stress.

This was the third time in my life that I'd been at close quarters to people pointing guns. The first had been a year before when I had looked up the gaping barrels of a shotgun wielded by a man who I knew had already used it once before to kill someone. The second had been a few days ago, in that field near Périgueux when an automatic had been levelled at Thumper. There is a particular terror in this experience, much more acute than being in some other form of danger where your safety or survival depends to some extent on your own abilities and or dexterity. When there is a gun pointing your way, you are very close to your maker indeed, your life depending entirely on the movements of the other person.

There are people who know the facts and statistics for different kinds of guns: how many millimetres the trigger has to move, the number of pounds of pressure that need to be exerted on the trigger, whether it is automatic or semi-automatic, how many bullets are held in the magazine, what kind of bullets there are, and the kind of charge that drives them and at what velocity. I know nothing about these things. All I know is that you can't dodge a bullet, and you can't outrun one, and if one hits you it does a great deal of damage or kills you. Humphrey Bogart would have punched him on the nose. Clint Eastwood would have taken the gun out of his hand and then punched him on the nose.

But I didn't do anything stupid, and I didn't do anything sudden.

'Do you want me to put my hands up?' I asked.

'Don't try to be funny, Parker.' Actually, I wasn't trying to be funny. I was trying to stay alive.

'I wasn't trying to be ...'

'Shut up!'

'Just calm down,' I said to him, my voice shaking slightly. 'I'm going to put the money on the floor here, and then I'm going to get out of the car, and then you can drive away with the money, and the picture, and even with my IOU, and have a wonderful life. OK?'

'I said shut up!' he shouted, very agitated. I shut up, knowing that agitation is not good for the stability of triggers.

'Keep still and don't move or by God I'll kill you.' I kept still and didn't move and while I was doing that, he got out of the car slowly, pointing the gun at me all the time. Then holding the gun in two hands he started going round the front of the car, still pointing it at me through the window. I had no illusions about the possibility of the glass deflecting a bullet, and I continued keeping still and trying not to do anything stupid.

Finally he was outside the passenger door, pointing the gun at my left ear. 'OK, open the door and get out.' I did what I was told. 'Get in your car.'

When I was sitting in the driver's seat, he put his left hand in his jacket pocket and brought out a pair of handcuffs. My heart began to race with the knowledge of what he was going to do.

'Put one side around your left ankle and lock it,' he said, his voice still shaking.

'What happens if I don't?'

'I'll shoot you in the knee or elbow or somewhere equally agonising, and you'll pray that you were dead.'

I did what he wanted. 'Now pass the chain over the steering column and lock the other side to your right ankle.' I did that too. He brought out another pair of handcuffs.

'Are those the same ones you used to kill Wheezy?' I asked.

'Shut the fuck up! Put your hands through the steering wheel.'

'All this just for three quarters of a million pounds. Is that how much Wheezy wanted? Or did he ask you for more, a couple of million, maybe?' He hit me with the revolver, the barrel and the protruding sight raking across my face while the impact rattled my teeth and sent a blinding flash of pain through my head. I didn't ask him any more questions.

The other handcuffs went onto my wrists in such a way that I could not pull my hands free of the steering wheel. And my feet were locked to the column further down. When the cuffing was complete, Cornwell put the gun back in his pocket and walked to the back of his car. I craned my neck round to watch him open the boot and take out a length of rubber hose. I lost sight of him as he went behind my car to attach it to the exhaust pipe, but a few seconds later I could see him again, feeding the pipe in through a two-inch gap in the back window.

He closed all the other windows, then leaned past me, turned the ignition key, started the engine, and then bent the key backwards and forwards until it broke off in the lock and I couldn't turn it off. Then he stepped back and looked at me.

'What, no triumphant speech? No gloating about how clever you are and how stupid I am?' I said, my voice sounding a great deal more bold than I felt. Inside me, all was panic and terror.

'Fuck you!' he said and slammed the door shut. I knew that this was not entirely about the painting, and very little to do with the money. This was revenge brought on by the purest form of hatred. I had spoiled his plans, humiliated him in public and outsmarted him. Each was unforgivable; together they were grounds for murder.

I turned my head and saw that he had walked over to his car and was leaning against it. For a moment I couldn't work out why he didn't drive away, and then I remembered. He had to hang around until I lost consciousness, so that he could take off the handcuffs and try again to make it look like a suicide.

In those first moments, an odd thought passed through my mind. I was pleased I had specified a car with a catalytic converter, so at least I wasn't being poisoned by all the poisonous metals in petrol exhaust.

But I was most certainly being poisoned by the carbon monoxide that was being pumped inexorably into the car by the engine with a phut-phut-phut sound, and there seemed to be absolutely nothing that I could do about it. Having seen the bruises on Wheezy's wrists and ankles, I knew there was no point trying to get out of the handcuffs. I tried banging my head against the side window, but I didn't have the leverage to exert any real force, and all I did was aggravate the pain that had almost paralysed me since he hit me in the face with the gun.

Then, despite the panic in my soul, my heartbeat began to slow, and I began to feel drowsy. I knew that it was due to the effect of the toxic exhaust gas, and that I should, if anything, be struggling more frantically now. But the drowsiness was sapping my will, and I was beginning to see pictures and images in front of my eyes, in particular that of a young girl with a wide mouth and wild red hair with flecks of straw in it.

I smiled at Silvie, and knew that it was time to do the one thing that Wheezy must have overlooked. I let my head fall forward onto the steering wheel and blew a satisfyingly loud and long blast on the hooter.

After that things moved pretty swiftly. I heard but could not see some sort of commotion outside the car, and a few seconds later Guy the Gorilla opened the door of my car and began unlocking the restraints on my hands and feet. I was puzzled. Hadn't Guy the Gorilla died at London Zoo many years ago? But then, lying on the gravel next to the car, my head started to clear and I began to realise that my bodyguard was worth every penny, and more, of the money that I paid him.

After five minutes of deep breathing I felt back in the land of the living and ready to carry this thing through.

'You were very prompt. Thank you,' I said to Thumper, who was looking at me with a rather worried expression on his face.

'Why didn't you hoot earlier? I think you may have to go to hospital for a check-up,' he said.

'No, I'm OK, really. I had to be sure that he was prepared to go through with it. But maybe I did leave it a minute or two too long, come to think of it. Where is the bastard anyway?' I said, looking around for Cornwell.

'I smacked him and put him in the boot of his car. He's quite safe there.' I shuddered at the thought of one of Thumper's 'smacks'.

'He's got a gun,' I warned.

'He had a gun,' Thumper corrected me, patting his side pocket.

'Good. Ready to complete the job?'

'Of course.'

'Remember the script? Right, let's do it.'

We went round to the back of the Jaguar and Thumper opened the boot lid. As the boot light came on I saw Cornwell lying dazed and shocked, a puffiness around his cheek and eye suggesting that the smack Thumper had given him was a rather good one.

'Hello,' I said pleasantly, 'it's time for you to come out of there.'

'What are you going to do?' The hatred and fury seemed

mysteriously to have disappeared, and he appeared to be eyeing Thumper with extreme nervousness.

'We're going to kill you. Terminate your existence in the same way that we would stamp on any psychopathic insect.' I deliberately kept my voice flat and unemotional. I did not want him to think this was a joke or anything he could talk his way out of.

'You can have the painting, the money, even the car! Everything!' His voice cracked, and I could see that he was beginning to fear for his life. 'Why ... why can't we talk about this?' he stammered.

Thumper leaned in and using one hand, yanked Cornwell from the boot, carried him over to the driver's seat of his Jaguar and shoved him down. And while he did this, I was explaining things to the man, ticking the points off on my fingers.

'Why? Four reasons. Firstly, you killed Wheezy. Secondly, you tried to kill me tonight. Thirdly, you tried to have me killed in France, and fourthly we want the painting and the money and no-one around to interfere with us about it. Let's do it, Thumper. Let's snuff this creep and get out of here.'

It took a couple of minutes to handcuff him into position as he had done to me, and then transfer the rubber hose from my car to his. And while Thumper was doing this, I was at the car's fuse box, removing the fuses that operated the lights and the hooter, so that Cornwell would not be able to attract attention to himself as I had done.

Cornwell was clearly shocked and very frightened now. When I leaned past him, started the engine, and then broke off the key as he had showed me earlier, he lost all control and started blubbing frantically. I felt a moment of compassion, which was almost instantly dispelled by the image of what he had done to little Wheezy Wallis.

'Come on then, let's bugger off,' I said to Thumper, and then I shut the door on Cornwell.

We got into my car, the engine of which was still running quietly, and drove off.

Chapter Thirty-Two

We didn't go far, of course. Just a hundred metres or so down the road where I parked the car and stalled it by shoving it into third gear and letting out the clutch quickly. Then we walked back silently to the cemetery gates to find Cornwell's car rocking and bucking as the man inside, convinced now that we had actually left him to die, gave way to uncontrollable panic. I thought of what he might be doing to his wrists and ankles, but felt no pity for him.

We waited quietly for a few more minutes, until the thrashing around inside the car began to subside, and then I went round and opened the door.

Cornwell was wide-eyed with panic and terror, and I was repelled by the appalling smell in the car. His trousers were soaked and he stank terribly. There was no trace whatsoever of the handsome, assured gallery owner, nor even of the evil psychopath who had tried to kill me. He sat there gulping air and shaking uncontrollably.

'He's crapped his pants,' I told Thumper with disgust. I pulled the bonnet release catch and Thumper then went round to the engine where he shorted something in the electronic ignition system and the engine died.

Cornwell, his eyes rolling with fear, started sobbing with relief, still handcuffed to his seat. He had truly thought he was about to meet his end.

'I've decided to give you a choice. You can either die now, in the same way that you killed Wheezy Wallis, or you can make a confession on tape that will send you to jail for life. I don't mind which you decide, but make it snappy because it's late and I would like to get to bed at some stage tonight.' There was no trace of humour in my voice.

There was no real contest, and when he started to talk into my tape recorder, he knew he was talking to save his life. I often wonder now what I would have done had he refused, and I have never really been able to decide whether I would have let him die in that car or not. Thumper would have had no compunction about doing it. He could have quite happily wrung Cornwell's neck.

The story as it came out, was rather as we had imagined, except for a few details about Margaret Forbes. It had started six months before when she had come to him with the fake painting, except that she believed it to be genuine, having found it amongst her deceased father's possessions. Cornwell, knowing a good thing when he saw one, and being in financial trouble besides, fostered a relationship with the woman, and took the painting to Beaumanoir for authentication. Beaumanoir recognised it as a fake immediately but Cornwell, realising the amount of money that could be made, bribed him to declare it genuine.

He then brought it back to England, announced the 'discovery', and reached a deal to split the proceeds with the gullible Miss Forbes, who had in the meantime fallen seriously in love with the handsome charmer. Cornwell had sat back, hoping to see his financial troubles disappear for ever.

The fly in the ointment was little Wheezy Wallis, who contacted him shortly after the announcement in the newspapers, and informed him that he had the original painting and would be prepared to sell it to him for a million pounds.

Had he bought the painting from Wheezy, everyone would have been happy. Cornwell and Miss Forbes would have shared something like five million pounds, and the Wallis clan would have gone off to live in luxury on the Costa del Sol. Cornwell was too greedy, however, to see a million pounds walk away with a little runt of a burglar, and had killed him as he had tried to kill me, by luring him to that dark spot in Highgate with the promise of a suitcase-full of cash. He had waited until Wheezy had passed out, removed the handcuffs, and had nearly got clean away with it, except for the sharp eyes of the pathologist in St Pancras.

I made sure that Cornwell's confession made no mention of

201

my name, or any aspects of the story which had to do with me. The admission about killing Wheezy would be enough to send him to prison and I had no need for further personal revenge or retribution. The immensely satisfying scene in the auction room that morning had poured salve on my wounds.

Thumper and I then went over the Jaguar carefully, wiping any part of it that could have carried our fingerprints, and then we went over it again, to make sure. Then we left Cornwell, still securely handcuffed to his seat, with the confession cassette on the back seat, and we went off to call the cops.

The ignition of my car was still switched on, and we started the engine by rolling the car down the hill.

It was actually Thumper who made the call. Adopting a startlingly accurate Glaswegian accent, he told the boys in blue exactly where to find a murderer and reminded them to listen to the tape.

Oh, I should mention that we left the Bretton on the back seat too. It would, I presumed, eventually end up in the possession of Miss Forbes, who would no doubt benefit from its full value this time, since Cornwell would be in the clink. It did, after all, really belong to her.

On the other hand, I did take the bag full of money.

'What are you going to do with the cash?' Thumper asked me on the way home.

'I think I'll give half a million to Herbert and the Wallis family, as a kind of compensation for Wheezy's death. Then I thought I would give a hundred and fifty thousand to Miss Dupont, as compensation for all the terrible things she was put through. And then there's fifty grand each for you and Frankie, for helping out and putting your arses on the line for me. How does that sound?'

'It's very generous, but what about some for you?'

'I don't need any more money,' I said.

The telephone rang in my hotel suite at just after five in the morning, when I had had about an hour's sleep.

'Unnnnnnnngh?' I said into the receiver.

'Is that you, Parker?' Theo Bernstein's voice barked.

'It is,' I admitted.

'Where have you been all night?' he said.

'What are you talking about, Theo?' I mumbled sleepily.

'I am asking you where you were last night. Answer please.'

'I was here, of course.'

'Is there anyone who can verify that?'

'Of course. Miss Dupont is here, and has been with me all night. Then there's the hotel staff who can tell you what time we went to bed.' (I had made sure of that.)

There was an exasperated sound on the line.

'Why? What's going on, Theo? Why are you asking me these questions?'

'We found Rupert Cornwell in Highgate, handcuffed in his car and sitting in a pile of his own excrement. With him was a cassette onto which he had recorded a full confession to killing Wheezy Wallis.'

'Wow! That's incredible. Why did he do it?'

'You know nothing about all this, of course?' There was a worrying note of sarcasm in Theo's voice.

'Me? Of course not,' I said solemnly.

'You know nothing about a convoluted tale of stolen paintings and extortion?' The sarcasm was becoming stronger.

'Not a thing,' I insisted. 'What makes you think that I do?'

'Only that Cornwell claims that you and some kind of gorilla tried to kill him and then obtained the confession from him under duress.'

'That's preposterous!' I exclaimed indignantly.

'He also claims you stole three quarters of a million pounds from him; in fifties, in a suitcase,' Theo said.

'Sounds like the man's gone loony,' I suggested. 'You know me, Theo; do you think I'm capable of attempted murder and of stealing huge amounts of cash?'

'Yes. This has every sign of your involvement in it. It's complicated, it's messy, it's bizarre and, most important, it's irritating – and that convinces me that you were involved.'

'Except that I have been here all night.'

'So you say.' Theo sounded weary.

'So we all say, at least ten of us.'

'I'm going to get to the bottom of this, Parker. I want you down here at the station in a few hours' time. Bring a lawyer if you want to. We are going to have a very long chat about this and that and one thing and another. Understand?'

'I hear you, Theo.'

'You'll be here by eleven o'clock or I'll send people to drag you here in chains.'

'Yes, Theo.'

'And bring a toothbrush, since you might be staying with us for a while.'

'Do you provide toothpaste?' I asked.

'I'm not joking, Parker. You're for the high jump.' He slammed the telephone down.

Actually, Theo didn't fool me. I knew he had not the slightest shred of evidence of my involvement in anything. All he had was the ramblings of a man trying to recant his confession, although one had to admit that the circumstances were decidedly odd. Had Theo had anything real to go on, I would have been arrested immediately and hauled off to the cells.

Even when the French police proceeded with the prosecution of their suspects for the attempted murder of Eve and me, Theo would still have absolutely no hard evidence of any involvement on my part with the events surrounding Cornwell and the painting. He would suspect everything, and understand quite a lot, but not a jot of it could he prove.

I suspected that I would be facing a difficult few hours at the police station later that morning, but nothing that Pendleton and I couldn't handle.

In the meantime, there was some serious journalism to be done. As soon as Theo hung up, I dialled Bloch's number.

'Arnie,' I said, 'it's Parker. Hold the front page.'